WHEN LIES CRUMBLE

The Carter Mays Mystery Series
by Alan Cupp

WHEN LIES CRUMBLE (#1)
SCHEDULED TO DIE (#2)

WHEN LIES CRUMBLE

A CARTER MAYS MYSTERY
ALAN CUPP

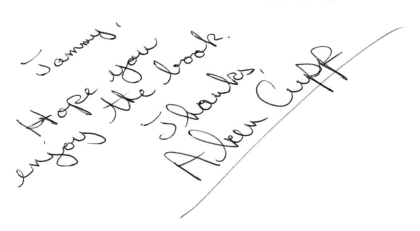

Tammy!
Hope you
enjoy the book.
Thanks,
Alan Cupp

HENERY PRESS

WHEN LIES CRUMBLE
A Carter Mays Mystery
Part of the Henery Press Mystery Collection

First Edition
Trade paperback edition | January 2015

Henery Press
www.henerypress.com

ISBN-13: 978-1-941962-63-3

Printed in the United States of America

ACKNOWLEDGMENTS

I want to thank the following people for their support, encouragement and assistance in making this book possible.

My wife, Dawn
My sons, Jesse & Austin
Coyal & Trudy (my parents)
Rhonda Purdon (sis)
Brooke Meisberger

Special thanks to Kendel Lynn for believing in me
and her invaluable guidance.

Above all, I give thanks to God for blessing me with
everyone mentioned above and so much more.

ONE

At seven minutes before the scheduled start of his six-thirty wedding, Tyler Moore had yet to be seen by anyone at the church. Billy, the best man, stood outside on the front steps of the massive cathedral and nervously took a long drag on his cigarette.

The light June breeze scattered ashes on his black tux. He brushed them off with his hand while he continuously scanned the street for his buddy's car.

After one last puff, Billy dropped the cigarette to the concrete and ground at it with his shiny black shoes before stepping back inside the church.

Jasper Bedford met Billy in the narthex feeling both concerned and agitated. "Any sign of him?" Jasper asked.

Billy shook his head.

"You're sure you guys didn't do anything stupid last night at the bachelor party that would cause him to be late?"

"No sir, Mr. Bedford," answered Billy. "We dropped him off at his place about two-fifteen. He may have been a little buzzed, but that's it."

"I've called his cell phone eight times and it keeps going to voice mail."

Darlene Bedford's heels clicked as her long slender legs carried her across the tile floor to her husband and Billy. A size six red dress clung to her body that had held up extremely well over her forty-eight years, the result of consistent exercise and a couple of surgical procedures. "Is he here?"

Jasper turned to face his wife and shook his head.

"Jasper, I'm getting really worried about him, and Cindy is freaking out."

Mr. Bedford glanced down at his Rolex and stroked his white goatee while he pondered what he should do. The last thing he expected from his soon to be son-in-law was not showing up.

He would have sooner expected it from his flighty daughter. Tyler had always demonstrated all the qualities Jasper desired for his daughter's mate.

He was a hard worker, ambitious, dependable, and loyal. As a result, the thought that something terrible had happened to the young man kept creeping back in Jasper's mind.

Without saying anything to his wife or Billy, Jasper walked away and entered the expanse of the elaborate sanctuary. Pipe organ music filled the air while four hundred people sat in the pews, waiting for the ceremony to begin.

Jasper approached two men on the back pew and tapped them on the shoulders.

Russell Hopkins and Dan Yielding both looked around to see their boss motioning for them to follow. Without hesitation they stood, straightened out their suit jackets, and exited the sanctuary behind Jasper.

When they reached the quiet of the narthex, Jasper stopped and placed his hand on Russell's arm as they huddled close. "I want you two to drive over to Tyler's condo and see if he's there. Call me the minute you arrive."

"Yes, sir," they both replied.

"What are you doing?" Darlene asked, as she approached her husband.

"I sent them to check out Tyler's condo."

"What are we going to do? We have four hundred people waiting for a wedding that is supposed to begin in three minutes." Jasper motioned for Billy, who promptly walked toward his boss.

"Billy," began Jasper, "I want you to go in there discreetly and tell the minister the wedding is going to be delayed and keep the organ player going."

"Yes, sir, Mr. Bedford." Billy went off to do as instructed.

Jasper put his hand on the small of Darlene's back and nudged her down the hall. "Honey, you need to go make sure Cindy is keeping it together. Assure her that everything is going to be okay."

"You're right. She was on the verge of a nervous breakdown when I left her a few moments ago."

Darlene Bedford disappeared around the corner, leaving Jasper alone to ponder the whereabouts of his only child's fiancé. After eight months of planning, organizing, and spending an exorbitant amount of money, this was not how he envisioned this wedding. Something had to be wrong. This was not characteristic of the young man his daughter had fallen in love with and Jasper himself had grown to admire and respect.

Pacing back and forth, Jasper contemplated where Tyler could be. Had he been involved in a car crash? Had he became suddenly ill, maybe the result of alcohol poisoning or something? Bachelor parties can get out of hand sometimes. Or was it a case of nerves? That was doubtful. Tyler Moore displayed nothing but confidence and steadfast behavior since being hired as a young accountant for West Lake Properties and Development three years ago.

He quickly proved to be a valued and reliable asset to the company. So when the young man showed an interest in dating Cindy, not only did Jasper approve, he encouraged the relationship. Tyler was a loyal, solid young man and Jasper saw a bright future for him in the company, perhaps even the innermost workings of the company.

After a half hour of pacing the floor until he grew tired of the sound of his shoes echoing,

Jasper peeped inside the sanctuary to check the crowd. The multitude sat restlessly waiting, whispering their speculations on the cause for delay. Everyone was growing tired of pipe organ music, including the organist himself.

Jasper's cell phone rang and he quickly retreated to the narthex and checked caller ID. It was Russell. "Tell me something good," answered Jasper.

"I'm afraid I don't have anything good to report, sir," replied Russell.

"What do you mean?"

"We're here at the condo. Nobody answered, so we let ourselves in."

"Yeah, and?"

"He's not here and it looks like he's not coming back."

"Not coming back?" Jasper replied. "What do you mean?"

"It appears as though he has packed up and gone. His clothes, computer, personal belongings, everything is gone. The only thing left is the furniture and his cell phone."

"He left his cell phone?"

"Yes, sir, and it shows thirteen missed calls, eight of them from you."

Jasper forcefully rubbed his temple with his fingers while he processed the information. "So you're telling me he's just picked up and left town?"

"That's the way it looks," answered Russell.

"I can't believe he'd just skip town. That doesn't make sense." Continuing to rub at his temples, Jasper thought for a moment. Suddenly he perked up as a thought passed through his mind. "Is his car there?"

"No, the car's not here."

"Okay, listen. Tyler drives a company car. All the company cars are equipped with a GPS we can track from the computers at the office. Get over there and find his location. When you get it, call me."

Jasper hung up and walked down the hall.

When he arrived at the room where the bridal party waited, he knocked lightly and hoped Darlene would come to the door. No such luck. The door swung open and there stood his pretty little girl, decked out in her seven thousand dollar wedding dress, her hopeful eyes red and teary. "Is Tyler here?"

Slightly shaking his head, Jasper reluctantly answered, "No, sweetie, not yet."

"Daddy, you have to find him. I think something terrible must have happened."

Taking a huge, prolonged sigh, Jasper prepared to tell his daughter what he dreaded saying.

"Dad, what is it?"

"Babe, I don't think that Tyler is going to make it," he quietly uttered just as Darlene approached the two of them.

Cindy's eyes fixed in on her father's, visibly distressed by the words that just left his mouth. Her sad, nervous eyes transformed to convey the shock and insult that such a horrendous thought deserved. "Why would you say that? Have you talked to Tyler?"

Darlene placed her hands on her daughter's bare, tan shoulders and gave her husband a perplexed look. "Jasper, what is it?"

"I just got off the phone with Russell. He and Dan were over at Tyler's condo." He hesitated.

"Yeah, so?" Cindy asked.

"Russell said that Tyler packed up his stuff and is gone."

Darlene moved in front of her daughter. "Packed up his stuff?"

Cindy repositioned herself between her parents. "Of course his stuff is packed. We're going on our honeymoon."

"No honey, I mean everything is gone; all of his clothes, his personal belongings, his computer, everything but the furniture and his cell phone."

"That doesn't make any sense." exclaimed Darlene.

Cindy moved to a chair and slowly lowered herself into it, staring at a blank spot on the wall.

Her five bridesmaids in their red satin dresses, who had migrated toward the conversation, surrounded their distraught friend to console her.

Watching his daughter, Jasper became increasingly agitated by Tyler's apparent action. The nerve of that guy to abandon his daughter. His face became red and tight as his eyes narrowed, feeling helpless in comforting his little girl.

Darlene took her husband's hand and led him into the hall. "Jasper, what are we going to do? Our daughter is devastated. We have four hundred of our friends and relatives waiting for a wedding that doesn't seem to be taking place, not to mention food for all of them at the reception hall. You really think Tyler just took off?"

"Yeah, it looks that way. I'm going to kill him when I find him."

Darlene's eyes shot down the hall for anyone who may have heard. "When you find him? Do you know where he is?"

"I've got the guys heading over to the office to get a location off the GPS in his car."

"And you think you'll be able to find him?"

"Oh, I'll find him. I guarantee you, I'll find him."

TWO

Later that evening, after all the wedding guests had dispersed, going back to their homes to speculate and gossip about the blown wedding, Jasper Bedford arrived at his eight thousand square foot home located on one of the prime lots in his gated community; a community his company developed.

Darlene had driven Cindy to the downtown apartment Jasper leased for his daughter's twenty-first birthday, to spend the night consoling her in a way only a mother can. The poor girl was overwhelmed with emotions ranging from hurt, humiliation, and embarrassment to pure rage.

As he passed through the door leading from the garage into the house, Jasper started to punch in the security code on the keypad mounted to the wall.

It was then he realized the alarm had already been deactivated. He stared at the display screen, wondering why or how the alarm was off. Years had passed since anyone neglected to activate the alarm when leaving the house. If there had been one thing his family learned over the years, it was to never leave the house without setting the alarm.

He paused, before slowly crossing the floor of the mudroom and stepping into the kitchen. His eyes shifted side to side as he made his way to the drawer where he kept a small revolver. Quietly, he opened the drawer and removed the gun.

Room by room, Jasper traveled throughout his house, searching for the intruder he sensed in the depths of his gut. Walking down the hall to his home office, Jasper flinched at the sound of his cell phone.

Quickly, he sought to quiet the ringing and answered with a low whisper. "What?"

"We've got a location on the car," replied Russell.

Keeping his eyes moving about the house and his voice low, Jasper asked, "Where?"

"O'Hare Airport."

Jasper released a sigh of frustration.

"What do you want us to do?" Russell asked.

"Get over there and find out anything you can about where he may have gone. Who knows, maybe his flight hasn't left yet. I'll send a picture of him to your phone that you can use to question anyone who might remember him."

"Okay. We're on our way."

Jasper flipped his phone closed and continued his path down the hall. When he reached the door of his office, carefully, he pushed it open and flipped on the light. Immediately his eyes landed on the open safe normally hidden by the bookcase, now pulled away from the wall. Jasper moved toward the safe to take a closer look.

Reaching inside, he pulled out the only thing that remained, a document that had not been there before: the prenuptial agreement Tyler Moore so willingly signed.

Jasper flung the papers across the room and slammed shut the safe door, letting out a barrage of obscenities. "I'll kill him."

Tossing the revolver on his cherry desk, Jasper pulled out his cell phone and called Russell.

"Yes, sir," answered Russell.

"Russell, if you find Tyler at the airport, take him to the office immediately. You can hurt him if you need to. As a matter of fact, I want you to hurt him, badly. But don't kill him."

"And if we don't find him there?"

"Find out whatever you can and then call me. I'm on my way to the office now."

"You got it," replied Russell.

Jasper hung up and then immediately called Tate Manning, Jasper's main accountant. He had been with Jasper for nearly thirty years and had all access to the company's finances.

Tate answered on the second ring. "Hello."

"It's Jasper. I need you to meet me at the office right away."

"Yeah, sure. Hey, did you ever find out what happened to Tyler? I feel really bad for Cindy. Is she okay?"

"She'll be fine. I just need you to get to the office as soon as possible."

"I can be there in a half hour," replied Tate.

After hanging up with Tate, Jasper retrieved a glass and a bottle of scotch from the mini bar in the corner of his office. He had been seriously duped and he was not happy about it. Now he had to find out how much damage had been done. So far, the monetary loss equaled around thirty grand from the wall safe, not to mention the money spent on the wedding that never happened. Jasper threw his head back and drained the shot glass. How had he not seen this coming? The fact that he had been caught completely off guard bothered him much more than the money that had been stolen. Had he grown soft? Careless? He poured himself another shot and downed it.

Tate Manning was waiting in the parking lot of the five-story building owned by West Lake Properties and Development. The first four floors were leased to other companies for office space. WLP&D occupied the entire top floor. Tate exited his Jaguar when Jasper's Mercedes rolled into the lot. The two men met at the front door where Jasper waved his keycard in front of the scanner, unlocking the door.

Walking through the lobby to the elevators, Tate asked, "What are we doing here, Jasper?"

They halted in front of the elevator doors and Jasper pushed the up button. "I need you to check all of our accounts."

"What for?"

"Tyler wiped out my safe at home and seeing how he had considerable access to our finances, I want to see what else he may have done."

The doors opened and the two of them stepped inside the elevator.

"Tyler ripped you off?" Tate asked.

"Yep. I had about thirty grand in the safe and now it's gone."

"And you're sure it was Tyler?"

"Well, gee, Tate, let's think about this for a moment. Me, my family, and everyone who works for me, was at the wedding. My state of the art, top-notch home security system somehow ended up disarmed. Then I find my wall safe, which is hidden behind a book case and is also state of the art, wide open with nothing in it but a prenup agreement with Tyler's signature. Tyler, the same guy who has come and gone from my home at will for the last couple of years, not to mention the fact he's worked for me for three years and had access to the company's finances. Tyler, the very same low-life who left my poor heartbroken daughter crying on what should have been the happiest day of her life. Yeah, Tate, I'm pretty sure Tyler had something to do with it."

Tate held up both hands. "Okay, already. I get it."

Still annoyed, Jasper responded, "Good. I'm glad we got that settled."

The doors opened and the men stepped off the elevator into the expanse of West Lake Properties and Development. The cubicles in the center of the room were typical of any business office. They passed through the common area until they reached a set of heavy glass doors separated from the rest of the office. Again, Jasper passed his keycard across the scanner, releasing the lock, and allowing them to enter the inner sanctum of WLP&D. Very few people had access to this area.

They went to Tate's office and Tate used his keycard to open the door. Once inside, Jasper settled into one of the brown leather chairs positioned in front of Tate's neatly organized desk.

Tate lowered himself into his custom made chair and turned on his computer. Neither man spoke while they waited for the computer to boot up. After typing in a password for three different security checkpoints, Tate could view the records he needed to see. Soon his jaw dropped open and a panicked look took over his bearded face.

Upon seeing Tate, Jasper sprang to his feet and walked around the desk to look over Tate's shoulder. "What is it?"

Tate said nothing in response as he frantically typed.

Peering over Tate's shoulder, Jasper studied the monitor. The financial damage jumped considerably from the thirty thousand from his home safe.

"Jasper, he's screwed us over. Bad." Tate exclaimed.

"Son of a..." Jasper's voice trailed off as a sick feeling came over him.

Tate punched at the keyboard. "There were several wire transfers made today; most of them to various offshore bank accounts. The first one started around four-twenty this afternoon, right when everyone was getting ready for the wedding."

Suddenly, Jasper noticed something. "Hey, Tate, isn't that your sign-on?"

Tate swallowed hard. "Yes, it looks like it, but you know I didn't have anything to do with it, right?"

Jasper studied the nervous eyes of his accountant. "I didn't say you did. But I'm wondering how he got your sign-on and password. Seems pretty careless on your part, don't you think?"

Tate went into a nervous mumbling. "Jasper, I don't know how he would have done that. I'm very careful with that information."

"Well, apparently you're not that careful now, are you?"

Tate's eyes shifted to the computer screen and he began to type rapidly.

Jasper continued staring at his longest-term employee, questioning if there could be something more to be concerned about. Could this have been a joint effort between Tyler and Tate?

Perhaps, Tate planned on skipping town, too, but didn't get out before Jasper contacted him.

Tate jumped up in his chair and pointed at the monitor.

Jasper's eyes moved from their suspicious analysis of Tate to the data on the screen. There, at the end of Tate's thick finger, Jasper saw his own name next to three more transactions. Panicked, Jasper read every piece of information showing. The more he read and realized, the more enraged he became. Jasper picked up the desk phone and hurled it across the room, shattering it into pieces as it took out a chunk of drywall. "He got into those files?" Jasper yelled. "How did he even know about those? There's no way he could have known."

Releasing a heavy sigh, Tate spoke up. "Well, obviously he did know about them. He knew a lot more of what we do than you thought he did."

"Someone screwed up and let something slip. How else would he know?"

"Yeah, but Jasper, everyone on the inside knows better than that. All these years, nobody ever slipped up. Your own daughter doesn't even know."

"True, but she never worked here at the company like Tyler did. It wasn't hard to keep her in the dark. But Tyler had the opportunity to develop friendships. He hung out with some of the guys who have dual roles working for me. It only takes a couple of drinks to loosen up someone's lips."

"He was closest with Billy," Tate offered.

"Yeah, I know. I already thought of him."

Pacing back and forth, Jasper asked, "So what was the total he got us for?"

Tate typed and clicked, assessing the damage, and writing down numbers on a scratch pad to make sure he didn't forget anything. Finally, he leaned back in his chair, expelled a deep sigh, and answered the man's question. "Six point seven million."

Jasper was not prepared for that high of an amount. "Six point seven?" Tate nodded as Jasper struggled with the number.

"Six point seven million," Jasper said again, shocked.

"It could have been a lot worse, Jasper," said Tate. "Fortunately Tyler didn't know everywhere to look or he could have completely wiped us out. I mean, I know that's a fair chunk of change, but in the grand scheme of things, we can recover relatively quickly, in a year or two."

Jasper found little comfort in Tate's 'glass is half full' outlook. He had been robbed and made to look like a fool. Some twenty-seven year old kid comes in, charms his way into the family, and royally screws him out of nearly seven million dollars.

"I still don't get how he got our log on information and passwords," said Tate. "It's not like anyone else knows that stuff."

"Did you ever key in your password while he was in here?" Jasper asked.

"No. I'm very paranoid about that. You're the only one with that information," said Tate.

"Well, obviously, neither of us is paranoid enough."

Tate started to say something, but then hesitated. Finally, Tate asked, "Jasper, since Tyler knew about the inner workings of the company, what are the chances Cindy now knows?"

The question pierced through Jasper, exposing one of his only fears. She had shown no indication that she knew anything. Still, given the close, intimate relationship with Tyler as her fiancé, it could have been discussed. Jasper pondered the possibility for a moment.

"I don't think she knows," he said. "For one, she's never once brought it up. As clueless as she can be, she never likes to think something is being kept from her. Second, if Tyler had told her what he obviously knew, it would have jeopardized everything for him. Because the moment Cindy asked me about it, which she most definitely would have, it would have exposed him. No, I think his goal all along has been this little caper he pulled off today. He had nothing to gain by telling her and everything to lose."

Tate nodded in agreement with Jasper's logic. "So what are you going to do?"

"About Tyler?"

"Yeah," replied Tate. "Do you think you'll be able to find him? He's obviously planned this out pretty well. I can't imagine he didn't have an extensive plan to disappear."

Jasper shook his head. "I don't care how well he planned it, I'll find him. If we have to cover every continent of the globe, I'll find him. And when I do, that six point seven million will not come close to being worth the pain and agony he will experience."

THREE

Sunday morning Jasper got out of bed, having not slept more than a half hour. Thoughts of his daughter being up all night crying on her mother's shoulder while Tyler was off somewhere with nearly seven million in stolen money ate at Jasper until he couldn't sleep.

His men spent hours at the airport Saturday night, questioning people, showing Tyler Moore's picture, trying to get some lead on his destination. They came up with nothing.

The idea that nobody in the entire airport could remember talking to or even seeing Tyler was mind-boggling. Not one luggage handler, ticket agent, or employee of the countless airport shops remembered Tyler.

Jasper checked recent activity on Tyler's company credit card to see if perhaps that could give them any leads. What he discovered pissed him off that much more. Tyler had maxed out the card, but not on anything that would disclose his whereabouts. He made several donations to local causes, political campaigns, and TV evangelists with questionable ethics. The causes and politicians he donated to on behalf of the company were ones he knew Jasper loathed and would never support. Every donation was made out of spite; just another way to screw Jasper.

Exhausted, discouraged, and unable to think on anything else, Jasper slipped on his robe and walked downstairs to the kitchen for coffee. Today's pot would be extra strong. He had to stay focused. Every day, every hour that passed without them gaining any ground toward finding Tyler, would make it that much more difficult to find him at all. Six point seven million dollars can do a lot to make a person disappear.

In addition to Russell and Dan, Jasper assigned his entire security team to do nothing but find the thief. He sent some of them to do a thorough search of Tyler's condo and then on to his office at WLP&D. After that, they were to work the streets, questioning business associates, neighbors, friends, or anyone who might have some insight to the real Tyler Moore.

Russell and Dan were also directed to question Tyler's closest friend, Billy. Jasper instructed them to use aggressive methods to ensure full disclosure. A decision Jasper hated to make because Billy had always been a valued asset during the nine years he worked for Jasper. But the stakes were high, and exhausting every possibility was the only choice. If Billy passed the test, Jasper would be sure to make it up to him.

While the coffee brewed, Jasper called his wife's cell phone.

After three rings, she answered.

"Hey Babe, how's Cindy doing?"

"Well, neither one of us got much sleep," replied Darlene.

"Join the club. You haven't even heard the best part yet."

"What? What happened?"

"Our son-in-law to be ripped us off."

"He did what?"

"I came home last night and found my office safe missing the thirty thousand dollars I had in there."

"No."

"Yeah. The only thing there was his copy of the prenup."

"That can't be," Darlene exclaimed.

"Oh, but it can be, and that's just a drop in the bucket to the nearly seven million he stole from the company yesterday."

"Jasper? Seven million?"

"Close enough. The guy duped us; you, me, Cindy, all of us."

"I can't believe he would be capable of doing that."

"You haven't heard the worst part yet," continued Jasper. "Some of that money was taken from our hidden accounts."

Rarely was Darlene Bedford at a loss for words.

Jasper continued. "This guy used our daughter to rip me off. God only knows how long he's been planning this. The whole relationship was a sham."

Darlene finally broke her silence. "How did he know about the hidden accounts?"

"I don't know."

"Do you think he passed on any of that information to anyone else, like the DA's office?"

"I don't know. I have Tate moving files and deleting some stuff today. It's hard to say what this guy's done to me."

"Cindy's going to be devastated when she finds out her engagement was only about money," said Darlene.

"Make sure you don't mention the hidden accounts," reminded Jasper.

"Jasper, do you really think you need to tell me that? Haven't we protected her from that knowledge all these years? Why would I say anything now?"

"Sorry. I just don't need anything else to worry about now."

"Yeah, well, neither do I. You act like this isn't affecting me as much as it is you."

"Alright, I get it," said Jasper. "I'm sorry I brought it up."

"So where are you on finding him?" Darlene asked.

"We've hit a bunch of dead ends."

"You mean you aren't any closer to finding him than you were last night?"

"No, not really."

"Jasper, you have to find him."

"I know that," Jasper shot back. "Do you think that I'm not doing everything I can?"

"What happened with the GPS?"

"We found his car at O'Hare."

"O'Hare? Jasper, he could be anywhere by now. He could be in Europe, South America, anywhere."

"You're not telling me anything I don't know."

Hostile silence followed the exchange as both sought to end the conversation. Jasper spoke first. "Give my love to Cindy and tell her that she's much better off without this loser."

"It's easier for you to say that to me than it is for her to hear it while she's clutching their eight-by-ten engagement photo."

Giving up on saying anything more to his wife, Jasper mumbled a hasty goodbye and hung up.

Darlene hung up her phone and tossed it in her purse while she uttered a few choice names for her husband. Still wearing the pajamas she borrowed from her daughter, Darlene took a deep breath, stood up, and went upstairs to talk to Cindy.

Knocking softly on the bedroom door, she waited for an invitation before entering. Cindy was sitting up in her bed, surrounded by an absurd amount of pillows. Her normally beautiful blue eyes were bloodshot and puffy from a night of continuous tears. Her nose was red and irritated from the box of tissues she used to wipe at it all night. She barely looked up as her mother sat on the bed beside her.

Darlene reached up and gently pushed the mess of long blonde hair away from Cindy's face. "Sweetie," began Darlene. "There's something I need to tell you."

The statement drew a nervous look from the heartbroken girl. "What is it, Mom?"

"I just got off the phone with your dad. He told me Tyler stole money from us, personally, and from the company."

Cindy gasped. "He stole money?"

"Yes. I'm sorry, Cindy."

Cindy shook her head back and forth in denial. "No. That can't be. I couldn't be that wrong about someone. There has to be something more we don't know about. How does Dad know Tyler is the one who stole the money?"

Darlene started to answer, but stammered. "I don't know all the details, honey. But apparently he transferred a large amount of money from company accounts, well over six million dollars. It was all done yesterday."

Cindy stood up and paced around the room. "Mom, somebody else has to be behind this. The man I fell in love with is not capable of this. Maybe Tyler's in trouble or something."

Not wanting to antagonize her daughter, Darlene said little in response.

"I have to find Tyler," said Cindy with a renewed sense of urgency. "I think something bad has happened to him. Someone probably used him to get to us, and now that they've got what they want they'll probably..." Cindy broke down crying.

"Cindy, listen to me," said Darlene. "I know it's difficult to believe, but sometimes you just don't know someone as well as you think you do." Immediately, Darlene's mind went to her husband.

"Mom," said Cindy, poised for defense. "I know Tyler, and this is not about him wanting money. All along he's been very adamant about us making it on our own without any financial help from you and Dad."

"Cindy, your dad went home last night and found someone had broken into his safe. The only thing in there was Tyler's copy of the prenuptial agreement."

The mention of the prenup caused Cindy to stop pacing and look at her mother. A moment passed while she processed the news. Then, as before, she began shaking her head. "That doesn't mean anything. It stands to reason if someone was using Tyler to steal from us, they would do everything they could to make it look like he was guilty."

Frustrated by her daughter's denial, Darlene stood up and headed for the door.

"Mom," called Cindy, "I know you don't agree with me, but I'm going to prove it to you."

Darlene turned and gazed at her broken, desperate daughter. "I hope you can," she said before leaving the room.

FOUR

Jasper's black Mercedes kicked up a cloud of dust as he drove onto the property where a new apartment building was under construction. He parked, got out and shook his head, annoyed by the millions of dust and gravel particles adhered to the recently polished paint of his car.

Stepping over building materials scattered across the quiet, vacated site, he made his way into the large concrete building, currently six weeks behind schedule. Most weekends the place would be teaming with workers earning double time trying to catch up on a project delayed by county zoning and three weeks of horrible weather. However, Jasper gave everyone the weekend off in honor of his daughter's wedding. Just one more way Tyler Moore was costing him money.

In the rear of the building, Jasper heard the faint sound of groaning and voices. The noise became louder and clearer as he approached the back corner, where he saw Russell and Dan flanking Billy, who was tied to a support beam.

Dan looked back first when they heard Jasper.

Billy, who was slouching with his head down, eventually looked up. His left eye was swollen shut and the rest of his face revealed a blue and yellow tint from the repeated blows he had taken. Crimson drops of blood trickled from his broken nose.

"Mr. Bedford," said Billy, his voice weak and strained. "I swear to you I don't know anything about Tyler. I swear it." His voice cracked and he began to sob a little. "You have to believe me."

Jasper motioned for Russell to walk with him, getting out of earshot of Billy. About forty feet away they stopped to whisper. "What do you think?" Jasper asked.

Russell's eyes focused on Billy while he spoke. "We've been at it for two hours now. He's taken a lot of punishment. I don't think he knows anything. I think he's more shocked than the rest of us."

"How confident are you?" Jasper asked.

"Very. Billy's a good guy, but he's not very tough. If he knew anything, I expected him to crack forty minutes ago."

Jasper looked away, biting at his lower lip, and cursing Tyler for forcing him to do this to Billy. After a brief hesitation, Jasper walked over to Billy, with Russell following him.

Billy looked up, bleeding, bruised, scared. "I swear, Mr. Bedford, Tyler screwed us all over. I didn't do anything."

Nodding his head, Jasper answered, "I know. I believe you, Billy. I'm sorry about this. I promise I'll make it up to you."

Looking at Dan, Jasper said, "Cut him loose, carefully."

Instant relief could be seen on Billy's face as Dan pulled out a knife and cut the ropes holding Billy's battered body to the beam. Russell caught the small-framed man and slowly lowered him to the ground.

"Thank you, Mr. Bedford," Billy managed to get out before breaking down into full-blown sobbing.

"Take him home and get him patched up."

Jasper turned and walked back to his dust covered car. As happy as he was to think Billy had not betrayed him, he still wasn't any closer to finding Tyler.

FIVE

Carter Mays sat at his desk logging his mileage for last week, when Cindy Bedford entered his office. He looked up, pleasantly surprised by the attractive young girl standing in front of him. Cindy's slender frame closed the short distance of the office and she extended her hand toward him.

"Hello, Mr. Mays," she said as he took her hand. "I'm Cindy Bedford and I want to retain your services. A friend of mine recommended you. Her name is Tasha Teague. She hired you to catch her husband cheating."

"Hello, Miss Bedford," replied Carter. "Yes, I remember Tasha. Please have a seat."

As the young lady settled into the sage green upholstered chair, Carter stole a quick appreciative glimpse of her long, shapely legs. Catching himself, he immediately refocused on his prospective client's purpose for being there.

"How may I help you?" Carter asked, lowering into his black desk chair and setting his hands on the desk.

"I want you to find someone," she answered.

"Who is it, and when did you last see this person?"

"It's my fiancé. We were supposed to get married two days ago, but he disappeared."

Carter leaned back in his chair and scratched at his three-day beard. "Nobody heard from him at all?"

"No."

"When was the last time someone saw him?"

"Friday night, or I guess technically it would have been early Saturday morning, after his bachelor party."

"What did the police say?"

"I haven't been to the police."

Carter's eyebrows rose slightly. "Why not?"

"My parents thought it would be a waste of time."

"Really? So they advised you to hire a private investigator?"

"No. I'm doing this on my own."

"What did they advise you to do?" Carter asked.

"My father said he'd take care of it."

Carter leaned forward again. "I'm sorry, I'm a little confused. What kind of work does your father do?"

"He owns West Lake Properties and Development."

"Oh, the huge building over on Sherman Avenue?"

"Yes, that's his company."

"Okay, so your father is in real estate development. How exactly is he going to take care of it?"

"He has people working on it."

"He's hired an investigative company?"

"No, he has people within the company trying to find Tyler."

Carter let out a snicker, drawing a curious look from Cindy.

"Did I say something funny, Mr. Mays?" Cindy asked.

"I'm sorry ma'am; it's just I'm trying to understand what's going on. You tell me your fiancé didn't show up for his wedding, and nobody has seen him since, but no one went to the police. Instead, your dad, a real estate developer, asked his employees to look for your fiancé. My first inclination is to wonder if your dad really wants to find this guy."

"I can assure you he does," said Cindy defensively.

"What makes you so sure?"

"My father is convinced Tyler stole money from him."

Cindy's last sentence stirred a whole new level of interest from Carter, who stood up and moved around to sit on the front of his desk. His solid arms folded in front of his lean muscular frame. "He stole money?"

"I said my father thinks that Tyler stole money, from his company," Cindy repeated.

"But you don't?"

"No, sir, I don't. I think someone may have used or forced Tyler into this and now I fear for his safety."

Carter met her eyes. "And it's not conceivable you could have been wrong about this guy?"

"The whole time Tyler and I have been together, he never showed any interest in my family's money. He was always stubborn about not excepting handouts from my parents. He even insisted on signing a prenuptial agreement."

"Did Tyler work for your father's company?"

"Yes, for nearly three years. That's how we met."

Carter studied the girl for a moment, wondering just how gullible she could be. "How much money are we talking about?" Carter asked.

"I don't know. What do you charge for your services?"

The question baffled Carter before he realized there had been a miscommunication. A boyish dimpled smile spread across his face. "No, I mean how much money was stolen?"

"Oh," replied Cindy, just now grasping the question. "I don't know the exact figure, but over six million dollars."

Carter stood up and placed his hands on his hips. "Someone steals over six million dollars from your father's company and he doesn't call the police?"

Cindy's response indicated it was the first time that thought had crossed her mind. However, she didn't dwell on it and returned to her business at hand. "So are you interested?"

"Are you sure you don't want to try the police first? It would save you some money."

"I'm not concerned about the money, Mr. Mays. Are you interested or not?"

Carter thought for a moment. "Okay, I'll do a little digging and see what I can find. I charge four hundred dollars a day, plus expenses, and I need the first two days up front."

A brief but satisfied smile came across Cindy's face as she reached in her purse to pull out her checkbook. "Will you be starting right away?"

"Actually, I'm meeting with a client this afternoon. I probably won't start until tomorrow."

"That's the soonest you can start?"

"If I start later today, it's still going to cost you four hundred. Wouldn't you rather I wait until tomorrow and get a full day for your money?"

Quite sternly, Cindy answered, "I told you before, Mr. Mays, I'm not worried about the money." She tore out the check and handed it to him.

"Yes, you did tell me that. It's just that most people don't really mean it when they say it."

"Well, I do."

Carter glanced down at the check made out for three days. "I can see that. By the way, call me Carter. I'm not very formal."

"Do you have a couple of business cards?" Cindy asked.

Carter moved behind his desk and retrieved two cards to give her. One she dropped into her purse and then proceeded to write on the back of the other one. When she finished, she handed it back to him. "Here's my home and cell number. I would like to hear what progress you're making each day."

Taking the card, Carter glanced at it, placed in inside his shirt pocket and nodded. "I can do that."

"So you'll be starting on it today?"

Carter nodded in agreement.

"Let's start by getting some info on Tyler."

Cindy reached into her purse and retrieved an envelope. "I've collected a lot already. You can read through it, and then ask me any additional questions you may have."

Taking the envelope, Carter opened it up and found three different pictures and two sheets of paper with extensive information including height, weight, full name, social security number, address, home and cell phone numbers, banking information, educational background, and political preferences. "Wow, you came prepared," commented Carter.

"I tried to include everything I thought would help."

Carter continued reading. "You've got down here that he was in the Boy Scouts," he said, humored by its inclusion into the bio.

"Like I said, I wrote down everything. I'd rather come off as stupid than to leave anything out."

"No, I'm sorry, I wasn't implying it was stupid," said Carter. "It's just very thorough."

"I want to find my fiancé, Mr. Mays. I mean Carter."

"That's great." Carter remarked, trying to smooth over any bruised feelings. "All this is a big help."

Cindy stared at him for a moment before asking, "Where do you think you'll start?"

"I'd like to take a look at his place; see if I can find anything."

Immediately he noticed a look of disappointment on Cindy's face. "Actually, his condo is pretty much empty."

"Empty?" Carter repeated, surprised by the revelation. "You mean like totally vacated?"

"I haven't been there yet. My father said the furniture is there, but everything else is gone. Oh, his cell phone was there."

"Your father went to Tyler's condo?"

"No, but the guys who work for him did."

"And all they found was furniture and Tyler's cell phone?"

Cindy confirmed with a nod.

"Any reason why he would have left his phone? Did he typically have it with him?"

"He always had his phone with him. I've never called him when he didn't answer, until Saturday. That's another reason I think he's in danger."

Carter returned to his seat and studied his newest client. "So, these guys who work for your father, when they're not out looking for your missing fiancé, what's their job?"

"I don't know exactly."

"I mean, are they in charge of security for the company?"

Shrugging her shoulders, Cindy answered, "I suppose. I'm not really sure. Why? How would that help find Tyler?"

"Just curious," replied Carter, feeling both concerned and intrigued by the mystery of Mr. Bedford and his employees. "I'd still like to look at the condo. Can you let me in or give me a key?"

"You can use my key," said Cindy, reaching into her purse. "Here you are," she said, handing him the key.

"Thanks. I'll make sure you get it back."

"Is there anything else you need from me?"

Carter held the bio up in front of his face and shook his head. "Nah, I think this will get me started. I'm sure I'll have more questions for you as things come up."

"You have my number. I'll expect to hear from you sometime this evening to update me on your progress."

Carter stood and extended his hand toward her as she stood. "Yes ma'am," he said with a smile. "Hopefully, we can get this resolved quickly, which brings me to one last question."

Arching her neatly groomed eyebrows, Cindy waited.

"People tell me they want to know the truth about whatever it is they're hiring me to do. Sometimes, however, when the facts turn out to be something that doesn't line up with what they expected, they get nasty with me. Some people have even tried to withhold payment from me. Are you prepared to accept my findings, whatever they prove to be?"

Without hesitation, Cindy answered, "Absolutely."

"Okay, then, I'll be in touch."

Cindy turned and walked out of the office as Carter caught himself staring again.

SIX

Following his afternoon meeting, Carter drove to Tyler Moore's condo. Located in a pleasant neighborhood across the street from a neatly manicured city park filled with joggers and dog-walkers, Carter parked in front of the white brick building. Tyler's unit was on the top floor of the four-story building. It wasn't what one would consider to be accommodations for the rich, but it was certainly at the very top end of Carter's price range. Carrying a small gym bag, Carter stepped onto the elevator and held the doors long enough to allow two young, attractive women carrying shopping bags, the opportunity to ride up and avoid waiting for the next one.

Both offered an appreciative smile and thanked him.

"Which floor?" Carter asked.

"Three," both women answered simultaneously.

The doors closed and Carter nodded at the five bags the women were holding. "Must have been a good sale," he commented.

The taller one with auburn hair answered, "It was a good sale. We did pretty well."

Carter grinned and said, "I'm sure whatever the two of you bought will look fantastic on you."

Both women smiled. The brunette leaned back against the wall and slightly tilted her head to the side. "Are you new to the building?"

"No, just paying a visit."

"That's too bad," she replied with a flirty grin.

Carter watched as the highlight of his day exited the elevator and went to the unit directly across the hall. Each woman looked back and waved goodbye as the doors closed.

On the fourth floor, at the end of the hall, Carter located Tyler's unit and began to insert the key Cindy gave him. However, he noticed the door jamb had been damaged, and the door wasn't even closed all the way.

His eyes scanned the hall before entering.

Standing just inside the condo, Carter took in the surroundings. The possibility that whoever forced their way in still remained, kept Carter alert and constantly shifting his eyes.

Taking calm, quiet steps, Carter made his way through each room until he confirmed nobody else was in the condo. Able to relax, he could now focus on the details of the place. Lowering his gym bag onto the bed, Carter unzipped it and removed everything he needed to dust for prints and went to work.

Across the street from the condo, two men sat in a black SUV. The passenger, a stout balding guy, listened intently through the small headphones he wore.

Sitting behind the wheel, an older, but much leaner man, sporting a long red ponytail, noticed his partner's increased interest in whatever was coming through the headphones.

He lightly backhanded the man and asked, "What is it? Do you hear something?"

The guy waved off his buddy's inquiry and kept listening.

The driver threw a harder backhand. "What is it, Mick?"

Mick looked up long enough to answer. "Someone's inside moving around."

Immediately, the driver reached for the binoculars resting on the seat and peered through them at the fourth floor windows of Tyler's condo."

"You see something, Roy?" Mick asked. Roy ignored him and kept his focus on the windows. Mick now delivered his own backhand into Roy's shoulder. "Answer me, jackass. Do you see anything?"

"No," snapped Roy. "Not yet."

"Call Mr. Bedford," said Mick, as he continued listening.

Roy pulled out his cell phone and dialed. While he waited for an answer, he took another look through the binoculars. Just then he saw someone pass by the fourth-story window.

"Hello," Jasper answered.

"Yeah, Mr. Bedford, this is Roy. There's someone inside Tyler's condo."

"It's not Tyler?"

"No, sir, it's not Tyler," replied Roy, drawing a curious reaction from Mick.

"How do you know it's not Tyler?" Mick whispered.

Roy handed the binoculars to Mick and pointed toward the top of the building, before returning his attention to his boss on the phone. "I'm sorry, Mr. Bedford, I didn't catch that."

Mick leaned over as far as he could. Finally, Roy shoved Mick back to his side of the car. "No sir," answered Roy. "I don't know who it is. It appears to be just one guy. I can't really see him well enough to get a description. Do you want us to intercept him?"

Roy listened for a solid minute, then replied. "Got it. We'll call you when we find out anything." He hung up and looked at his partner. "He wants us to stay back, follow the guy and find out what we can. Maybe he'll lead us to Tyler."

Peering through the binoculars, Roy asked, "So, can you tell what he's doing in there?"

Mick shook his head. "Not really. I hear a little movement, and then it gets quiet, then more movement."

"I've got to get a better look at him. Slide over behind the wheel and be ready to pick me up. I'm going inside."

After lifting several prints from various surfaces in the condo, Carter carefully packed up his newly acquired clues and prepared to leave. He took one more stroll through the place to make sure he didn't miss anything obvious. He remembered Cindy saying Tyler left his phone behind, yet he didn't see it. Carter guessed the men working for Mr. Bedford had taken it.

With nothing more to see, Carter picked up his bag and left the condo. As he walked down the hall, a man with a red ponytail rounded the corner and arrived at the elevator at the same time. The man smiled and said hello. Carter responded with a courtesy nod men often offer to acknowledge another man.

Stepping onto the elevator, the stranger asked, "Lobby?"

"Yeah, thanks," answered Carter.

With Carter staring straight ahead, he heard the man speak. "Heading to the gym?"

Carter glanced at his fellow passenger who was pointing at the bag. "Oh, the bag? Yeah, I'm on my way to work out," he lied.

"Where do you work out?"

"A friend of mine has some equipment in his basement. We get together a couple of times a week to work out."

As the elevator doors opened, both men stepped off. Then Carter noticed an older woman walking toward him carrying a bag of groceries. He stopped, leaving the talkative stranger a little baffled as to what he should do.

The guy slowed down and glanced back at Carter, who was getting back onto the elevator. Taking slow steps away from the elevator the man asked, "Change your mind about working out?"

"No. I forgot something upstairs."

Forced to maintain his path, the man with the ponytail offered one more nod as he walked away. "Hey, have a good workout," he yelled.

"Thanks," Carter said with very little enthusiasm toward the chatty stranger.

Carter held the door for the woman who had just entered. "Going up?"

She smiled, appreciative of the gesture, and replied, "Actually, I'm not. I'm on this floor."

The doors closed and Carter pushed the third floor button. When he arrived, he crossed the hall to the door opposite the elevator and knocked.

When the brunette answered the door, she looked pleasantly surprised to see Carter. "Hey, it's the elevator guy," she said to her friend in the background.

"Hi," said Carter. "I'm sorry to bother you."

"You're not bothering me," she said. "What can I do for you?"

"I'm looking for someone," said Carter.

"Your friend?"

Carter smiled. "Well, actually he's not really a friend. He has a condo upstairs." Carter held up a picture of Tyler.

"Are you a policeman or something?"

"Private investigator," replied Carter. "I was wondering if you knew him."

"Come on in," she said, stepping out of the way.

Carter entered the room, passing through the fragrant smell of the brunette's perfume. She led him into the living room where the redhead sat with a book in her lap.

"Hi again," offered the redhead.

"Hi. Good book?"

"Yes, it is. Did you stop by to ask about my book?"

"He's looking for that Moore guy who lives upstairs," the brunette said, to clarify.

"So you know him?" Carter asked.

"Not really. I've talked to him in the elevator a few times; just small talk. Is he in some sort of trouble?"

"Nobody knows where he is," said Carter. "By the way, what are your names?"

The brunette answered first. "I'm Carina."

"And I'm Alley," answered the redhead.

Carter confirmed the spelling for each one as he jotted it down on a notepad.

Carina crossed the room to her purse where she pulled out a business card and gave it to Carter. "Here, have one of my cards."

"Thanks," he said, taking the card and reading it. "So you're a photographer, huh?"

Carina answered with a nod, "Yes, I am."

Carter glanced around the room at the framed photos hanging on the walls. "Are these your work?"

"Yes, except for that one over there. That was done by a friend of mine."

Carter paused for a moment to take in each photo. "I like them. You do good work."

"Thank you," replied Carina.

"Anyway, back to Tyler Moore," said Carter. "Can you remember anything at all about him that may help me get a better idea of who I'm looking for?"

Both women stared at the floor in front of them while they thought. Finally, Alley spoke up. "He was a big Notre Dame Football fan."

Alley's mention of Notre Dame prompted an enthusiastic reaction from Carina, who pointed to her friend and said, "Yeah, you told me he liked Notre Dame."

"How do you know? Did he wear a lot Notre Dame apparel?"

"No, not really," said Alley. "Now that I think about it, he never wore it. I think that's how I first realized he liked Notre Dame. He had on an Illinois shirt, so I commented on it. That's when he told me that he actually loved Notre Dame. He said he knew the name of every player on the team. I told him that I grew up in Mishawaka and asked him if he went to Notre Dame. Then he just started looking uncomfortable and changed the subject, started talking about the weather. It was kind of weird."

"Hmm," grunted Carter as he took notes. "He didn't even answer your question?"

"Yeah, he did. He said he went to University of Illinois. Then he started talking about the weather. One moment we're having a normal, casual conversation, the next moment I feel like I'm intruding in his personal life. Definitely weird."

"Is there anything else?" Carter asked.

"No, I don't think so. After that, I sort of kept my conversations with him fairly brief. We'd say hi, but that's about it."

"That's all I ever said to him," added Carina. "I guess you could say he was kind of distant."

"Sorry to waste your time," said Alley. "That's all we've got."

"Oh no, don't apologize. This helps. And even if you didn't have anything to tell, I could never view talking to you two as a waste of time. This is the highlight of my week."

Both women smiled as Carter stood to leave. Carina escorted him to the door. Carter pulled out a business card and handed it to her. "If you think of anything else, call me."

Carina opened the door and allowed just enough room for Carter to get by her. "And if you ever need a photographer, call me," she said.

"Is that the only reason I could call you?" Carter asked.

The question produced another flirty smile and she shook her head as she leaned against the door. "No. You can call for no reason at all, if you'd like."

"I'll do that," he replied. Then his eyes shifted one last time to Alley who appeared entertained by their obvious interaction. "Thanks again, Alley."

"You're welcome. I'm sure I'll be seeing you again in the near future," she quipped.

Carter took another look at the beautiful brunette directly in front of him. "I'll talk to you later."

"Okay," she replied, while playing with her hair and biting her lower lip.

Stepping across the hall to the elevator he pressed the button and took another glance behind him at Carina who was slowly closing the door and waving goodbye.

He stood there wondering if perhaps she was still watching him through the peephole. The elevator arrived and he stepped on, turned around and smiling stared directly at the peephole, just in case she was watching As he drove off, Carter was too distracted by thoughts of Carina to notice the black SUV tailing him.

SEVEN

By some spectacular stroke of luck, the parking space directly in front of the diner opened up just as Carter arrived. The black SUV cruised on past and eventually circled the block. A bell rang out as Carter opened the door and entered the half-full establishment. In the back booth along the wall, he saw his uniformed friend Bobby waiting with a cup of tea. Bobby barely looked up when Carter slid into the booth.

"What's up, buddy?" Carter said.

Bobby took a sip of tea. "Why don't you tell me, since you're the one who asked me to meet you here?"

Carter dropped an envelope on the table. "I need you to run some prints for me."

"You know I'm not supposed to do that," replied Bobby.

Carter rolled his eyes. "Yeah, whatever. I lifted some pretty good ones, so it shouldn't be hard."

Bobby took the envelope. "What's it for?"

"A missing person case."

"How's business?"

"Steady. Why? Are you thinking of quitting the force to come work for me?"

Bobby snickered. "Work for you? I'd be your competition and probably put you out of business within a month."

Carter laughed.

The waitress arrived and Carter ordered a chicken salad sandwich and iced tea. She wrote it down and walked away.

"Aren't you eating anything?" Carter asked.

Bobby shook his head. "Nah, trying to drop a few pounds."

"So seriously, you ready to come work for me?"

"Seriously, I'm not. I like having a pension, and health insurance, steady income. Plus, I have four weeks of vacation now. And unlike you, I have a bunch of mouths to feed."

"I have Booker to feed," said Carter.

"The dog doesn't count."

"He's a German Shepherd. Do you have any idea how much food he eats?"

"I've got Robbie. It's been scientifically proven you can't fill the stomach of a fifteen-year-old boy. I could feed you and your dog cheaper than I can feed that kid. And that's just Robbie. Behind him, I have Blake, Sylvia, and Kyle."

"You know they have this thing called birth control?"

"Funny. But don't worry, we're done."

"Are you sure you don't want to try to get a sister for Sylvia? I feel sorry for her being the only girl."

"Are you kidding? She has the two older brothers eating out of her hand and is definitely the boss of Kyle."

Carter smiled. "Yeah, Sylvia is a cutie."

"You need to settle down and start having kids. What are you, thirty-five?"

"Thirty-three, thank you. I haven't found the right girl yet."

"How's that possible? You dated half the women in Chicago."

"You're a bonehead. However, I did meet one today who's got me intrigued."

Bobby tilted his head back and arched his eyebrows. "Oh really? She intrigued you, did she?"

Nodding, Carter answered, "She's hot."

"I think you're too focused on the 'hot' part. You need to just find a good woman to settle down with."

"Wow, you must think I'm pretty shallow."

"I didn't say that. You've dated a lot of hot women, but you're still single. Maybe you're not destined to marry a hot woman."

The waitress brought Carter his food. He picked up his sandwich and looked at his friend. "I refuse to continue with this asinine conversation. I didn't meet you to discuss my personal life."

Bobby laughed out loud. "Feeling the stinging pain of truth, huh? It's making you uncomfortable, isn't it?"

Carter took a huge bite food and mumbled, "Shut up."

Bobby picked up the envelope. "So when do you need this?"

Carter swallowed his food and took a sip of tea. "ASAP."

"As if I didn't already know that was going to be your answer. Should I just email you?"

"Yeah, that's fine."

Bobby reached for his wallet. "I've got to scoot," he said.

Carter held up his hand. "Don't worry about it. I got the check."

"Oh, thanks, man."

"It's the least I can do for helping me out," replied Carter.

"Ain't that the truth," said Bobby. "I risk my job for you and you buy me a cup of tea."

"Don't worry. You'll find some premium White Sox tickets in your mailbox in the near future."

Bobby smiled and patted his friend on the shoulder. "That's mighty nice of you, pal."

"Yeah, well, I'm a giver," replied Carter.

"I'll catch you later," said Bobby, walking away.

"Later."

The black SUV slowed and eventually stopped along the curb while Carter pulled into the parking garage of his office building. Mick exited the vehicle and walked in the entrance far enough where he could keep an eye on where Carter parked.

When Carter stepped onto the elevator, Mick appeared and followed him inside.

Carter pushed the second floor button and looked at Mick. "Three please," requested Mick.

Carter pressed the button and leaned against the wall as the doors closed. He glanced at the bulky guy with the comb-over and thought about how much more he enjoyed his elevator ride with Carina and Alley. Then he noticed the bulge beneath the man's jacket. "You a cop?" Carter asked.

Startled, the man looked up. "Huh?"

"I asked if you were a cop. I noticed you're carrying," he said, pointing at the bulge.

Mick looked down at his side. "Oh, no. I'm not a cop. I'm in corporate security."

"I see," said Carter.

"You're very observant," said Mick. "Most people never notice."

"It's kind of my job."

"Oh really, what do you do?" Mick asked, as a bell rang and the doors opened.

"Private investigator," answered Carter.

"No kidding? My sister was just asking me yesterday if I knew anyone. She thinks her husband is running around on her. Do you have a card?"

Carter stopped and reached into his pocket while Mick held the doors open. "Sure. Here you go."

Mick accepted the card. "Thanks. I'll give this to her. Have a nice evening."

"Yeah, you too."

As soon as the doors closed, Mick pulled out his phone to call Mr. Bedford. However, his location in the elevator kept him from receiving a clear signal. Once he reached the outside evening air, he pulled out his phone again and walked toward the SUV where Roy waited.

Jasper Bedford answered right away. "Hello."

"Mr. Bedford, this is Mick."

"What do you have?"

"The guy Roy called you about is a private investigator. His name is Carter Mays."

"What was he doing in Tyler's condo?"

"I don't know, sir. I would guess he's looking for him too."

"Do you know who hired him?"

"No, sir. He did meet with a cop at a diner when he left Tyler's. We're not sure, but we think he may have given something to the cop; maybe an envelope."

"Find out everything you can about him. Follow him home, see where he lives, then go back to his office and find out who he's working for."

"Yes, sir. I'll let you know what we find."

Mick finished his conversation and got into the SUV, where he filled Roy in on what was going on. Then it was a matter of waiting for Carter's next move.

EIGHT

Carter pulled into the driveway and parked in front of the detached two-car garage positioned to the rear of his two-story Victorian style house. Stepping out of the truck, he stopped to grab the six pieces of wood molding he had purchased on the way home from his office. Entering through the back door, Booker greeted him with an enthusiastic welcome, circling Carter's feet as he maneuvered the eight-foot long pieces through the door, past the kitchen and into the living room that was under renovation.

A ten-by-ten piece of thick canvas covered the hardwood floor in front of the fireplace where the new molding was to be installed. A variety of tools including a chop saw, air compressor and nail gun lay scattered on the canvas. A folded eight-foot stepladder leaned against the wall.

Carter carefully placed the wood across two sawhorses and knelt down to pet his dog. "How you doing, boy?" Glancing up at the wall above the mantle, he admired the work he had completed so far. Two years had passed since he purchased the house and he was nearing the end of renovation. Soon he'd put it on the market and hopefully turn a nice profit, as he had on his previous two houses.

Moving into the kitchen, he opened the pantry, filled Booker's food bowl, and gave the dog fresh water. With Booker diving into his dinner, Carter opened the freezer and pulled out a box of mixed vegetables and some of the walleye he caught on last year's fishing trip to Lake Erie. As he prepared dinner, his mind drifted between the disappearance of Tyler Moore and Carina. Though he preferred to dwell on Carina, he kept coming back to the Moore case. It was Cindy Bedford's dad that really intrigued Carter. Who would allow themselves to be robbed of six million dollars without calling the police? The only answer to that question is someone who didn't want the police meddling in their business. It would have to be someone who had even more to lose if the police became involved.

With his fish baking in the oven and the vegetables cooking on the stove, Carter moved down the hall to his den and sat down at his computer to check his email.

He watched a funny video his brother forwarded to him and read an email from his folks in Phoenix, telling him how incredibly hot it was there.

Four years had passed since his father retired from the police force and moved to Arizona, and they're still talking about the weather. Carter chuckled and said out loud, "I told you it was going to be hot."

As he read through his emails, another message popped up in his inbox. An email from Bobby; the very reason Carter had checked his messages. Unfortunately, it did not contain any information concerning the fingerprints Carter had lifted, but rather an excuse as to why Bobby had not been able to get to them yet.

Apparently, Carter's former boss, Captain Tillman, put Bobby on some official urgent assignment as soon as he arrived to work, thus delaying getting the results Carter hoped to have before calling Cindy Bedford with his first night's update.

After checking the progress of his fish, Carter called Cindy as she had requested.

She answered on the first ring. "Hello."

"Hi Cindy, this is Carter."

"Yes, I know. What did you find out?"

"Well, not much yet. I just started this afternoon," he replied, hearing the high expectations in her voice.

"What do you mean, not much?"

"These things take time. Did you expect me to have found him already?"

"I expected some progress," she said with an unpleasant tone. "What did you do?"

"I went to his condo and searched it."

"And?"

"I was able to get some fingerprints."

"Whose fingerprints are they? Do you think it could be the people who are behind this?"

Carter was amazed by the girl's confidence that her fiancé was the victim in this whole thing. He wondered if he had made a mistake by taking the case. "I don't know who the fingerprints belong to yet. I'm waiting to hear."

"Is that all you have? Mystery fingerprints?"

Now Carter was definitely second guessing his acceptance of the case. He tried to remain calm and remember she was under stress and probably heartbroken. "I talked to some of his neighbors." The thought of Carina took some of the edge off the conversation.

"Did they have any useful information?"

"Nothing specific," answered Carter.

A loud, obvious sigh of disappointment followed.

"I do have a question for you," said Carter.

"What?" Cindy asked.

"Did Tyler like college football?"

"Football? What does that have to do with anything?"

"Trust me, it may help. Did he?"

"Yes, he does," answered Cindy. "I would appreciate it if you wouldn't speak of Tyler in the past tense, as if he was dead."

"I apologize. I meant nothing by it," assured Carter. "Who is his favorite team?"

"That would have to be Illinois. That's where he went."

"What about Notre Dame? Did he like them?"

"Mr. Mays, I really don't see why any of this matters."

"I'm just trying to get to know a little bit about your fiancé. It can be a big help."

Another sigh of frustration came through the phone. "He never mentioned Notre Dame," Cindy finally said. "Illinois was his favorite team, just like my dad."

"Your dad likes Illinois?"

"Yes. He and Tyler both graduated from Illinois. They even belonged to the same fraternity. Tyler often watched the game with Dad. If Tyler would have been a Notre Dame fan, Dad never would have hired him. My dad hates Notre Dame."

"Really?" Carter inquired. "Why does your dad hate them?"

"I don't know, Mr. Mays. He just does. Always has. Is this going anywhere? I mean, I would really like to know that I haven't wasted my money hiring you."

"Miss Bedford," began Carter, in a calm but firm tone. "You hired me to find your fiancé. I am trying to do that. But I am not going to justify or explain my methods of investigation to you. If you think you can get someone better suited for this job, then I will return your deposit, minus today's fee, and you can hire someone else. However, if you want me to continue, then please answer my questions without the hassle and attitude you've given me this evening."

Silence abounded and Carter took the opportunity to check on his dinner while Cindy contemplated her response. He could almost hear her boiling on the other end.

Finally, she surrendered. "Fine," came her snippy reply.

Slipping on an oven mitt, Carter removed his fish from the oven. "Good. I'm glad we're able to come to terms. I really am trying to help you."

"Okay," said Cindy, softening. "Is there anything else?"

"Not at the moment. I hope to have results from the fingerprints by tomorrow. I'll keep you updated."

After hanging up, Carter finished his preparations and sat down to enjoy his meal. He couldn't understand the whole Notre Dame thing. The conflicting viewpoints concerning something as seemingly irrelevant as Tyler Moore's favorite football team seemed peculiar enough to not dismiss it. Perhaps there were two different Tylers. On one hand, you have the Illinois graduate who shares the common ground with his boss and future father-in-law. On the other hand, you have a guy who casually and unguardedly discloses he loves Notre Dame Football, then appears uncomfortable and changes the subject.

When dinner ended and the dirty dishes were loaded into the dishwasher, Carter decided to spend some time on the fireplace molding.

While he measured, cut and nailed, Carter speculated on Tyler Moore and the mysterious Mr. Bedford. Exhausting a host of possibilities explaining the disappearance of Tyler, Carter switched his brain into exploring more pleasant thoughts of Carina. He contemplated calling for a moment, but it was getting late and he didn't know when would be too late to call her. Perhaps she had an early morning photo shoot tomorrow. He didn't want to start off on the wrong foot.

Growing too tired to operate a saw or nail gun, Carter called it a night and went to bed. Passing by the den, he stopped to check email one last time.

His eyes perked up when he saw a new message from Bobby with an attachment.

It turned out the fingerprints in Tyler's condo belonged to four different men, none of them being Tyler Moore. Each man identified by the prints had a criminal record of some type, ranging from assault to larceny to arson.

When he clicked on the attached photos, Carter immediately recognized two of the men. The first guy he recognized, Michael Hawthorn, was the stocky man Carter gave his business card to in the elevator in his office building. And then there was Roy Makowski, the chatty, pony-tailed guy from the elevator in Tyler Moore's building.

"I've got to start taking the stairs," Carter said to himself. Then thoughts of Carina popped into his mind. "Well, maybe not."

No doubt these were the so-called employees who worked for Mr. Bedford. Obviously, Mr. Bedford is looking for certain qualities in his employees other employers would shun, adding a whole new level of intrigue to Mr. Bedford.

Carter studied the faces and facts regarding all four men. Chances were good he may run across the other two before this case was resolved. At least now he would have some warning. Based on their records, Carter knew this was not just another case and things could get dangerous.

Checking all the locks and peeking out the window for any strange cars on the street, Carter made his way upstairs to his bedroom and shut the door, locking it. Booker settled down on the rug, as was his custom. After brushing his teeth and stripping down to his boxers, Carter placed his 9mm on the nightstand beside him. Being uncertain of what he was getting involved with left him feeling extremely cautious. Within four minutes, he was asleep.

As Jasper and Darleen Bedford prepared to go to bed, the phone rang. Darlene passed by it with her long flowing nightgown, leaving it for her husband to answer. "Hello."

"Mr. Bedford, this is Mick."

"What do you have?"

"We found out who hired the PI."

"Who?"

"Your daughter."

Immediately Jasper's hand moved up to the side of his head and began rubbing at his troubled temples.

"Mr. Bedford, you there?"

"Yes, Mick, I'm here. I heard you."

"We found a file she gave him with all kinds of information and a few pictures. There was also a check she had written."

"Crap," Jasper exhaled. "Anything we didn't know?"

"I snapped digital shots so we can compare notes."

"That's good, Mick. What about the guy?"

"We know where he lives. Roy Googled the guy and checked out his business website and some other sources. According to his site, he spent time in the Marines as an MP, he's ex-Chicago PD, has a bachelor's degree in criminology and started this agency about three years ago."

"Alright. That's all for now. You guys can go home."

"Thanks, Mr. Bedford."

Jasper dropped the phone on the bed. "Our daughter is trying to kill me."

Slipping under the sheets, Darlene looked at her husband. "Why do you say that?"

"She hired a private investigator to find Tyler."

Darlene quickly sat up in bed. "No."

"Yep. The guy was snooping around Tyler's condo today."

"What are you going to do?"

"I'm going to talk her into dropping it."

"What if she doesn't? You know how stubborn she can be."

"Then I guess I'll talk to this investigator and see if I can't persuade him to drop the case."

"And if he doesn't want to cooperate?" Darlene asked.

"I'm sure I can persuade him one way or another."

Jasper went to the bathroom to take some aspirin for his sudden headache. When he returned, Darlene suggested an idea.

"What if you let this guy keep looking?"

"What?" Jasper replied, pulling the sheet up over him.

"What if you don't interfere with this guy's investigation? He might be better equipped than the guys you have looking. He might lead you right to Tyler."

"I don't know. I'm not crazy about anyone, especially an ex-cop, snooping around. He might not find Tyler, but uncover something else by accident. I don't need that right now."

"Still, it's worth keeping in mind."

Jasper used the remote to turn off the light and tried to go to sleep. An hour later, he remained awake, still with a headache, and listening to his wife snore.

NINE

Tired and irritable, Jasper knocked on the door of his daughter's apartment. Russell and Dan flanked each side of him as he waited for the door to open.

Eventually, Cindy answered the door, wearing short, tight workout shorts and a sports bra. Beads of sweat adorned her tan, toned body. Dan stared for a moment before he noticed his boss' eyes burning through him, at which time he quickly looked away.

"You guys wait out here in the hall," commanded Jasper.

Cindy stepped to the side to let her father enter.

"For crying out loud, Cindy, put some clothes on before you answer the door."

With a frown she shot back, "What? I'm working out. This is what people wear when they work out."

"No, that's what people wear when they want to be noticed."

"Well, maybe I do want to be noticed," she snapped.

Jasper squelched any further comment. Cindy's modesty or lack thereof, was not the purpose of his visit. He had more important issues to discuss. "Let's sit down. I need to talk to you."

Cindy sat on the sofa, while her dad chose the chair directly across from her. "What's up?" Cindy asked.

"I understand you've hired a private investigator."

Cindy replied, "Yes, I have. How did you find out so fast?"

"Why would you do that?"

"To find Tyler," she answered, with a condescending attitude. "Why do you think?"

Ignoring the tone, Jasper said, "I told you that I would take care of it, didn't I?"

"Yes. But I thought it wouldn't hurt to have additional help."

"We don't need additional help. I have all my guys working on nothing but finding Tyler. You're wasting your money."

"I don't care about the money," said Cindy.

"Of course you don't. It's my money."

"Is that all you care about, the money?"

Jasper took a deep breath and tried to remain calm. "No. I'm telling you that you don't need this PI to find Tyler. We'll find him."

"What have you done to find him?"

"We're searching every avenue, sweetie. I promise you."

"Do you have any fingerprints?"

The question left Jasper momentarily speechless. "Fingerprints?"

"Yes, fingerprints. The investigator I hired already has fingerprints from Tyler's condo."

"Whose fingerprints?" Jasper asked.

Cindy hesitated. "He doesn't know yet, but he will today."

"What's he going to find out from fingerprints, that Tyler used to live there? That's brilliant."

"Maybe it will tell him who is behind this whole mess."

Jasper shook his head in disbelief. "You're so naïve. You honestly believe Tyler didn't screw us all over? You think this is some type of conspiracy?"

"Yes, I do. That's why I hired this guy, because you are so closed minded and convinced it's Tyler, you won't even explore any other possibilities."

"Unbelievable," Jasper exclaimed with half a laugh. "Tyler's bet on the dumb blonde really paid off well for him."

Immediately Jasper regretted his words and could see the hurt in his daughter's face. Tears welled up in her pained blue eyes. "Honey," began Jasper. "I'm sorry, I didn't mean that."

"Please leave," she said, trying not to cry.

"Sweetie?"

"I don't want you here," Cindy said, getting up and walking toward her bedroom. "You can let yourself out."

The door slammed and Jasper stood there, wishing he could rewind thirty seconds. He stared at the door and contemplated trying to smooth things out with her. Eventually, his head dropped and he released a long breath, as he decided to let it go for now.

When Jasper exited the apartment, Russell and Dan were waiting at the end of the hall. "Come on," he said, barely making eye contact.

"Where to?" Russell asked.

"We're going to go see the PI."

Carter unlocked the door to his office and took his seat behind the desk. His eyes immediately went to the bottom right desk drawer resting slightly open. It was only open a half of an inch, but it was a half-inch more than he would have left it. Carter had few quirky habits, but he was anal about closing drawers all the way. A characteristic he had since childhood. His dad used to intentionally leave a drawer barely open, knowing his son would stop whatever he was doing to go close it. Eventually, when he realized his dad was doing it just to mess with him, Carter decided to ignore it the next time. And in spite of the fact he knew his dad was messing with him, he couldn't resist getting up and closing the drawer.

Glancing around the room, he noticed a file cabinet drawer resting slightly open. Carter thought one drawer, maybe, but two drawers, never. Someone had been snooping around his office. He stood up and walked around, looking for anything out of place or missing. Examining the lock and door, Carter realized the perpetrators were very adept at picking locks.

After a thorough search, Carter determined nothing was missing. Whoever had been in his office was merely snooping and not there to steal anything. If he had to make a guess, Carter figured the two guys watching him yesterday were responsible. For a brief moment, he pondered reporting the break-in to the police.

However, he didn't see the benefit. Filing a report would eat into his day and be a waste of time, based on the fact nothing had been taken.

Sitting behind his desk, Carter switched on his computer.

He wondered if his after-hours visitors tried to get into his computer. The security he had set up made it highly unlikely they would have succeeded, but he reviewed the history to make certain. Everything looked okay for the most part, so he proceeded with the business of the day.

Using the information on Tyler Cindy provided, Carter surfed the Internet, searching for anything of relevance. In the past, Carter had some success in finding someone simply by Googling his or her name. However, this wasn't one of those times. First of all, there are far too many guys named Tyler Moore.

Thinking about the fingerprints he found last night, Carter found it alarming that none of the prints belonged to Tyler. Obviously, the place had been wiped down before Jasper Bedford's men arrived, indicating that perhaps something criminal had happened to Tyler, and the perpetrators didn't want to leave behind any clues.

The other and more probable possibility was that Tyler didn't want to be found.

The office door opened and Carter watched a distinguished man in his fifties, sporting a white goatee and expensive suit, enter his office. Two men followed behind. Carter recognized them as the other two owners of fingerprints left in Tyler Moore's condo: Bedford's men.

The man with the goatee offered a smile and extended his hand. "Carter Mays?"

Carter stood and shook the man's hand. "That's me."

"I'm Jasper Bedford, Cindy's father."

Not giving any indication he already knew that, Carter asked, "What can I do for you, Mr. Bedford?"

"May I sit down?" Jasper politely asked.

"Absolutely," Carter answered.

Jasper and Carter both sat in their respective seats while Russell and Dan remained standing. Carter barely made eye contact with them.

"Mr. Mays, I'm here to talk to you about Cindy and this loser boyfriend she asked you to locate."

"Boyfriend? I thought he was her fiancé."

"I stand corrected. However, it really doesn't matter at this point. He's gone."

"That's what she tells me," said Carter. "Do you have any idea where he might be?"

"No, I don't, and at this point I don't care. Tyler Moore has greatly hurt my daughter."

"So you're not looking for him?"

"She's better off without him."

"You didn't answer my question," said Carter.

Jasper's smile began to fade. "Excuse me?"

"I asked if you were looking for him and you didn't answer my question."

"Frankly, I don't see what finding him would accomplish."

"I thought you might want your money back."

Jasper's face tightened. "What money?"

Carter smiled. "Mr. Bedford, if someone stole millions of dollars from me, I know I would want to find them."

Jasper played dumb. "Millions of dollars? What are you talking about?"

"Cindy told me you believe Tyler stole over six million dollars from your business."

Jasper chuckled. "Mr. Mays, one thing you'll need to know about my daughter is that although her intentions are good, sometimes she gets her facts distorted."

Keeping his eyes honed in on Jasper's, Carter asked, "Are you telling me he didn't steal money from you?"

"Tyler was heavily involved in a couple of deals that could be very lucrative for the company. He was well-liked by the people we're trying to do business with, and having him suddenly disappear could jeopardize those deals, and cost me a significant amount of money. My distraught and often confused daughter came up with her own interpretation of those facts."

Carter leaned back in his chair and placed one leg on the desk. "Oh, I see. That makes sense."

"Do you have any children, Mr. Mays?"

"No, I don't."

"When you do, you will learn that no matter how old they get, they never really listen to what you tell them," Jasper joked.

"I thought it was odd someone would steal that amount of money and you not even call the police," said Carter, still studying his guest's eyes. "But then, I would have thought you'd call the police even if he didn't steal any money."

"I didn't see the need. Skipping out of a wedding isn't exactly a crime."

"True. But then again, you're talking about a guy who worked for you, and was hours away from being your son-in-law, just suddenly disappearing. I would think you'd be worried about him, as both an employer and a father-in-law."

"To be honest," said Jasper, "I had a hunch Tyler might be getting cold feet."

"Oh yeah, why?"

"He was acting different. Me, the guys he hung around with, we all noticed it." Jasper turned around toward his men behind him. "Isn't that right, guys?"

"Yep," said Dan.

"Oh by the way, forgive my manners," said Jasper. "These are two of my valued employees, Dan Yielding and Russell Hopkins."

Carter offered a subtle nod and hello. He already knew their names from the email Bobby sent him. He remembered arson was one of Dan Yielding's job skills. "What exactly is their role in your company?" Carter asked.

"Their roles?" Jasper repeated. "They serve as consultants."

"Mr. Bedford, I'm still not clear on the purpose of your visit," commented Carter.

Jasper leaned forward, resting his forearms on the desk. "Mr. Mays, I'd like you to drop the case."

"Why?"

"Tyler Moore has proven to be a great disappointment to me, my wife, and most of all, to our daughter. Right now, my daughter is heartbroke, disillusioned, and doesn't know what's best for her."

"And you do?"

"Absolutely. I'm able to look at this objectively. The further away he is, the better off she'll be."

"Here's the thing," began Carter. "Your daughter hired me to do a job. I accepted, and I don't believe it would be right for me to simply drop it based on her father's wishes."

"I respect that," said Jasper with a smile. "However, I feel so strongly about this, I'm prepared to pay you considerably more just to let it die."

"You're willing to pay me to drop your daughter's case?"

Jasper removed his checkbook and pen. "Yes, I am. How does two thousand sound?"

"I'm sorry, Mr. Bedford, I can't do that."

"You're right. How about five thousand?"

"This isn't about the money," insisted Carter.

"You're right, Mr. Mays. It's not about the money. The fact is, if you continue this investigation and find Tyler Moore, you're just going to drag out the hurt and inevitable truth that he doesn't care anything about her. I would rather Cindy be able to move on with her life and put this behind her."

"I'll admit that I don't know your daughter that well, but I have the impression even if I did drop her case, she'd hire someone else. Are you planning on paying off every PI in the city?"

Jasper contemplated Carter's analysis of his daughter.

"Okay, then, let me make you another proposition," Jasper said. "You remain on the case for another couple of days, but don't do anything. Then tell her you found him, and he wants nothing to do with her, or that he's gay living with some guy in Hawaii, or anything that will make her never want to see him again. I'll still pay you the five thousand, and you keep any money she's already paid you."

"That's unethical," said Carter.

"It's not if you look at the big picture and see you're actually doing her a favor," said Jasper. "Plus, you're getting a nice chunk of change."

"This may come as a surprise to you, Mr. Bedford, but all of my decisions aren't driven by money."

Jasper sat back in his seat, obviously becoming frustrated. "Mr. Mays, you need to work with me here. I'm trying to help."

"It seems more like you're trying to sabotage your daughter's effort to find the man she loves."

"I'm trying to do both," claimed Jasper, getting a little less friendly. "Tyler Moore is a lowlife and the last thing my daughter needs."

"If he's such a lowlife, why was he working for you?" Carter asked, humored by the irony of Jasper, who surrounded himself with ex-cons, referring to Tyler as a lowlife.

Taking a deep breath, Jasper answered, "Until recently, I didn't realize what kind of man he really was. Had I known, I would have definitely intervened sooner."

"Mr. Bedford, if you want to come back later today with Cindy, and she agrees she no longer wants me to investigate this matter, then I will happily refund all her money. However, until that happens, I'm obligated to continue."

Jasper looked down for a moment, cradling his head in his hand and rubbing at his temples. Finally, he looked up and glared at the uncooperative detective. "Mr. Mays, I think it's only prudent I warn you that Tyler Moore associated with some unsavory people, and if you go sticking your nose into their business, you may suffer greatly for it. I would hate to see that happen to you."

Not loving the threatening tone he was hearing, Carter leaned forward to address his guest.

Out of the corner of his eye, he noticed Dan placing a fresh cigarette in between his lips and was preparing to light up. "Please don't smoke in here," said Carter, firmly. "I wouldn't want you accidentally starting any fires."

Dan froze, with the lit lighter just inches from the cigarette. He looked at Carter and then glanced at his boss. The tension grew as everyone realized Carter may know more about them than they thought.

Jasper shook his head slightly and Dan put away the lighter, but continued to hold the cigarette between his lips as his annoyed eyes narrowed.

"As I started to say," continued Carter. "I think I'm starting to get a pretty good idea of exactly what kind of men Tyler ran with. However, I'm not easily intimidated."

"Not easily intimidated, huh? Mr. Mays, there have been a lot of macho men like yourself who ended up in some nasty and dangerous dilemmas. I hope you're prepared to live or die with your decision."

"I think we're done with this conversation," said Carter.

Jasper rose to his feet. "You've disappointed me, Mr. Mays."

Russell and Dan kept their eyes on their boss, ready to respond to any direction he gave them.

Carter sat up in his chair and watched for any sign something unpleasant was about to take place.

"That wasn't smart," said Jasper.

"Thanks for stopping by," said Carter.

After they left, Carter expelled a long sigh. What had he gotten mixed up in now? It was obvious that Jasper Bedford was not a typical businessman. How deep and how dangerous this situation could go was uncertain.

TEN

On the way to West Lake Properties & Development, Jasper contemplated how he was going to deal with Carter Mays.

On one hand, he could just let it play out and hope the detective didn't stumble upon any sensitive information. However, Mr. Mays' comment to Dan about starting a fire indicated that perhaps he had already uncovered some detrimental information. Another option was to eliminate Mays from the picture all together, something Jasper was slow to do.

That kind of action always carried a certain risk, although there had been a few times where the result had been worth it.

Jasper's concentration broke when his cell phone rang, a number he didn't recognize. "Hello?"

"Hello, Jasper."

Stunned by the voice, he checked the display on his phone again. It was a local area code. "Tyler?"

"I guess you've been looking for me?"

"Yeah, you could say that," replied Jasper, trying to keep his composure.

"I'm sorry things went down the way they did. I feel just terrible about Cindy."

"Cindy's fine," Jasper lied. "She's already over it."

"Really? Well, that's good then."

"Where are you, Tyler? We need to talk."

"Yeah, I figured you'd want to talk. That's why I called. It's not what you think."

"How do you know what I think?" Jasper asked.

"Well, I didn't show up for the wedding and then you discover some money is gone."

"Some money," said Jasper with a sarcastic snicker. "You took close to seven million."

"I can explain," he said.

"I can't wait to hear it. You want to meet me at the office or would you prefer the house?"

"Actually, neither one of those locations work for me. I was thinking somewhere more public."

"Public? If it's not what I think, then why the need for somewhere public?"

"I saw what you did to Billy, and he had nothing to do with any of this."

The fact that Tyler had knowledge of Billy agitated Jasper. Had he been right under their noses while they were running all over looking for him? "If you say it's not what I think, then you have no reason to worry."

"Just the same, we'll meet on my terms or not at all," insisted Tyler. "There's the library on Irwin Avenue. Meet me at four o'clock this afternoon on the second floor in the children's section. Come alone or don't bother. I know everyone who works for you, and if I see a familiar face other than yours, you'll never see or hear from me again."

Jasper flipped his phone closed.

"Was that Tyler?" Russell asked.

Jasper nodded his head as he stared off into the distance. "Yep, that was him."

"What did he say?"

"He said this whole thing is a misunderstanding and he wants to meet to explain."

"What's the plan?" Dan asked.

"He wants me to meet him at the library at four. Alone."

"That gives us some time to set something up," said Dan.

Jasper toward Dan. "Really? You think you can nab him?"

Dan nodded his head to confirm.

"That's interesting, because the whole time you clowns have been out looking for him, apparently he's been watching you. He knew what you did to Billy. But now you say you can set something up to catch him."

Neither Dan nor Russell said anything in their defense.

"No," said Jasper. "You guys are going to sit tight and wait a few blocks away. I'll go to the library alone. Once he's there, he shouldn't be hard to pick up. But I want to make sure we don't do anything to spook him ahead of time."

Considering that none of the numerous prints in Tyler Moore's condo belonged to Tyler, it seemed pretty clear to Carter that Tyler did not want to be found, or indeed there had been some foul play and someone wanted to cover their tracks.

After meeting Bedford and his so-called employees, Cindy's theory that someone had done something to Tyler seemed to be more of a possibility. If for some reason Bedford didn't approve of his soon-to-be son-in-law, perhaps he intervened and tried to make it look as if Tyler skipped town.

He called Cindy and invited himself over to talk. He wanted to know more about the relationship between her fiancé and her family. Carter also wanted to see what Cindy knew about her father. How would she feel about her father's visit to Carter's office?

He found it difficult to believe Cindy was oblivious to her father's suspicious behavior. In the brief time he had known of Jasper Bedford, Carter had developed serious reservations about the man's character. Could Cindy be that oblivious not to recognize the obvious, or was she just very good at playing dumb? Cindy answered the door wearing khaki shorts and a tank top.

Again, Carter couldn't help but notice the legs.

She invited him in and led him through the short entrance into the open space of her living room. "So did you learn anything from the fingerprints in Tyler's condo?"

WHEN LIES CRUMBLE   **59**

"I can tell you none of the prints belonged to Tyler."

She turned to look at Carter. "Who do they belong to?"

"Apparently, they belong to your father's employees who went there to look for him."

"Don't you find it odd there weren't any prints from Tyler?"

"Yes, I do."

"Why do you think that is? Foul play?"

"I'm not sure yet."

"Have a seat," she said.

They sat on the cream leather sofa.

"Would you like something to drink? I have coffee, tea, soda, or bottled water."

"No, thank you," replied Carter. "Nice place."

"Thank you," said Cindy.

"What do you do for a living?"

"I'm in advertising. Of course I'm off this week because I was supposed to be on my honeymoon."

Carter scanned the room, taking in the décor. "You must be doing quite well."

"My dad pays for this place," she said bluntly and unashamed. "So you told me on the phone you had more questions for me. Is there a reason you couldn't ask me over the phone?"

"No, but I wanted to come over for another reason, however we'll get to that in a moment."

The vagueness of his comment appeared to perplex Cindy, but she continued. "What do you want to know?"

"What kind of relationship did Tyler have with your family? Did they get along?"

"Absolutely," she answered. "My parents loved Tyler."

"And he liked them as well?"

"Definitely. Why?"

"Because your dad doesn't want me to find Tyler. He stopped by my office this morning and wanted me to drop the case."

Cindy sat up straight on the sofa. "My dad tried to get you to drop my case?"

Carter nodded. Cindy stood up and began pacing, her long tan legs taking her back and forth in front of the sofa. "I can't believe he would do that. He must have left here this morning and went directly to see you."

"Your father was here this morning?"

"Yes. He was trying to get me to fire you and let him take care of everything. We got into it and I walked out of the room and told him to let himself out."

"If your dad really liked Tyler the way you claim he did, why doesn't he want him found?"

"Because he thinks Tyler used me to get to his money."

Carter scratched at his scruffy face. "Yeah, about that, he said Tyler didn't steal any money. He said you misunderstood the situation."

"All I know is that my mom said he stole money from us," replied Cindy.

"What else did your mom tell you?"

"She said they found Tyler's car at the airport parking lot."

"When did she tell you that?"

"I think it was Sunday."

"Why didn't you tell me that when you came to see me?" Carter asked, slightly annoyed.

Cindy shrugged her shoulders. "I guess I forgot."

"You remembered to tell me he was in the Boy Scouts, but not a key piece of information like that? Did you not include that because it makes it look like Tyler left on his own?"

"No, that's not it. By the time I came to see you, my dad's men already checked out everything there. I didn't think it would be a productive use of your time for you to explore where they had already been."

"That's not for you to decide. You're supposed to give me all the information you have and let me take it from there."

Cindy held her eyes closed as she apologized. "Alright, I'm sorry. I should have told you."

"What prompted them to look at the airport?"

"It was a company car. They all have GPS."

"Is the car at the airport or did your dad's employees get it?"

"I don't know for sure, but I think they probably got it."

Carter shook his head, frustrated by being kept in the dark. "Are there any other key pieces of information you haven't shared with me?"

"No, I swear," promised Cindy, regret clear in her sad blue eyes. "I'm sorry."

"Okay, forget it. Let's move on."

Cindy sat back down while Carter contemplated the best way to ask his next question. Finally, he spoke. "If your dad were to find Tyler, do you think he would try to harm him?"

"Harm him? You mean like beat him up or something?"

"Something more serious," replied Carter.

"Why would you ask me that?"

"It seems only natural that a father would be tempted to take revenge on anyone who hurt his little girl."

"Yeah, maybe, but you make it sound so ominous, like my dad might do something criminal."

"And you don't think that's a possibility?" Carter fished.

"No," Cindy answered adamantly. "My dad's a stable, educated, and successful businessman. Plus, he's considerably older than Tyler. Nothing against my dad, but I don't think he's that much of a threat. Sometimes he comes off as domineering, but at the end of the day, he's still just a middle-aged business man."

The longer he listened to Cindy speak, the more Carter began to believe this girl was truly in the dark. If she was playing dumb, she deserved an Academy Award. Carter was now faced with whether or not he should try to open Cindy's eyes to the kind of man he believed Jasper Bedford to be, or to let it go for now. Any accusations toward her father might end in losing her cooperation and possibly even the case. So for the moment, he decided to drop it. He could always bring it up later.

"Do you know at which airport parking lot they found Tyler's car?" Carter asked.

"No. I could ask my dad, though."

"That's okay," replied Carter, wanting to keep Mr. Bedford as far removed from the investigation as possible. "When was the last time Tyler was here?"

"You mean, here, in my apartment?"

Carter nodded.

"He was here the Thursday before our wedding."

"Have you cleaned since then?"

"I don't clean. I have a woman who comes every Wednesday," answered Cindy.

Of course you do, thought Carter. No doubt Daddy Bedford pays for that, too. "May I see your bathroom?"

Cindy looked offended. "Do you always ask people if they recently cleaned before using their bathroom?"

"I don't need to use your bathroom," clarified Carter. "I asked to see it."

Cindy's expression transitioned from offended to confused. Nevertheless, she led Carter down the hall and pointed him to the first door on the right.

Carrying a small bag with him, Carter pulled out a pair of latex gloves and lifted the toilet seat.

"What are you doing?" Cindy asked, firmly.

"I'm checking for fingerprints."

"Why?"

He stopped what he was doing long enough to explain. "Since I didn't find any of Tyler's prints at his place, I thought I'd try here. If he used the bathroom, chances are good he lifted the lid, something you would never do. And unless you have a lot male visitors using your bathroom, any prints I may find should belong to Tyler."

"That's clever."

"Thanks," said Carter nonchalantly as he dusted for prints.

"But why do you need Tyler's prints? You already know who he is."

"It's just helpful to have as much information as possible."

With Cindy watching, Carter lifted a solid print from the seat.

"Wow, that's pretty cool how you do that. I've never seen that done before."

"It's the small details that usually break open a case," he replied as he put his stuff away.

Cindy backed out of the door to let Carter pass and then followed him to the front door. "Is that all you need?"

"That'll do for now. I'll keep you posted on any developments," promised Carter as he left.

Jasper entered the library at 3:53 p.m. and went up to the second floor where the children's section ran along the entire length of the south wall.

Huge slightly tinted windows allowed for natural light. Walking among the small children accompanied by young moms, Jasper browsed the shelves trying not to look as awkward as he felt. His cell phone rang, drawing looks from twin girls sitting cross-legged in the orange padded chairs. He didn't recognize the number on the display. He answered and walked a few steps away for privacy. "Hello?"

"You're early," said the familiar voice.

"Does that surprise you?" Jasper asked. "You know I tend to be early everywhere I go."

"No, it doesn't surprise me."

Jasper glanced around the expanse of the second floor. "So where are you, Tyler?"

"I'm close. Did you come alone?"

Looking out the window at the street below, Jasper answered, "You ought to know. You're watching me, aren't you?"

"You didn't answer my question."

"Yes, I came alone," he said. "Are you going to be man enough to meet me face to face, or are we going to play phone games all evening?"

"We'll meet. I'm just being careful," said Tyler.

"Are you afraid of me, Tyler?"

"Absolutely. I know what kind of man you really are."

Jasper spoke low and calm. "Oh you do, do you? What kind of man do you think I am?"

"You're a very dangerous man."

A frustrated snicker escaped Jasper's throat. "Dangerous? Where would you get a goofy notion like that?"

"I'm not your naïve little daughter," said Tyler. "I know exactly what kind of man you are."

Scanning the building across the street, Jasper desperately hoped to catch a glimpse of Tyler. "Oh, now I think you've misjudged me."

"No, I don't think so. And all those hidden accounts you thought I didn't know about confirm what I'm talking about."

"You mean those accounts you hacked into and stole from me?" Jasper said, feeling frustrated and vulnerable. "Why don't you cut this crap and come talk to me face to face?"

"On the third floor, along the east wall, there's a young girl sitting at one of the computer desks. She has dark hair, black shorts, and a red t-shirt. Go find her. Her name is Elizabeth."

"What?" Jasper snapped. "Are you going to come talk to me or not?"

"I am," assured Tyler. "I just had to make sure you didn't bring anyone with you."

Jasper let off a string of choice words which drew disapproving stares from some of the moms who heard him. He nodded a half-hearted apology at them before walking away from the children's section. "Listen, Tyler, I don't appreciate you making me jump through hoops."

"I'm not trying to antagonize you, Jasper. But quite frankly, you scare me, and this is the way I feel comfortable in meeting you. If you want, we can forget the whole thing and you'll never hear from me again."

Jasper paused and bit at his lower lip. "Alright. What am I supposed to do when I find this girl?"

"Tell her who you are. She has something for you that will help clear this up. Once you've had the chance to look over it, we can talk."

Tyler hung up, further aggravating Jasper. He smacked his phone closed and took off for the staircase.

Once he reached the third floor, Jasper walked toward the east side of the library. Off to the right, staring at a monitor with her chin cradled in her hand, sat a young girl, about fifteen, who fit Tyler's description. She appeared bored, waiting for something.

Jasper slowed his pace and tried to calm down. The last thing he wanted was to scare this kid.

She noticed Jasper approaching and perked up.

"Hello," said Jasper, smiling. "Are you Elizabeth?"

"Yes," she answered shyly.

"I'm Jasper. Do you have something for me?"

The young girl smiled and started to stand up. The girl's eyes grew wide and frightened, prompting Jasper to turn around to see four men appear from behind a row of shelves and rapidly approach Jasper.

As soon as Jasper saw the badges hanging around their necks, he knew he'd been royally screwed. "Guys," he pleaded, "this isn't what it looks like."

"It never is," said one of the officers.

The man who was standing slightly in front of the others and obviously in charge, removed a pair of handcuffs from somewhere behind his back and addressed Jasper. "Chicago PD. Sir, you're under arrest for illegal contact with a minor and sexual importuning."

Looking scared and embarrassed, the girl began bawling. One of the officers sought to calm her.

"This is a huge misunderstanding," claimed Jasper. "I don't even know this girl."

"Is that why you called her by name?"

Jasper started to respond, but knew it was pointless. Tyler set him up beautifully and he walked right into it. One more reason he was going to really enjoy getting his hands on Tyler. Now Jasper was motivated more than ever to find him.

"Sir, please turn around and place your hands behind you," requested the lead officer.

Jasper did as he was told and felt the cold metal clamp down on his wrists. He looked at the young girl who was still sobbing uncontrollably. "Miss, tell them you don't know me."

"Don't talk to her," commanded the policeman.

"Listen to her. She'll tell you that we don't know each other."

As the policeman began reading Jasper his rights, one of the officers led the young girl away.

Jasper grew more enraged at his own blind stupidity and began to swear.

When the man finished delivering the speech he had recited so many times, he asked Jasper, "Sir, do you understand these rights as I have explained them to you?"

Jasper glared at the man and replied, "Screw you."

Unfazed by the hostile response, the officer said, "I'll take that as a yes."

Led through the library in cuffs, Jasper avoided eye contact with the host of people staring. As they rounded the corner, an angry man charged them.

Jasper only noticed the man's presence about a half second before he felt the force of the man's fist connect with his cheek.

Two of the officers lunged at the enraged man and pinned him against the wall.

Fighting to get another swing at Jasper, the man yelled, "You sick, twisted pervert. What do you think you were going to do to my daughter? My god, she's fourteen years old."

As the police subdued the girl's dad, Jasper saw the young girl in the clutches of her weeping mother.

Surely, she could tell them this was all a mistake. With his head throbbing from the punch he took, he called out to her. "Elizabeth, tell them. Tell them you don't know me. Tell them this is a mistake."

The mother stepped in and blocked her daughter from Jasper's line of site and began screaming at him. "Don't you talk to my daughter. Don't you ever talk to her again."

"I'll kill you, you sick bastard," yelled the struggling dad from beneath the pile of bodies holding him down.

A crowd of library patrons began shouting names at Jasper, the man they understood tried to meet up with a girl forty years younger, and Jasper shot back with his own choice obscenities.

The lead officer grabbed Jasper by the arm and steered him away from the volatile scene. "Shut your mouth and move," ordered the policeman.

The street noise was considerably quieter than inside the library. Jasper scanned up and down the street, to see if perhaps Tyler was nearby, smirking as he watched the show he had so cleverly produced. There was no sign of the coward.

Inside the back of the unmarked cruiser, Jasper sat uncomfortably with his wrists bound behind him and his head bearing the pain of a father's revenge. All he could think about was how incredibly stupid he had been to allow this. It was mind boggling to him Tyler Moore had played him so easily, not once, but now twice. How had this happened? Jasper leaned forward and pressed his head against the metal screen barrier that separated him from the front seat. He had always been so careful. For years he'd managed a successful operation, undetected by anyone. Never an investigation. Never any questions about his business dealings. He had been smart every step of the way, never allowing himself to get so greedy or so emotional that it clouded his judgment. Now everything was in jeopardy.

He glanced out the window and saw the girl's dad being led out of the building by the two exhausted officers. One talked on his radio while the other held onto the angry, hurting, and crying man. Following behind was the girl Tyler used as bait, still at her mother's side. The whole family was a sobbing mess. For the moment, Jasper put himself in the father's position. If that had been Cindy, no doubt Jasper would have reacted the same way.

Tyler orchestrated the whole thing with perfection. He set up the scenario and everyone fell for it. Jasper hoped this would give Tyler a false sense of security, because it was far from over.

ELEVEN

Jasper Bedford sat alone in a holding room at the police station. He stared at his reflection in the large wall mirror, confident people on the other side stared back at him, discussing his guilt. How ironic for him to serve time for something he didn't do after years of running his operation completely unnoticed. Jasper shook off the notion he could actually be found guilty. It looked bad on the surface, and would be extremely embarrassing for a while, but surely this wasn't going to stick. How could anyone believe he would be interested in some fourteen-year-old girl?

Two men entered the room, both wearing stern expressions on their faces. The first man was in his early fifties, carrying about thirty extra pounds around the middle, a light colored mustache and very little hair left on his oblong head. He introduced himself as Officer Patrillo. The second man, the lead officer at the arrest, was leaner, younger, probably late thirties. His boyish round face and short, dark hair combed neatly to the side made him look more like an accountant than a cop. His name was Officer Royce. Patrillo sat in the one folding chairs across the small table from Jasper, while Royce leaned against the wall.

"Mr. Bedford," began Patrillo, "Officer Royce tells me you claim this is all a misunderstanding. I'd like to hear your side of the story."

"Where's my lawyer?" Jasper asked.

"He's on his way," replied Patrillo. "I just thought you might want to go ahead and clear the air."

"Not until my attorney gets here," insisted Jasper.

"If this is all a misunderstanding, why do you need a lawyer?"

"I've got nothing to talk about right now."

Patrillo looked up at Royce, who shrugged.

"I guess he's got nothing to say," said Patrillo.

"I guess not," replied Royce.

Patrillo stood and took two steps toward the door, then stopped. "Oh yeah," he said. "I almost forgot to tell you."

"What?" Jasper asked with little interest.

"I just got a call from my men who are at your house right now."

Jasper's eyes quickly made direct contact with Patrillo's. "My house? Why are they in my house?"

"Based on today's events, the judge was nice enough to issue a search warrant for your home and office."

Jasper felt the color vanish from his face, as Patrillo continued.

"Anyway, they're looking around when lo and behold, what do you think they found?"

Nervous, but fighting to hide any observable traits of fear, Jasper shrugged his shoulders. "I don't know. What?"

"They found your laptop."

"My laptop?" Jasper repeated, confused. "I don't have a laptop at home."

"Really? That's funny, because they found it in your office, hidden in the back of a cabinet under your wet bar. And what's really interesting is all the pictures they found on it; pictures of very young girls doing very inappropriate things."

"You thought you were being smart, huh?" Royce said. "You thought if you had a computer designated to your secret Internet activities, nobody would ever find out what you're doing."

Patrillo leaned over, resting his hands on the table. "Yeah, the desktop PC in your office looks clean. At first glance, someone might believe this is a big misunderstanding. But my guys are good, and once they found that laptop, the truth got a lot clearer."

"I'm telling you, I don't own a laptop," said Jasper, getting hostile. "I swear this whole thing is a mistake."

"Oh come on, Mr. Bedford," said Royce. "We found a laptop hidden in your home office, one with an email trail and a chat room history, then you show up today to meet the same girl you've been chatting with online and you're going to have the audacity to tell me this is just a misunderstanding?"

"It's a setup. I've never even been in a chat room."

"A set up?" Patrillo repeated with a snicker.

Jasper realized they provoked him into a conversation without a lawyer. He sat back in his chair, folded his arms across his chest, and looked away. "I want my attorney here."

The two officers looked at each other. Royce offered a satisfied grin.

"Alright," said Patrillo. "We can continue this when your attorney gets here. But with the evidence we have right now, you better have a really good one."

When the door closed, Jasper wanted to pick up his chair and fling it into the mirror. The situation was beginning to look dire. He couldn't understand why Tyler had gone to the trouble to set him up. He already stole a large sum of money. Why not just disappear to enjoy the new wealth? The whole thing seemed vindictive and personal, which dumbfounded Jasper. He and Tyler had a great relationship during the last three years, right up until the day of the wedding. Jasper had treated him with respect, and even grown to genuinely love the young man. Now it seemed Tyler was going out of his way to bury him. The only explanation he could fathom is that Tyler figured this was the only way he could get away with the money and not spend the rest of his life hiding. Never had Jasper felt so betrayed.

Jasper caught himself and quickly shut off any emotion toward Tyler except for anger. Anger would be his focus, what fueled his drive to find Tyler and retaliate.

The door opened and a very large uniformed officer appeared. He escorted Jasper to a small conference room with a table and two chairs. Dylan Fitch stood in the middle of the room, waiting to meet with his client.

A Yale grad, Dylan had represented Jasper for nearly twenty years now. He was the senior partner and majority owner of the firm Fitch, Gladstone, and Baker. His custom made suit and designer eyewear reflected his polished, expensive taste. Dylan enjoyed the finer things in life and pursued them with a vengeance. He collected practically every toy a man could want including a Porsche, Harley motorcycle, Hummer, a mammoth houseboat on Lake Michigan, and at least one of every cool electronic gadget available. Just five years younger than Jasper, Dylan had never married. His philosophy being there were far too many beautiful women out there to settle for just one.

Jasper entered the room and the officer closed the door to give the men privacy.

Dylan approached Jasper and extended his hand. "I got here as soon as I could. Do you want to sit down?"

Jasper nodded and took a seat.

Dylan moved to the other side of the table and opened his briefcase as he sat.

"Okay, here's what I know so far," said Dylan. "They've charged you with gross sexual imposition and attempted sexual contact with a minor. As I understand it, more charges are pending based on what they found on your computer."

"It's not my computer," said Jasper.

Dylan arched his eyebrows. "It's not yours?"

"No," said Jasper.

"If it's not yours, Jasper, then whose is it? It was in your office, your home. Are you telling me Darlene is into young girls?"

Jasper wanted to slug Dylan for such a stupid comment. "I've been set up. The whole thing is a set up."

"Who's setting you up?" Dylan asked.

"Tyler Moore," replied Jasper.

"Tyler?" Dylan repeated. "What makes you think Tyler is setting you up?"

"He's the one who told me to talk to the girl in the library."

"What? You talked with him? When? I thought he had disappeared."

"He had, but he called me this morning and said he wanted to meet, to sort things out."

"Did you tell the police that?"

"No, and I'm not planning to, either," answered Jasper. "If they know about Tyler, then it's going to lead to a whole bunch of questions. They're going to want to know why he disappeared."

"Why did he disappear?" Dylan asked.

Jasper stared at his lawyer for a moment. "Tate didn't tell you?"

Dylan shook his head and leaned forward to hear.

"Tyler stole money from me and the company. That's why I'd rather not even mention Tyler's name. I can't very well tell them he stole from me, because then they'll start focusing on my finances, and you know I can't afford for that to happen."

"Why not? West Lake is a legitimate company with legitimate assets. It's completely separate from the other stuff."

"He didn't steal from just West Lake. The majority was from the other stuff. West Lake doesn't have that kind of cash."

"What?" Dylan exclaimed. "I didn't know he knew about the other stuff."

"He didn't, or least he wasn't supposed to know."

"Well that just made things more complicated. How much did he steal?"

"Close to seven million," replied Jasper.

Dylan let out a long whistle.

"Wow, that's a big chunk of change. I bet you spent every waking moment trying to find him."

Jasper pointed his finger directly into Dylan's face.

"You have to get me out of here. I hired you to keep me out of trouble, and I've made it very easy for you over the years because I've been smart and avoided it. Now is when you start earning all the money I pay you."

"It's not going to be easy," warned Dylan. "The courts like to make an example out of people who face the charges you're facing."

"How soon can you get me out of this hole?"

"The judge is scheduled to set bail first thing in the morning," said Dylan.

"In the morning?" Jasper repeated, not thrilled with the thought of a night in jail.

Dylan held out his hands. "That's the best we can do right now. And I'd bet my practice the judge is going to set a very high bail to try to keep you in here."

"I can't stay in here. You've got to get me out. Call Tate and have him ready to pay my bail as soon as possible. You also need tell Russell to lay low for a while. Tell him to keep someone on the investigator, but don't do anything else."

"What?"

"It's best if you don't know the details. Just do it."

Dylan nodded in agreement and began to pack up his stuff. "Do you want me to call Darlene for you?"

Jasper wasn't keen on the idea of his good-looking, womanizing attorney having any contact with Darlene. He had noticed the flirtatious way they interacted at social gatherings in the past, and quite frankly, he didn't trust either of them. "No, I don't," he said adamantly.

Dylan tapped on the door and the huge guard opened the door. Dylan said goodbye and Jasper walked with the guard back to his holding cell.

TWELVE

Carter pulled up outside the entrance of the airport parking lot. It was the fourth one he visited that day and he hoped that by some stroke of luck, the attendant would remember seeing Tyler Moore last weekend. He turned on his truck's flashers and walked up to the tiny structure that housed the attendant.

A young guy, not much older than twenty manned the booth and greeted Carter with a curious look. "Can I help you?"

"Hi," said Carter with a disarming smile. "I hope so."

The guy's gaze moved over to Carter's truck and then back to Carter. "You broke down or something?"

"Oh, no, nothing like that. I just wanted to ask you a question." Carter reached into his pocket and pulled out a picture of Tyler. "Do you remember seeing this guy over the weekend?"

The kid glanced at the picture and shook his head. "I didn't work this weekend. But hey, you might check with Buddy."

"Who's Buddy?"

"He's a shuttle driver," replied the kid, pointing across the parking lot. "That's him. I'm pretty sure he worked last weekend."

Carter thanked the guy and walked across the blacktop, trying to anticipate where the shuttle was going and cut Buddy off before he could exit the lot.

Four aisles over, Carter stopped and waited while he watched Buddy, at the far end of the aisle, help a woman transfer her bags from the shuttle to her car. A moment later the shuttle approached and eventually stopped in front of Carter.

The door opened up and Carter stepped onto the empty shuttle. "Are you Buddy?" Carter asked.

"Yep, that's me," answered the older gentleman. "Who are you?"

"My name is Carter Mays. I'm a private investigator."

"What do you want?" Buddy asked, nervously stroking his thick mustache.

Carter showed the driver Tyler's picture. "Have you ever seen this guy?"

Buddy removed a pair of reading glasses from his shirt pocket and slipped them on.

He tilted his head back to study the picture. "Yeah, I saw this guy. Last Saturday. I remember, because it was the end of my shift. As a matter of fact, I worked two hours over that day covering for a guy who was late."

"What do you remember about him?"

"It was my last run of the day. I saw him pull in and park all the way in the very back. I don't know why he wanted to park so far away. There were a lot of closer spaces. Anyway, I went to pick him up. But he said he wasn't ready to go just then and that he'd get the next one. I told him it could be twenty minutes before another shuttle came. But he said he didn't care. So I went on and parked the shuttle and got ready to leave."

"Can you tell me the next driver that picked him up?"

"That's just it. The next driver didn't pick him up."

"What do you mean?"

"After I clocked out, I hung around a while and shot the bull with Wanda who was working the booth. I noticed Eddie come in. Eddie was the next driver to come in after me. Anyway, he was dropping folks off and cruising around the lot when I saw him stop for that fella you're looking for. But I'm pretty sure the guy passed up that ride, too. He just didn't seem in much of a hurry. I figured he must have had a later flight."

"Do you know if he got on the next one or not?"

"I didn't hang around much longer. I guess he got a ride."

"About what time of day was that?"

"I'd say five-thirty or six."

Carter thanked the man and stepped off the shuttle. After Buddy drove away, Carter stood in the middle of the vast parking lot and looked around. He noticed four security cameras mounted on light poles across the parking lot.

Walking back to the booth where he started, Carter once again approached the young man working the window.

The guy looked up from his hotrod magazine.

"Hey," said Carter, smiling. "It's me again."

The guy set his magazine aside. "Yeah?"

"I'm sorry, what was your name?"

"My name is Sid," answered the young man.

"It's nice to meet you, Sid."

The guy nodded, but said nothing more.

"Sid, I was wondering if you had access to the video these security cameras capture."

"We keep everything from the current month in here. After that, it goes down to our main office where it's stored for one year."

"Cool," replied Carter. "Is there any way that I could take a look at last Saturday's footage?"

"Oh, I don't know, man. I really don't know if I'm supposed to let anyone see that. I'm pretty sure they don't want me to let anyone who isn't an employee inside the booth."

"What if I gave you thirty bucks?"

"Fifty," Sid, quickly countered.

Carter paused a moment, to make Sid believe fifty was the absolute most he could get. Finally he said, "Alright, fifty."

Carter pulled out two twenties and a ten and handed it to Sid, who waved him inside the small booth.

Stepping inside the ten by twelve building, Sid led Carter to a small monitor resting on top of a counter. Below the counter, Sid searched through a short, two-drawer file cabinet and retrieved a couple of disks. Soon, Carter was viewing last Saturday's history. Fast-forwarding through the morning and early afternoon, Carter finally arrived at the point where Tyler Moore entered the parking lot. The camera captured the image of Tyler driving to the furthest point in the parking lot and backing in the space. And, as Buddy had described, the video showed Tyler passing up two chances to take the shuttle.

Shortly after the second shuttle drove away, Carter watched as Tyler exited the car with no luggage and in one swift display of athleticism, scaled the fence and walked out of camera range.

"Huh," said Sid, watching the video over Carter's shoulder. "That's weird. Why would he do that?"

"I don't know," answered Carter rewinding the action for another viewing.

Carter thanked Sid for his help and exited the booth.

"No problem, man," said Sid. "Thanks for the cash."

As he headed back to his office, Carter contemplated why Tyler Moore would drive to the airport parking, leave the car and walk away. More than likely he knew the company car had GPS and they could track him. Probably wanted to send his pursuers off on a wild goose chase. But where did he go when he jumped the fence? Maybe he had another car waiting or left town by train or bus. Perhaps he hadn't left town at all. The one thing that did seem evident, Tyler Moore was acting on his own and not being forced into something as Cindy suspected.

When he arrived at his office, Carter did a quick scan to see if he had any uninvited visitors again. He had rigged various spots in his office that if disturbed, would reveal intruders. Everything appeared undisturbed.

Sitting down at his computer, Carter logged on to check his email. As he had hoped, there was a new email from Bobby regarding the print he lifted from Cindy's apartment. When he opened the attachment, he was surprised by what he saw. The print came back as belonging to someone named Steven Conway, only Steven Conway looked exactly like Tyler Moore. The file consisted of only one misdemeanor possession charge for marijuana when Conway was eighteen. Without the drug charge, there would be no fingerprint record at all. The file listed South Bend, Indiana as the last known address. That explained the Notre Dame connection Alley and Carina had mentioned.

"Ah, Carina," muttered Carter. A smile came across his face as he realized he hadn't called her like he planned. He contemplated calling her at that moment, but decided against it. He preferred to wait until he was home and could focus on nothing else but talking to her. For the moment, he had more questions that needed answers. He printed off the email and put it in the case file.

THIRTEEN

During his drive home, Carter called Cindy. He wasn't sure how she would take the news her fiancé used a bogus identity during their entire relationship. This revelation might kill her desire to find him, which would make her dad happy.

He tried her cell phone, but didn't get an answer. Then he tried unsuccessfully to get her at home. He left a brief message both times, so she would know he called.

Thoughts of Carina entered his mind again and Carter decided he couldn't wait any longer to call her. Besides, traffic was backed up to a crawl and it didn't appear he'd be getting home anytime soon.

"Hello," came that sweet, sultry voice he remembered from his first meeting with her on the elevator.

"Hi, Carina?"

"Yes?"

"This is Carter Mays."

"Hi Carter Mays," she said. "Nice to hear from you so soon."

"Do you consider this to be soon?"

"Not too soon," she said. "Is this a business or pleasure call?"

"Pleasure. I've been thinking about how much I'd like to take you to dinner."

"That sounds nice. I'd like that."

"Is there sometime toward the end of this week..."

Another call interrupted Carter's train of thought. He glanced at the display and saw it was Cindy. "Carina, I'm sorry," he said.

"I'm getting a business call. Would you mind if I call you later?"

"Not at all," she said. "Business is business."

"Thanks, I'll call you tonight."

Carina said goodbye and Carter switched over to receive the other call. "This is Carter."

"Hello, Carter. This is Cindy. I'm sorry I didn't get your call before."

Carter sensed something was wrong. Cindy's voice was weak and cracking as she spoke. "Is everything okay, Cindy? You sound upset."

"I am upset," she replied.

"What's wrong?"

"It's too embarrassing to talk about. It's my dad."

"Your dad? What happened?"

"He's been arrested."

Immediately Carter speculated why Jasper Bedford had been arrested. Had Cindy finally seen the truth and now felt completely humiliated she hadn't seen it before?

"Arrested for what?" Carter inquired.

"He..." Cindy paused while her emotions overcame her.

All Carter could hear was sniffing and crying noises. He waited patiently while she regained her composure.

"He was arrested for trying to meet with a fourteen-year-old girl for sex."

Wow, Carter thought. Hadn't seen that coming. There was a list of criminal offenses he would have guessed, but not that one. A successful man with a daughter left at the altar, who was now dedicating all his time to finding the guy who abandoned her. The timing seemed odd. But then again, it seemed every day that Carter heard on the news that some middle-aged guy was trying to meet with some underage girl who turned out to be the police.

He couldn't understand the mentality of these men. Surely they heard of the same countless arrests that had taken place over the years. Did they not wonder if they were being set up for the same fate? Or are these men so driven by their lust they throw every reasonable consideration out the window for the chance to be with some young girl?

"This is so humiliating," added Cindy.

"Are you alone right now?" Carter asked.

Still sniffing, Cindy answered, "Yes. Why?"

"I hate for you to be alone when you're obviously upset. Where's your mom?"

"She's at home, probably getting drunk. As a matter of fact, that's what I should be doing."

"Cindy, I really don't think getting plastered is going to help."

"It won't hurt."

"I don't know about that," replied Carter. "People make rash decisions when they mix a stressful situation with excess alcohol."

"You're sounding kind of preachy, Carter. I didn't figure you for the preachy type."

"Look, I'm not too far from your apartment. Why don't I stop by and we can talk?"

"Have you found out anything about Tyler?" Cindy asked.

Carter hated the thought of sharing his new revelation about Tyler's bogus identity with Cindy in her fragile state. He might try to avoid that until a little later. Another bombshell may put her over the edge. "I'm looking into some things. I don't have anything solid yet."

"Nothing?" Cindy said, not hiding her frustration.

"If it's okay, I'm coming over."

"Feel free to pick up some booze on the way over. I'm not sure I have enough."

"Sit tight and stay away from the liquor," said Carter. "I'll be there within a half hour."

When the traffic finally began moving again, Carter took the next exit in order to head back downtown to Cindy's. He called Carina as he drove to finalize their date plans. He would pick her up Saturday evening at six-thirty for dinner.

The closest parking space to Cindy's building was a block and a half away. Carter parked and walked to the building entrance. Out of the corner of his eye, he noticed a vehicle slowly pass by with two men inside. The driver sported a long ponytail draping down below his fedora hat. It was the chatty guy from the elevator.

Keeping his eyes forward, Carter did not show any indication he spotted Bedford's men. He did wonder how long they'd been following him, and made a mental note to start watching his back closer.

Not knowing their intentions left him feeling uneasy. Were they simply watching him or planning something? For now they just drove by, no doubt to circle the block and find a place to park within view of the main entrance. Cindy answered the door with a half empty wine glass in her hand.

Carter's eyes moved down to the glass and then back up to Cindy's red, watery eyes. "Is that your first glass I hope?"

"Nope," replied Cindy. "It's my fourth."

"I told you to stay away from the liquor," said Carter as she let him in.

"And I told you to pick up some booze on the way over," Cindy shot back. "I guess neither of us is good at taking direction. Besides, who are you, my dad?"

Carter looked at her and shook his head.

"Oh yeah," continued Cindy. "If you were my dad, you'd be down at the junior high looking for a date," she said in disgust.

Walking away from Carter, Cindy plopped down on the sofa and curled her feet up beside her hips. The short shorts she wore rode up to reveal the entire length of her shapely left leg.

Carter's eyes instinctively fixated on the fleshy display, before forcing himself to look elsewhere. It was extremely brief, but he thought she might have caught him looking nonetheless.

"So have you talked with your dad?" Carter asked as he sat on the opposite end of the sofa.

She snickered. "Have I talked with my dad? I've got nothing to say to him. I was already mad over his interfering in my business with you. Now I find out he's a pervert. No, I haven't talked with him and I'm not going to."

"Maybe you should hear his side before you make snap judgments."

Cindy stared at Carter, wrinkling her brow. "I got the sense from you earlier that you didn't particularly like my dad. Now you're defending him."

"I'm not defending him. I just think you need to hear his side of the story before you write him off."

"They busted him in the library talking with a fourteen-year-old girl, whom he called by name. My mom said the police found a laptop hidden in his office with a ton of nasty little pictures on it, along with a bunch of emails he exchanged with the girl from the library. I'd say those are pretty clear indications he's guilty as sin."

Cindy threw back the glass and drained the remainder of the wine. When she swallowed the last swig, she stood and crossed the room to the table where she left the bottle.

Carter watched her pour the last little bit into her glass and return to the sofa.

Before she put the glass to her lips, she paused. "Oh, I'm sorry. Where are my manners? Would you like a drink?"

"No, thank you. Why don't you put the glass down? I think you've had enough."

She looked at him with a smirk on her face. "Okay, I'll put it down," she said, proceeding to swig the rest of the wine. When she finished she placed the glass on the coffee table. She grabbed a pillow and pulled it up to her chest, crossing her arms around it.

"That wasn't what I meant," said Carter.

"Sorry, I misunderstood," she claimed. "I'm having kind of a bad week."

"I guess you are," conceded Carter.

"I don't suppose you have good news about my fiancé?"

"No, I don't."

"What about the fingerprint you got from my bathroom? You don't have anything on that yet?"

Carter shook his head.

"You're kidding me."

Carter sought for some way to change the subject, but Cindy stared at him like she was analyzing him.

"Wait a minute," she said. "You know the print belongs to Tyler. He's the only one it could be. So why did you want it? What are you looking for?"

"I thought he might have some history that would help me learn more about him," replied Carter.

"What kind of history? You mean like criminal history?"

"Something like that."

Cindy continued staring until Carter responded, "What? Why are you staring at me?"

Her eyes narrowed as her mouth gaped open.

"You found something didn't you? You're holding out."

Normally, Carter was good at keeping it cool and not tipping his hand. However, Cindy seemed to be looking right through to the center of his brain. It was as if the alcohol gave her some ultra-sensitive insight. "What are you not telling me?"

"In light of everything you have going on with your dad, and the fact that you're somewhat inebriated, I think we should wait until tomorrow to discuss Tyler," answered Carter.

"I don't want to wait until tomorrow," insisted Cindy.

"Trust me. It can wait."

"I'm paying you and I want answers when I want them."

Carter let out a big sigh.

"Cindy, you don't need anything else on your mind now."

"Oh my god, it's something horrible, isn't it?"

"No, it's not like that at all. It was a simple marijuana possession charge when he was eighteen; a misdemeanor."

The revelation caught Cindy off guard. "He was busted for pot? That's it?"

Carter nodded and expelled a light breath of relief, confident that he had averted telling her the entire truth.

Unfortunately, she began looking through him again, tilting her head to the side in suspicion.

Carter rolled his eyes. "Now what?"

"Why didn't you tell me that to begin with? If it's not a big deal, then why all the mystery? Are you lying to me?"

"No, I'm not lying to you," he replied adamantly.

"There's something else. I know it." Cindy insisted.

"No, I'm telling you the only charge is the pot incident."

"Did he do any jail time for it?"

"He was sentenced to time served in the county jail, which amounted to two or three days," answered Carter.

"How would my dad not know about that? I know he runs background checks on all his employees. I don't think he would hire someone who had been busted for drugs."

"Maybe he did know," said Carter, thinking of the colorful backgrounds of Jasper's employees he'd met so far, and thus causing Carter to remember the two guys he had seen outside Cindy's building. He desperately wished Cindy would drop the subject. He could see the wheels in her brain spinning. Hoping to distract her, he spoke. "Hey, do you have something to drink?"

"I didn't think you wanted anything."

"I mean just some soda or even water."

"Yeah, sure," replied Cindy, moving toward the kitchen.

Carter stood and crossed the floor to the window where he peeked out the blinds to the street below. Just as he figured, his shadows were parked across the street, about a half a block from the entrance.

"What are you looking at?" Cindy questioned when she returned with a can of cola.

"I was checking out your view."

"Is diet okay?" she asked, holding the can out toward him.

Carter reached and took the can from her hand.

"Yeah, that will do. You don't look like you need to drink diet," he commented.

"I normally don't. I mostly drink water. It's healthier and good for the skin."

Carter's mind flashed back to a few moments ago when he was certain she caught him checking out her leg. He watched as she stumbled a little on her way back to the sofa. "It looks like you should have gone with water tonight instead of the wine," he said.

"Are you some sort of minister on the side? You're preaching at me again."

"Just an observation," replied Carter.

"I'm fine. I just tripped on the rug."

"So what does your mom say about this situation with your dad?" Carter asked as he followed Cindy to the sofa.

"She was crying when she first called me. But by the time we got to the end of conversation, she was cussing like a sailor and condemning him to hell. By now, she's probably consumed enough alcohol and medication to put her in a very deep sleep."

"Do you think you ought to be with her? You two could probably use one another right now."

Cindy scoffed. "Wow. You're like Mr. Private Investigator Slash Preacher Slash Freaking Dr. Phil."

Carter ignored the sarcasm.

"Okay, okay," she said. "Stop giving me the guilty stare. I'll go to my mom's."

Cindy stood up and began looking for her purse and keys.

"What are you doing?" Carter asked.

"I'm going over to my mom's like you suggested," said Cindy.

"You don't think you're driving, do you?"

"Yeah, I was. Let me guess, I'm too drunk to drive?"

"You are way too drunk to drive."

"Well, I certainly don't need a DUI. Although, that would go well with my father the sex offender and my fiancé the pothead."

"I'll drive you to your mom's," offered Carter.

"Isn't that out of your way?"

"I'll include it as one of the expenses for your case," he said with a smile. Cindy paused and stared at Carter. Waiting for some sort of reaction, Carter watched Cindy's blank expression, wondering if she had taken him seriously.

"You have a nice smile," blurted Cindy, still staring. "I don't think I've noticed that before."

He chuckled. "Thanks. And I was kidding, Cindy. I'm not going to charge you to drive you to your mom's."

"I don't care. Charge me whatever you want. I'll use my pervert father's money to pay for it." The bitterness in her voice was sharp and vengeful, as her attention fell off of Carter's newly discovered good looks.

So much for trying to lighten her mood, thought Carter.

"Okay, let's go," she said, heading for the door.

"Do you mind if I use your bathroom first?"

"Are you looking for more fingerprints?" Cindy asked with less than subtle sarcasm.

"No, I just need to use the bathroom."

"You know where it is," she replied.

Carter walked down the hall and entered the bathroom, turning on the light and the exhaust fan to mask his voice. Pulling out his phone he dialed and waited, while he soaked in the tasteful décor. A woman answered. Carter spoke low with his back to the door. "Patty? It's Carter Mays."

"Hey, Carter," said Patty, sounding as cheerful as Carter remembered when he worked out of the second precinct. "I haven't heard from you in a while. How have you been?"

"I've been good. And you?"

"I'm doing well, thank you," she answered.

"How are Hank and the kids?"

"Hank is still Hank and the kids are growing way too fast for me. Carrie is getting ready to start college this year."

"You're kidding me."

"I kid you not. She's going into pre-med on a full ride scholarship to Harvard."

"Harvard? Get out. She must have got her brains from her momma."

"You got that right," replied Patty. "So what can I do for you? I know you didn't call to catch up on my life."

"You know me well, Patty. I do need a favor."

"I'm listening."

"I'm downtown at the Sheffield building. Across the street from me on Lindale Street, there's a black SUV with two men in it. I need you to send a patrolman by to check them out. I think they may be up to no good."

"So basically, you want me to run interference for you?"

"Basically, yeah. But seriously, whoever you send, tell them to proceed with caution."

"I'll have someone there in four minutes," promised Patty.

"Great, I can always count on you."

Carter thanked Patty and hung up. He lingered in the bathroom for another minute, flushing the toilet and washing his hands before he exited the room to join Cindy.

After taking the elevator to the ground floor, Carter looked out the large windows as they walked toward the exit. A police cruiser with flashing lights sat across the street, directly behind the black SUV. He escorted Cindy out onto the sidewalk and moved down the street toward his truck. Carter glanced over to see both men inside the car, looking frantically past the officer who was questioning them, at their assigned subject walking away with the boss' daughter. Carter grinned and winked in their direction.

Carter unlocked and opened the passenger door for Cindy. After she was in, he closed the door and circled his truck, watching the interaction between Jasper's men and the cop. When he took his place behind the wheel, he saw something that made his heart skip a beat.

Cindy was perusing through the case file she found. Her brow wrinkled at the photo in front of her. She stared at the picture of her fiancé and the different name at the top of the paper. Carter cringed at his carelessness. He completely forgot he left her case file on the front seat, with her last name clearly marked on the tab.

She glanced over at him. "What is this?"

Carter wanted to take the file from her, but there would be no way to glaze over what she had already seen. "I'm sorry, Cindy. I didn't want to tell you this tonight with everything you're dealing with already."

"What is this?" Cindy asked, holding the emailed photo up in front of Carter's face. "Who is Steven Conway?"

"I'm afraid that's Tyler's real name."

Cindy began to speak but couldn't. Her hand covered her mouth as her eyes became watery. She swallowed hard. "Tyler isn't his real name? It was all a big lie?"

"I don't have a lot of details yet," explained Carter.

"My parents were right. He used me. Oh my god."

The tears came quickly and Carter searched for something to say to ease the broken woman's pain. There was nothing he could say. He reached out and touched her shoulder. "I'm sorry."

"When were you going to tell me this?" Cindy snapped.

Carter pulled his hand back. "I was going to tell you tonight, but then this thing happened with your dad and I felt like it could wait until tomorrow. I'm sorry."

"I can't believe this. My whole life is turning to crap."

"In light of this, do you still want me to find him or should I stop?" Carter asked.

"No, I still want you to find him, I guess," she answered.

"You don't seem sure," remarked Carter.

Carter watched the heartbroken girl stare out the windshield, trying to figure out what she wanted. Everything she knew and believed had been thrown back into her face. Did she still want answers? Did she still want to know how this man, whom she gave her all to and loved dearly, had been able to do this to her? Had it all been one huge façade? Were the feelings he showed and the promises he made simply been a calculated move to get money? Was there anything out of the whole relationship had been valid?

Finally, she fixed her gaze on Carter and gave a subtle nod. "I still want you to find him."

"Okay," replied Carter. "But if at any point you decide otherwise, I'll drop it."

He saw her eyes become more watery and her lip began to quiver. She tried desperately to hold it in, but the emotion overcame her and she broke down into sobbing.

Reluctantly, Carter reached out and gently placed his hand on Cindy's shoulder again. This time she fell into his chest, weeping and clutching his shirt. With the young woman buried in his chest, Carter's eyes shifted to his side view mirror to check on Jasper's men and the cop. He didn't want to hang around too long and risk having them on his tail again. Fortunately, he could still see the patrolman's lights flashing.

With his right hand busy holding his distraught client, Carter used his left hand to start the engine.

Cindy looked up.

"Let's get out of here," he said.

Cindy sniffed and slowly returned to her place in the passenger seat, wiping her eyes.

Carter glanced over at his client who was trying to regain her composure and appearing slightly embarrassed by her breakdown. He put the truck in gear, checked his mirror and pulled out onto the street.

The drive to Cindy's parents' house remained awkwardly quiet. Carter was tempted to initiate conversation on a couple of occasions, but decided to let Cindy have some quiet space. She would talk if she wanted to.

When they pulled up to the gated community, Carter rolled his window down to allow Cindy to do the talking.

The stern-faced guard stepped out of his small booth, carefully studying the unknown vehicle. Bending over at the waist he peered inside the truck. Immediately he recognized Cindy and a smile replaced his serious and suspicious expression. "Oh it's you, Miss Bedford. I didn't see you at first."

Cindy leaned slightly toward the driver side. "Hi, Kenny," she said, showing little emotion. "Please let us in."

"Sure thing, Miss Bedford," replied Kenny, pushing the button that opened the gates.

"Thank you," said Cindy half-heartedly.

Carter stopped in the circular pavestone driveway of the impressive Bedford estate. Cindy sat motionless, staring out the windshield while Carter waited for her to exit the truck. Finally he spoke. "Cindy? Are you going inside?"

Her gaze drifted over toward him. "Yeah, I am. Aren't you coming in with me?"

"I hadn't planned on it," he answered.

"I want you to come in for a little while," she said. Her eyes took long blinks while she waited for a response.

"I don't want to intrude on your family."

Cindy snickered. "Intrude on my family? It's just my mom in there and I doubt you'll even see her. I told you, she's most likely passed out for the evening."

"It's getting late."

"Come on. You're not going to turn into a pumpkin. I really don't want to be by myself right now."

Looking at the young woman's sad hurt eyes, Carter hesitated. Finally, he agreed. "Okay, I'll come in for a minute."

An appreciative half smile appeared on her pleasant face. "Thanks, Carter."

Up the walk to the front door, Carter followed his client, his eyes inadvertently drifting up and down her form.

Cindy placed her key in the door and entered without knocking. Immediately, she entered the code on the alarm keypad, taking no precaution to keep Carter from seeing it, 46422.

As they crossed the tile floor of the entry, Cindy cast her purse and keys on a marble top table, creating a considerable amount of noise.

Carter's eyes scanned the massive and well-decorated interior for any sign of Mrs. Bedford.

"I'll be right back," Cindy said as she ascended the staircase.

Carter strolled around the entry, staying close to the staircase. He felt uncomfortable, like an uninvited guest.

Maybe it was being in the home of a man he didn't particularly like or trust. He stopped in front of a painting of an Italian street scene, surrounded by a gold frame with accent lights illuminating from above.

He tried to make out the name of the artist, but couldn't. His knowledge of fine art was rather limited.

Cindy reappeared and descended the steps. Somewhere along the way she had kicked off her shoes, exposing her painted pink toenails. Her long blonde hair was now pulled back into a ponytail. When she reached the bottom, she passed by Carter and said, "I told you she'd be passed out." With a wave of her hand she motioned for Carter to follow.

Down the hall and into the expanse of a large, well-equipped kitchen, Carter tagged along behind his client.

Cindy immediately walked over to the wine rack and removed a bottle of white wine.

"Great," said Carter. "More wine."

Cindy ignored him and moved over to one of the cherry cabinets where she retrieved two glasses. Again she walked away and waved her hand for him to follow her.

Carter sighed as he trailed behind her once more down another hallway to a den at the back of the house.

Cindy sat on the caramel colored loveseat and placed the glasses on the glass coffee table. Without asking, she poured wine into both glasses while Carter watched from the entrance. She picked up both glasses, took a sip from hers while she held the other one up toward her guest.

"No thanks," replied Carter.

She shrugged and returned the glass to the coffee table. Then she patted the loveseat and said, "You can at least sit down and watch me drink if you're not going to."

Carter elected to sit down in one of the adjacent chairs. "I don't bite," said Cindy, just before she took another sip.

Carter leaned back in the oversized and cushy chair, resting his elbow on the armrest and leaning his head over onto his right hand. "So am I supposed to sit here until you pass out?"

Cindy giggled briefly. "I don't know. I don't know anything anymore. It's so funny. A few days ago, I was happy. My parents were normal. I was getting married to a guy I loved. Life was good.

Now, in less than a week, my dad is in jail for trying to screw a teenage girl. My fiancé, who apparently I never really knew, is off somewhere, probably assuming a new identity and smoking pot."

Tears formed in Cindy's pretty blue eyes and her head dropped.

Carter felt sorry for the poor girl whose life had been turned upside down. He moved over and sat on the loveseat, and put his arm around her. "It's definitely been a tough week for you," he said.

As she cried, Carter caressed her upper back with his fingertips, wishing he could say something to ease her hurt.

She glanced up at him, tears falling down her cheeks.

"You're going to get through this," he promised.

Suddenly Cindy moved up and kissed him on the lips.

The quickness of it left him speechless and staring at her.

She moved in and kissed him again, her mouth open and her hand grabbing him behind the neck. The kiss lasted much longer than the first one.

He pulled away. "Cindy, we can't do this."

Determined to continue, Cindy moved in for another passionate kiss, resting her leg across Carter's lap.

Carter pulled back, just before their lips touched.

"What?" Cindy asked.

"We can't do this," he said, his mouth and body in total disagreement with his conscience.

"Why not?" she asked. "Don't tell me you're not attracted to me. I've seen the way you look at me sometimes, checking me out." Taking his hand, she placed it on her thigh.

Her silky skin felt as good as he imagined it would. He wondered if she had really caught him admiring her or if she was just making assumptions.

No doubt a girl like her is used to most guys checking her out. He pushed her leg off of him and stood up. "First of all, you're my client."

Cindy stood and rested her forearms on his shoulders. "That's easy. You're fired." She smiled and began to kiss him again.

He grabbed her arms and pulled them away from him. "You're also drunk."

"I'm not drunk," she claimed.

Carter's arched eyebrows challenged her statement.

"Okay, I'm a little drunk. But I'm not so drunk that I don't know what I'm doing."

"Cindy," began Carter.

She interrupted him. "Come on, Carter. Kiss me. If you don't enjoy it, we'll stop."

"Cindy, enjoying it isn't the question here. Obviously, I would enjoy it. I'd be lying if I said I didn't. You're a beautiful, sexy young woman. But it's not right."

"It feels right to me."

"You're not in a good state of mind right now, Cindy. Between the wine and all the crap you're dealing with, your judgment is clouded."

Giving up, Cindy collapsed onto the loveseat and reached for her glass. "I guess I can add total rejection to my list of highlights this week."

Carter sat down next to her and took the glass from her hand before it reached her lips. "Why don't you lay off the wine?"

"You're no fun at all," she replied. "You look like a guy who would be fun, but you're definitely not."

"I think you should call it a night and go to bed."

Cindy expelled a long, weary breath. "Maybe I should."

Carter followed her from the room.

She glanced back once. His gaze bounced upward to her eyes. She grinned and continued her path.

When they reached the front door, she extended her hand toward him. "Good night, Mr. Mays."

He accepted her hand for a lingering handshake. "Get some sleep," he said.

She grinned mischievously. "Do you want to tuck me in?"

Carter smiled. "No, I don't think so. I'll call you tomorrow and we can talk about things."

"Don't call me too early. I'm feeling really sleepy."

"I won't. Goodnight."

"Goodnight, Carter."

FOURTEEN

The next morning, Jasper Bedford walked from the courthouse accompanied by his attorney, Dylan Fitch, and Tate Manning. Tate had posted Jasper's bail, which the judge set at a hefty $750,000. Jasper was not in a pleasant mood. They crossed the street to the parking garage where they arrived at Dylan's Porsche, parked diagonally across two spaces.

"Nice parking," commented Jasper.

"Hey, it keeps people from banging up my ride," said Dylan. "We need to get together this afternoon to discuss our defense strategy. What time is good for you?"

"Make it around two o'clock."

"That will work," said Dylan, getting behind the wheel of his car and slipping on a ridiculous looking pair of red and white leather driving gloves.

The tires of the Porsche screeched as Dylan pulled away. Jasper rolled his eyes as he and Tate watched the car disappear around the curve. "If he weren't such a good lawyer, I'd fire that pompous jackass," said Jasper.

"Well, you definitely need him right now," said Tate, as they approached Tate's car. "He's your best hope for getting out of this."

"I can't believe I'm in this mess."

"Yeah, you must have done something to piss off Tyler." Both men got into the Jaguar and Tate started up the motor as Jasper began to vent.

"That's just it. I've never given him any cause to do this. You know? I mean, I hired him into my company, gave him a good job, promoted him; welcomed him into my home and family when he started dating Cindy. I've treated him exceptionally well. Now he's trying to bury me."

"He's off to a good start," said Tate.

"Yeah, well, this isn't over. I'm not going to lie down and take it. I'm going to do some burying of my own."

"You better be extremely cautious right now. The last thing you need is to draw more attention from the police."

"Can you believe this crap? I've spent all these years undetected; never having any problems and now I'm fighting taking the rap for something I didn't do."

"Hey, I've tried to get you to drop all the other business and go totally legitimate with the company. We're big enough we don't need to depend on that anymore. Sooner or later, I'm afraid it's going to hang us."

Jasper gave Tate a disgusted look. "I just finished saying that the business isn't what's threatening me and you're back on your going legit soapbox."

"Jasper, I know that's not what's hanging over you right now, but with the police investigating, who knows what they might uncover. If you had taken my advice a few years ago, we wouldn't have to worry about what the cops found."

"You mean *you* wouldn't have to worry about it. You wouldn't have to worry about them uncovering the skeletons in your closet. I'd be the only one at risk, huh?"

Tate checked for traffic before emerging from the garage into the bright sunlight of the day. "That's not what I meant, Jasper, and you know it."

"And even if we did go completely legit tomorrow, it doesn't negate everything you've done to get where you are today. You don't go from the devil to the church choir just like that." Tate kept quiet and said nothing in response as he navigated his way through the busy streets.

"Besides, it's not like we haven't cut way back on our other business dealings. We're only doing three or four deals a year now," said Jasper.

"But we don't need it," replied Tate. "The company is strong enough not to depend on that anymore, especially if you put that extra effort in to the legitimate side of the business. I'm getting tired of the stress."

"Is your guilty conscience getting to you after all these years or are you just afraid of going to prison? Face it, Tate, you know you've become accustomed to a certain lifestyle, and I doubt you'd be able to maintain it without those extra deals. Yeah, West Lake is strong, but not strong enough to weather the lean times. Let's face it; the development and construction business is subject to ups and downs. We've got to have the other business to counteract those times. Like two years ago, when that huge job fell through and we were looking at having to cut some people from the company. It's because of other stuff those folks still have a job."

Tate scoffed. "It's funny how you can make it sound so righteous. And yet, somehow, you never wanted to tell your own daughter what you do."

"This conversation is over," said Jasper. "I don't need another headache on top of what I'm already looking at. So drop it."

Neither spoke for the rest of the drive to Jasper's house. Occasionally, both men would steal a glance at the other one, with Jasper analyzing the level of trust that existed in their strained relationship.

Tate pulled up in the drive to let Jasper out of the car.

"Thanks," Jasper said half-heartedly as he got out.

"You're welcome," Tate replied with the same lack of enthusiasm.

Jasper walked through the unlocked front door, taking notice that the alarm wasn't activated. Walking up the steps of the quiet house, he made his way down the hall.

Cindy walked out of the bathroom wearing a towel and combing through her wet hair. Startled, she stopped long enough to recognize the intruder as her father and turned away, disappearing into her old bedroom before Jasper could say anything.

He moved to the door of the bedroom and knocked. "Cindy?"

There was no response. He tried again, this time calling louder and knocking.

She continued to ignore him.

"Cindy, open the door," he barked, getting agitated. "We need to talk."

Loud music rang out from inside and Jasper gave up for the moment. Walking away, Jasper entered his bedroom and immediately noticed a nearly empty bottle of vodka on the nightstand. His wife was not in sight. He continued into the master bath where he found her reclined in their garden tub with a small pillow supporting her head and a washcloth covering her eyes. She didn't move or say anything upon his entry, although he was certain she heard him.

"Hey," he spoke softly.

Her head turned away from him toward the wall.

"I see you've been drowning your troubles," said Jasper. "Of course, that is your normal response."

A solitary finger communicated her reply.

"Nice," said Jasper. "Since you refused to come down to the police station or make any effort to contact me, I thought I should tell you that this thing with the girl is a complete pile of crap. I didn't do anything wrong. The whole thing was a set up."

Darlene said nothing as she continued to look away from him.

Jasper sat on the edge of the tub. "Tyler set this whole thing up. He's trying to bury me."

"Pretty convenient to blame this on Tyler," she said, still looking away. "I guess those other women in the past were Tyler's doing as well?"

"Look at me," Jasper demanded.

Darlene ignored him. Jasper's lips tightened as he looked up to the ceiling momentarily. Suddenly he threw his hand on top of his wife's head and plunged her beneath the bath water. Her hands instinctively grabbed him around the wrist to remove his hand, but he was too strong. She began flailing her arms and legs, trying to surface and get air.

Jasper pushed her under further, now holding her with two hands as he was being drenched with splashing water. Finally he let her up and she gasped for air, coughing and wiping the sudsy water from around her eyes.

Once she had her breath, she unleashed a barrage of obscenities on him, calling him a lunatic.

He grabbed her behind the head with one hand and slapped the other hand hard against her mouth.

Seeing the fear in her eyes as she braced to go under the water again, Jasper moved from his seated position on the edge of the tub, to kneeling on the floor, putting him in direct eye level with his frantic wife.

"Shut your mouth and listen to me," he yelled. "You're not going to sit here and disrespect me. I told you I was set up. This has nothing to do with anyone in the past. I never did anything or intended to do anything with this kid. I didn't even know she existed before I saw her in the library. That computer they found in my office was planted. I've never seen it either. For whatever reason, Tyler Moore is trying his best to bury me, so cut me a little slack. Got it?"

Crying, Darlene nodded her head in submission.

Jasper released his grip on her and she took in deep breaths, trying to recover.

Jasper stood up and removed his soaked shirt.

Darlene stared at the wet floor, lost in thought. Her gaze shifted to her husband.

"I'm not lying to you," he whispered.

She stood and reached for her towel, stepping out of the draining tub. "So what are you going to do about Tyler?"

He held his gaze on her, trying to determine if she was on his side or not. "I don't know. He has the upper hand on me for the moment. I don't know where he is and I'm sure the cops will be keeping close tabs on me."

Darlene approached. "If he's setting you up, then our first focus should be on proving that."

Jasper reached for his wife's hand. "Thank you," he said. "I need your support now more than ever."

"You've got it," she replied, one hand on his chest.

He kissed her. The stinging words he had used a moment earlier came back to him. "I'm sorry."

Darlene shook her head. "It's okay. You're under a lot of stress." Jasper wrapped his arms around his wife and hugged her tightly. Her arms encircled his lower torso. "We'll get through this," she said.

"I wish our daughter would hear me out," said Jasper. "She wouldn't even look at me when I came in. She ran off to her room and locked the door."

"She's here?" Darlene inquired.

"Yeah, she's here. You didn't know she was here?"

"I've been in our bedroom all morning. She must have come in after I went to sleep."

Sleep? More like she passed out, Jasper thought to himself.

"I wonder why she's here," said Darlene.

"Come to think of it, I wonder how she got here. I didn't see her car outside."

"I'll get dressed and go talk to her," offered Darlene.

"Good luck," said Jasper. "She doesn't want to hear anything negative about Tyler."

"That's too bad because that's what she's going to hear," said Darlene, walking inside her closet to get dressed.

By the time Darlene passed through the bedroom, Jasper had slipped off to sleep. She stopped and stared at him, hating the fact he could say some of the most hurtful things to her and yet she still loved him. Part of her wanted to lie down and snuggle up beside him. The other part of her wished he'd have a heart attack and never wake up.

When Darlene reached her daughter's old bedroom, Cindy was gone. A wet towel remained on the unmade bed; not typical behavior, even for her spoiled daughter. She obviously left in a rush. Darlene searched through the house. She tried calling Cindy's cell phone, but it went to voice mail. A quick check with Edgar the gardener, who was working diligently in one of the flowerbeds, confirmed Cindy had left a few minutes prior.

According to Edgar, he saw Cindy walking at a fast pace toward the front gate of the neighborhood where she got into an awaiting cab.

FIFTEEN

The drive to South Bend, Indiana was an uneventful one. Carter spent most of the trip reminiscing about the previous night, Cindy and the kiss. It was his most memorable interaction with a client. It played over and over in his mind, and he enjoyed each replay. Carter was proud of the fact he had responded with professionalism and sound judgment. He wondered how the incident would affect his next meeting with Cindy.

He drove past the pristine and tradition-rich campus of Notre Dame, watching students enrolled in summer classes moving about.

A few more miles and he came upon an older, but well-maintained neighborhood consisting of row after row of small brick ranch homes, identical in style, differing only in brick color and landscaping.

According to the police report, the last known address for Steven Conway, a.k.a. Tyler Moore, was coming up. Carter slowed his truck, reading each address, until he finally arrived. Parking on the street, Carter exited his truck, walked up on the porch, and rang the bell. Immediately the sound of two yappy dogs echoed from inside.

A woman carrying a baby on her hip answered the door. A toddler clung to the back of her legs, peeking around at the stranger on the porch. Two noisy Chihuahua dogs stood at her feet, acting as if they would lunge through the screen door and try to eat Carter. The woman appeared tired, frazzled, and interrupted.

Carter smiled and greeted her. "Hello, Miss," he said forcefully over the dogs. "My name is Carter and I'm looking for a friend of mine. His name is Steven."

The lady shook her head, causing her frizzy hair to fall down in front of her eyes. With her free hand she pushed it away and then switched her baby to her opposite hip. "I don't know him. You've got the wrong house."

Carter struggled to hear the woman over the barking dogs. "I haven't seen him in a few years and this is the last address I have."

"I've been here for seven years and I don't know him. You might try Mr. Peterson across the street. He's lived here forever."

Carter started to thank the woman, but she shut the door and returned to her hectic day before he could finish.

Crossing the street, Carter walked by the shiny Buick parked in Mr. Peterson's driveway and approached the door. He rang the bell and waited. A moment later he tried knocking. If Mr. Peterson was home, it didn't appear he was taking visitors today. Carter stood on the porch and faced the street, trying to determine his next move.

From the side yard, an elderly man appeared wearing a broadbill straw hat, Hawaiian shirt, khaki shorts exposing his pale legs and work gloves with fresh clumps of soil sticking to them. "I thought I heard somebody," he said. "What can I do for you?"

"Mr. Peterson?"

"That's me," he replied.

"Hello," said Carter, stepping out into the yard. "The lady across the street said you might be able to help me. I'm looking for an old friend of mine, Steven Conway."

The old man studied Carter for a moment. "He doesn't live here anymore. He moved away several years ago. And I'd bet my Social Security check that he's no old friend of yours."

Carter smiled and conceded that the old man was correct.

"More than likely, I'd say you're a cop or some kind of investigator."

"Right again," said Carter. "You're very perceptive."

"I'm a retired cop myself and I've used that same lame line thousands of times. Oddly enough, most people buy it."

"That's true. I think you're the first person to call my bluff."

"So what are you, a private investigator? You don't strike me as a cop."

"I used to be a cop; Chicago PD. Now I work for myself."

"Are you thirsty? I was just getting ready to take a break and have some lemonade."

"Sure."

"Follow me," he said taking of his hat and gloves and tossing them on the porch. Small beads of sweat rolled down his mostly bald head.

The inside of the house was neat and simply decorated. The hardwood floors showed some wear, but remained in decent shape. Pictures of the old man with a pleasant looking elderly woman sat on an antique sofa table.

"Is this your wife?" Carter asked.

The old man stopped and stared fondly at the pictures. "Yep. That's Betty. We were married for forty-two years. She passed almost two years ago."

"I'm sorry."

"Nothing to be sorry about, son. That's life. I was blessed to have that long with her. I couldn't have asked for a better wife."

As they entered the kitchen, Mr. Peterson motioned for Carter to sit down at the table while he washed his hands off in the kitchen sink.

"Do you have any children, Mr. Peterson?"

"Call me, Al. We had three daughters. One lives in California. My oldest one lives here and teaches biology at the University. My youngest one died in a car accident twenty years ago."

"I'm sorry," Carter said again.

"Yeah, me too."

Al retrieved two glasses from the cabinet and a pitcher from the refrigerator. "Do you like lemonade?"

"Yes, I do," answered Carter. "Thank you."

Al filled the two glasses, sat down across from Carter and took a long drink. "So you're looking for Steven, huh?"

"Yes, sir. What can you tell me about him?"

"He and his mom lived across the street for most of his childhood. He was just a baby when they moved in, probably not even a year old. She was a nice enough lady."

"What about the dad?"

Al shook his head. "Never any mention of him and I never asked. Although, I used to see, or should I say, Betty used to see, a man over there from time to time when she first moved in. I was usually at work. But Betty said this man would stop over and visit, oh maybe once a month, when Steven was little. Eventually though, he stopped coming around. I'm guessing Steven wasn't even two when he stopped showing up. I don't know if he was the boy's father or not."

"What kind of kid was Steven?"

"He was smart, always got good grades; generally a nice kid for the most part. His mother did the best she could with him, being a single mom. When his mom started having more problems, he seemed to have a bit of a chip on his shoulder. He became less personable. But I guess that's natural when you're that age and life deals you a lousy hand. For that matter, any age."

"What happened to his mom?"

"She had health problems," replied Al. "I think it was some kind of seizures, but I'm not sure. They were very private about it. Eventually, they moved. I don't know if money got tight and they had to move in with relatives or they needed a smaller place that would be easier to care for. Like I said, they were private about it. Betty took them a meal a few times. They were always gracious, but kept things pretty distant. They didn't volunteer information and we didn't pry."

"Do you know if the mom ever recovered?"

"No, she didn't. I remember seeing her name in the obituaries a few months after they moved. We would have gone to the service to pay our respects, but I didn't see it until the day after the funeral. It used to take me a couple of days to get around to reading the paper."

"How long ago was that?"

Al paused, looking down at the floor. "Oh, I'd guess seven to eight years ago. But you know how time flies, it could have been ten or twelve. It's getting harder for me to keep track of time."

"Do you remember where her funeral service was held?" Cater asked, taking a notepad and pen from the back pocket of his jeans.

Al shook his head, scratching at his chin whiskers. "Nah, not really. I would imagine it was either Taylor's or Buffington's. They handle most of the funerals around here."

"What was his mother's name?"

"Louise Conway."

"What kind of work did she do?"

"She worked as a secretary at the local Board of Education."

"Did you ever hear anyone mention the name Tyler Moore?" Carter asked.

"Nope," answered Al. "Doesn't ring a bell."

Carter paused for a moment while he took notes.

"May I ask why you're looking for him?" Al asked.

"He's missing," answered Carter.

"And you think this Tyler Moore might have something to do with it?"

"No. Up until recently, that's who I was looking for. Steven Conway and Tyler Moore are one and the same."

Al arched his eyebrows in interest. "Oh, I see. That certainly adds some mystery to things, doesn't it?"

"Yes, it does."

Carter drained the remainder of his lemonade, stood up, and pulled a business card from his wallet to give to the old man. "Thanks for your time, the information, and the lemonade, Al. If anything else comes to mind, please give me a call."

Al stood to accept the card and placed it in his shirt pocket. "I will do that," he promised. "Good luck on your case."

Al followed Carter out the front door.

Carter thanked him and said goodbye, while Al picked up his hat and gloves to go back to work.

Carter used his GPS to find the addresses of the two funeral homes that probably handled the funeral services for Louise Conway. Buffington's was the closest, so Carter went there first.

Like so many funeral homes, Buffington's Funeral Home was a large white house; built in the early 1900's, impeccably clean, resting on a well-manicured corner lot with ample parking. The parking lot was empty, bringing some relief to Carter who did not want to try to seek information during someone's funeral.

The first person he met was a young man around the side of the house who was buffing the high gloss black finish on a hearse. He appeared to be in his early to mid-twenties, wearing dress pants and a white dress shirt with the sleeves rolled up. His back was to Carter and he was singing low, listening to hip hop music through an MP3 player.

"Hello," said Carter, trying to get the young man's attention.

There was no response, so Carter moved in and tapped the guy on the shoulder, obviously startling the guy, as indicated by the awkward manner in which he quickly jumped around. Carter did well not to laugh, but couldn't completely suppress the smile from his face.

"Geez," the young man exclaimed. "You scared the crap out of me."

"Sorry about that," offered Carter.

The guy continued breathing heavy. "What do you want?"

"I was hoping to talk to the funeral director."

"He's inside," said the young man. "Go through that door and his office is the first door on the left."

"Thanks," replied Carter. "Sorry again about startling you."

Readjusting the earphones on his MP3 player, the guy turned around and resumed buffing the car.

Carter entered the funeral home and located the office. The door was open, so Carter stepped inside the doorway and knocked on the doorframe.

An older man, probably in his early sixties sat at two desks butted up against one another to form an L shape. The larger, expensive Mahogany desk facing the door made for a nice impression. The smaller desk running perpendicular served as a computer workspace. The jet-black color of the man's hair obviously came from a bottle and appeared extremely unnatural. His face was gaunt with large bags under his eyes, giving him the stereotypical look of an undertaker. Upon hearing the knock he immediately stood to greet Carter, extending his long bony hand as he spoke. "Hello, may I help you?"

"I hope so," answered Carter. "My name is Carter Mays. I'm a private investigator and I'm looking for some information."

A surprised look came over the man's face, but it soon faded and he introduced himself as Eli Buffington. "Have a seat," invited the man.

"Thank you," said Carter, sitting in the maroon leather chair.

"What kind of information are you looking for?"

"Do you remember holding a funeral service several years ago for a woman named Louise Conway?"

"Hmm," said Eli, folding his hands together. "It sort of sounds familiar. Let me look it up."

Turning his chair to the side, he typed in Louise Conway's name and ran a search. The layout of the office gave Carter a good look at the monitor, which he paid close attention to in case Eli was slow to share information.

"Ah, here we go," said Eli. "We did do her funeral."

"What can you tell me about it?"

"Like what?" Eli asked.

"Do you remember anything about it, like how many people came? Was it a one day deal or spread out over two days?"

Eli slipped on a pair of reading glasses and cocked his head back slightly to see the monitor. "We had a visitation in the evening and the actual funeral service the following morning. She was buried at Peace Valley Cemetery."

"Who made the arrangements?"

Eli looked at the screen and then frowned. "That's odd. I don't have a name listed."

"What do you mean?"

Eli pointed to a specific field on the display. "Right there," he said. "I always put the name of the person or persons that made the arrangements. That way I can keep in contact with them and send them informational mailers; a marketing tool, so to speak."

The thought of a funeral home marketing to people seemed a little morbid to Carter, but he figured business is business, no matter what line of work you're in.

Carter was poised to ask another question when Eli perked up, snapped his fingers, and pointed at the screen. "Now I remember," Eli exclaimed.

"Remember what?" Carter inquired, startled by the man's outburst.

"Yes, I do remember now."

"What?"

The man continued pointing toward the screen, jabbing his finger into the air as he spoke. "There was this guy who came in and said he wanted the very best funeral and he would pay for everything. He was a very nice man. He went with our premium casket and vault."

"You don't remember his name?"

Eli shook his head. "He never would tell me his name."

"What about an invoice or some type of payment records?"

"He paid cash," replied Eli. "And it was not a cheap funeral. He even had us hire extra musicians for the funeral."

"Really?"

"Yes, he insisted on having a flute and a violin in addition to our regular keyboardist."

"Did he say how he knew Louise?"

"He just said that he was an acquaintance."

"What about at the funeral? Did he seem like he was family, or friend, or what?"

"He didn't come to the funeral or the visitation," said Eli.

"He didn't?"

"I never saw him there. Quite frankly, the gentlemen seemed rather low key about his involvement, didn't want anyone to know about it."

Carter leaned back in his chair for a moment to process the new information. "Do you have any recollection of what he looked like? Anything particularly striking about him?"

Slowly the man shook his head while he lightly chewed on his tongue. "No, nothing distinct."

"Can you take a guess on how old he may have been?"

"Mid-forties, I suppose," said Eli with a half-hearted reply.

Carter pressed. "Dark hair? Light hair?"

"Dark, for what he had," said Eli, closing his eyes as if he were replaying the moment in his head. "It seems like he was getting a little thin on top and that he kept his hair pretty short. Oh, and I think he had a beard."

"Glasses?"

Eli shook his head and shrugged. "I don't remember. But I want to say no glasses."

"Tall or short?"

"About average."

"Heavy? Thin?"

Again Eli shrugged. "Maybe a little on the heavy side."

"And you never saw him again after he made arrangements?" Carter inquired.

"Nope."

"Did Louise Conway's son give any indication that he knew the man who paid for it?"

"He didn't have a clue. I remember he was really surprised and relieved that everything had been taken care of already."

"So the son was completely in the dark about who paid for his mother's funeral?"

Eli nodded. "Yes, sir. I remember he showed up at my office with a woman, his aunt or a friend of the family. She agreed to help him make the arrangements. He was barely out of high school and unsure of what to do. Then I told him about the gentlemen who had stopped by just hours before and taken care of everything. At first, I don't believe the son was too thrilled with some stranger butting into his family business. But after I showed him everything the man arranged, he seemed quite relieved."

"Do you remember the name of the woman with him?"

"No, I never got her name."

Carter stood up and prepared to leave. He reached down and picked up one of the business cards displayed on Eli's desk. "May I have one of these in case I think of any additional questions?"

"Sure thing, son," replied Eli.

"Thank you," said Carter handing one of his own business cards to the funeral director. "Here's my card in case you remember something else that may help. You're more likely to reach me if you call my cell instead of the office."

The two men shook hands and Carter exited the building, being careful not to startle the hearse driver again.

The local Board of Education was housed in the lower west section of a brand new building that served as the main headquarters for multiple community offices, not far from Louise Conway's old house. Carter entered the office where he was greeted by a rather feminine young man in his late twenties. "Hello, may I help you?"

"Hi," said Carter. "I'm looking for anyone who may have worked with Louise Conway. She was a secretary here roughly ten years ago."

"Hmm," thought the young man. "You're best bet is probably Angela. She's worked here a long time. I'll call her for you."

"Thank you," said Carter.

The young man picked up the phone and called Angela, explaining Carter's request over the phone. A brief moment later, a rotund woman with bright red hair and an excessive amount of make-up appeared, smiling ear to ear. She walked right up to Carter; her arm extended, and spoke. "Hello. Are you a friend or relative of Louise's?"

"Actually, no. My name is Carter Mays. I'm a private investigator."

Angela's smile quickly faded. "Oh, I see."

"Did you work closely with Louise?"

"Yes, I did," answered Angela. "May I ask what you're investigating?"

"I'm looking into the disappearance of her son, Steven," replied Carter.

"Really?" Angela asked in dramatic fashion. "That's awful. How can I help?"

Carter saw the reluctance in Angela's face immediately transform into cooperation. "I was hoping to learn anything about the family that may help me."

"Well, you do know that Louise passed several years ago, don't you?"

"Yes ma'am."

"It was such a shame. She seemed so young."

"Did you go to her funeral?"

"Absolutely," stated Angela. "The only thing that would have kept me from going would have been my own funeral."

"What do you remember about it?"

"Oh, it was a lovely funeral, very well done. They even had a violin and a flute playing the music. Louise loved to hear the flute."

"Did she ever talk to you about her romantic relationships? Boyfriends, anything serious?"

"She really didn't have any."

"Really?"

"Oh, she was a beautiful woman. I'm sure it wasn't from a lack of opportunity. But she was so focused on being a mom, she didn't really pursue a social life. It was all about Steven. Plus, she had health issues."

"How about Steven's dad? Did she ever talk about him?"

"Nope. She never brought him up, so neither did I."

"Did she start working here before or after Steven was born?"

"It was after. He was just a baby when she started."

"Do you know where she worked before she came here?"

"I know she moved here from Chicago. I think she worked as a secretary, but I don't remember where. She didn't talk about herself too much."

"Chicago, huh?"

Angela nodded.

"How old was she when she came here?"

"I guess late twenties. Beautiful girl."

"You wouldn't happen to still have an employee file for her still, would you?"

"No, I doubt it," answered Angela. "Even if we did, I couldn't let you see it."

Carter nodded indicating he already knew the answer. "That's what I figured, but I had to ask."

"I'm sorry. I'd like to help you any way I can to find her son."

"That's okay," said Carter, reaching into his pocket for a business card. "You have helped me. Here's my number to call me in case you think of anything else."

"I certainly will," promised Angela. "I hope you find him soon and everything is okay."

Carter thanked the lady and left to go back to Chicago.

SIXTEEN

Jasper Bedford arrived on time for his two o'clock appointment at his attorney's office with Darlene by his side. Dylan Fitch addressed her first, reaching for her hand. "Why Darlene, how wonderful it is to see you again. You're looking as lovely as ever."

Jasper passed on by to sit down on the leather sofa, rolling his eyes and leaving his wife and Dylan to exchange their borderline obscene pleasantries. Listening to them make small talk while his future and freedom hung in the balance, made Jasper want to kill both of them. He finally spoke out. "Hey, do you two mind? I'm about to be nailed to a cross and you two are playing catch up."

Dylan sat in the chair across from Jasper, while Darlene sat on the sofa with a noticeable space between her and Jasper.

Glancing briefly at her husband, Darlene gazed at her attorney and said, "Dylan, you're obviously still working out religiously. Where do you find the time while running a busy and successful law firm?"

"It's a matter of prioritizing," replied Dylan, flashing a smile her way.

Jasper glared at his wife and then at his lawyer. "Right now, I'm your priority."

Dylan went into his all business, lawyer mode. "Okay, Jasper, I've been giving this a great deal of thought and I think your best shot of getting out of this unscathed is to tell them about Tyler."

Jasper fell back into the sofa, clasping his hands on top of his head and letting out a disapproving sigh. "I don't like that idea."

"I know you don't," said Dylan. "But I'm afraid if we don't, they're going to hang you. The evidence is pretty damning."

"I told you the computer was planted," stressed Jasper.

"Yeah, and I've got people trying to find out if there were any fingerprints on it. If it was yours, it should have your prints."

"Exactly. And when they don't find my prints on it, which I know they won't, that should clear me."

"They still have you approaching the girl in the library, addressing her by name and asking her if she had something for you," reminded Dylan. "If a jury hears that, and you don't have a really good explanation, you're going to burn."

Jasper leaned forward, resting his forearms on his thighs, staring at the rug under his feet, contemplating his situation.

"You don't have to tell them the entire amount Tyler stole. Just give them the information you don't mind them knowing. They don't have to have all the facts. Tate should be able to move or delete the files you don't want them to find."

Darlene scoffed. "I don't get how you let Tyler lead you into such an obvious trap. Did it never occur to you when he gave you these instructions, that this could be easily misinterpreted?"

Jasper didn't even bother to look up as his wife questioned his judgment.

"I can't believe you actually went up to some strange fourteen-year-old and asked her if she had something for you," said Darlene with a subtle but condescending hint of laughter in her voice. "You are usually not that stupid."

Jasper sprang upright and glared at his wife.

Dylan intervened. "So Jasper, what do you want to do?"

Holding his gaze on his sassy wife, Jasper didn't acknowledge Dylan's question right away. Finally, he spoke. "I guess you're right. That is my best chance of beating this thing."

"Good," said Dylan. "We want to paint the picture of you as the victim here. We'll tell them about Tyler abandoning your daughter at the wedding, breaking into your home and office to steal your money. And then in a ruthless act of hatred, he tried to smear your name and reputation. We'll turn all the focus onto Tyler. And if we have any luck, we'll be able to link him to the emails that were exchanged with the girl."

"And you're sure that will work?" Darlene asked.

Dylan nodded. "As long as I'm being told everything," he said, staring at Jasper. "If there is anything you're holding back, I need to know now."

Jasper scowled. "I've told you everything just as it happened. I didn't do anything wrong here," he said adamantly.

"Sorry," replied Dylan. "I had to ask."

"No, you didn't," said Jasper.

He stood and walked to his window, just as cell phone rang. He checked the display. "Yeah, Russell," answered Jasper.

"Did I catch you at a bad time, Mr. Bedford?" Russell asked.

"No, you're fine. What do you want?"

"I thought I'd give you an update on the PI. I had Luke following him all day."

"And?"

"He spent the day in South Bend, Indiana."

"Doing what?"

"He appears to be questioning people."

"Are you sure he's not visiting family or friends? Maybe that's his hometown."

"Luke seemed fairly certain he was meeting these people for the first time. The guy made three different stops: a residential neighborhood, a funeral home and the local Board of Education."

"That's interesting," commented Jasper. "I don't suppose Luke heard what was said in these conversations?"

"No, sir. But he does have the addresses in case you need us to dig a little deeper."

"No, I'd rather not do anything too aggressive right now. My circumstance is too fragile. Where's Mays now?"

"Luke's following him back to Chicago."

"Okay. Have Luke stay with him, but not too close, and keep me informed. Thanks, Russell, and tell Luke good job."

"Yes, sir, Mr. Bedford."

When Jasper hung up, he turned to see Darlene and Dylan staring at him, their curiosity evident. "That was Russell. He's had Luke following that private investigator all day."

"Okay," said Dylan. "This is the second time I've heard you refer to this investigator. Who is he and what's he investigating? Did you hire him?"

"No, I didn't. Cindy hired him to find Tyler."

"Oh, and you're following him in case he succeeds. That's a good idea."

"Yes, it is," commented Darlene. "That's Jasper for you, always thinking."

Jasper didn't bother to acknowledge his wife's comment, though he could easily hear the "I told you so" tone in her voice.

"So has this investigator made any progress?" Dylan asked.

Jasper shrugged. "I'm not sure. He spent the day in South Bend interviewing people."

"South Bend, Indiana?" Dylan asked.

"No, Dylan, South Bend, Alaska. Stupid question."

Dylan chose to ignore the jab and get back to business. "Okay, we need to go over all the details of your phone conversation with Tyler. Plus, I'll check your phone records and find out where he called you from. Do you want to sit here or over at my desk to go over this?"

"We'll do it here," replied Jasper.

As Jasper sat down, Dylan pulled out his tablet to take notes. "Okay, let's get started then."

SEVENTEEN

On the way home from South Bend, Carter pondered the information he had gathered up to that point. Ideally, he would like to see Tyler Moore's college records. However, in the early years of his investigative career, he tried numerous times, unsuccessfully, to get the slightest peek at a person's records. Schools and businesses are very good about maintaining their employees' and students' privacy.

He figured Steven Conway had to have switched his identity before he began his college career. To pull off completely changing your identity, including a new social security number and all the documents needed to enroll into college, would require help and money. It was highly unlikely, given his age and limited financial resources that Steven Conway could have acted alone. The question was, who helped him? Another question, why would he switch identities? With the exception of the misdemeanor pot bust, there was nothing obvious in his past he needed to hide. Probably half or more of the politicians and top businessmen in the country had more baggage than Steven Conway. Carter also kept coming back to the mystery man who paid for Louise Conway's funeral. What's his significance in all of this? Could he have been Steven's father? There were definitely some interesting aspects to this case.

Feeling confident the University would never grant him access to Tyler Moore's file, Carter decided to check another source; a source he figured he could access with the help of his client. He dialed the phone as he drove.

"Hello," answered Cindy Bedford.

"Hi, Cindy. It's Carter."

"Oh, hi, Carter," she said, her tone softer than normal, almost timid sounding.

"Are you okay, Cindy? You don't sound the same."

She hesitated. "I've been dreading talking to you all day."

"Thanks," replied Carter with a snicker.

"No, it's just that I vaguely remember things, or rather I got a little out of hand last night, and you didn't see my best side."

"Look, Cindy, don't worry about it. It's fine."

"No, it's really not," insisted Cindy, sounding more like her normal assertive self. "I'm so embarrassed by the way I threw myself at you last night. At least, that's the way I'm remembering it. Is that the way it happened?"

Now Carter hesitated, not wanting to make his client feel more awkward.

"I wouldn't say you threw yourself at me," he said. "You were just being friendly."

"Yeah, friendly, like a ten dollar hooker. I swear to you I'm really not a sleaze. It was the alcohol and the stress from all this crap in my life."

"Cindy, I told you that it's okay. Let it go."

"I can't. I feel horrible I came on to you like I did. I don't know what your opinion of me was before, but last night certainly couldn't have helped."

"It's over. Okay?"

"And by the way, thank you," said Cindy.

"For what?"

"For being a gentleman," she answered. "Most guys wouldn't have passed up that opportunity. I mean, not that I'm all that."

Carter could hear the stress returning to her voice.

She continued. "I don't mean to make it sound like I'm this great, whatever, that …"

Carter laughed interrupting her. "Cindy, will you quit trying to explain yourself to me?"

"Well, I don't want to come off as thinking I'm some hot babe that any man would kill to be with. I'm not that conceited."

"You do realize the more you talk, the worse you're making yourself feel, don't you?"

A sigh of frustration came through the phone. "Yes, I know."

"How about if you quit talking and listen?"

"Okay, I'm listening."

"What kind of access do you have to your father's company?"

"Why?"

"I'd like to take a look at Tyler's employee file."

"I could get it, no problem," replied Cindy.

"That easy, huh?"

"Daphne, one of my friends from high school, works in Human Resources. I could call her and have it by this evening."

"Are you sure she'd be willing to do that?"

"Oh definitely; it wouldn't be a big deal at all. My friends are so pissed at Tyler right now, they'd do anything to help me."

"Cool. Should I swing by and pick it up this evening, or do you want to meet me somewhere?"

"Whatever's easiest," replied Cindy. "I'll be home all night."

"Okay, I'll check in with you before I drop by."

"What are you looking for anyway?"

"I'm not sure. I'll know it when I see it."

Carter ended the call and glanced in his rear view mirror to see if the silver sedan was still behind him. He saw it about four car lengths back. Carter first noticed it when he left the Board of Education in South Bend. After a stop for gas, one stop for fast food, and one other random stop, the car continued to shadow him. Clearly, he was being followed, and he felt certain it was by one of Jasper's boys trying to find Tyler Moore through his efforts.

Pulling off the interstate, Carter drove to a large shopping mall and parked. Getting out of his truck, he took notice of the sedan parking two rows over as he made his way to the main entrance. Looking in the reflection of the glass doors, he saw the guy following behind him. The man was average height with a stocky build sporting a buzz cut and sun glasses. "How many guys does Bedford have working for him?" Carter mumbled to himself.

As soon as Carter entered the mall, he picked up his pace and ducked inside a maternity clothing store before his pursuer had a chance to see where he went.

From behind a rack of maternity dresses Carter watched the guy pass by him, as he urgently scanned the horde of shoppers for his target.

From behind, Carter heard a female voice. "May I help you find something, sir?"

He turned to see a saleswoman smiling at him. "No, thank you," he said, keeping his voice low and his eyes on the man. "I'm just looking."

"We have a wonderful sale going on right now. Is this for your wife?"

"I'm not married," replied Carter.

"Girlfriend?"

"No," he answered, really wishing the lady would leave him alone. As he watched his follower turn around, Carter quickly backed up a step behind a clothing rack.

"Oh, a sister then or perhaps a friend?"

Getting annoyed by the woman's persistence, Carter finally answered her. "It's for my mom."

"Your mother?"

"Yeah, I'm having a little brother."

"Really?" The woman asked, taking a step back to look at Carter. "Excuse me for asking, but how old is your mother?"

"She's forty-five. She had me when she was twelve," he lied.

The lady gasped. "Twelve?"

Still watching the man make his way deeper into the mall, Carter continued laying it on thick.

"Yeah, I never really knew my father. My dad was forty when I was born and it never worked out between them. Now she's met a cool guy, but he's only twenty-one."

"Oh my gosh."

"Yeah, the whole thing's kind of weird, but they seem happy. As a matter of fact, they're going to be on the Maury Povich show sometime next month. So that's cool."

With the woman completely speechless and the man well off into the distance, Carter clasped his hands together and said, "Well, I'm not seeing anything here I like. Thanks anyway." Abruptly he exited the store and headed back to the parking lot, moving at a hurried jog.

As he approached the guy's car, Carter reached into his jeans and pulled out a pocketknife. Glancing around the parking lot, Carter waited for a woman to exit her car and pass by before he squatted down by the front tire. Unscrewing the valve cap, Carter used the small knife blade to depress the valve, deflating the tire until it was virtually flat.

Standing up and trying to look as inconspicuous as possible, Carter made his way back to his truck, only to see the guy standing outside the mall scanning the parking lot.

With Carter now standing, the guy's eyes locked in on him. Immediately, the man ran across the parking lot toward Carter. For a stout guy, Carter thought the guy moved really fast and decided he had better pick up his own pace if he was going to beat the guy to his truck.

Right before the guy reached the front of the truck, Carter got behind the wheel and shut the door, locking it just as the guy reached for the handle. Carter offered a smirk as he started the truck and pulled forward.

Suddenly the guy hopped up into the bed of the truck, sat down, leaning back against the tailgate and offered a smirk of his own to Carter, who was watching in the rear view mirror.

Carter slammed down on the brakes, making his uninvited passenger fall forward. He then jumped out of the cab. "Get your butt out of my truck," Carter demanded, walking toward the rear of his vehicle.

The man stood up in the bed and barked, "What did you do to my car?"

"Why have you been following me?"

"I asked you what you did to my car," repeated the guy.

"I don't have the time or patience for this," said Carter, getting extremely agitated. "Get out of my truck."

The guy placed his hands on the side of the bed and hopped out, directly in front of Carter. With his shoulders squared he got up in Carter's face and yelled, "Go fix whatever you did to my car."

Carter simply ignored him and turned to get back into the cab, when he felt the guy's hand grab hold of his shoulder. With one quick move, Carter spun around, grabbed the man's arm and slammed him up against the car in the adjacent space. Having a solid, controlling hold on the man's arm, Carter pinned the man down on the hood. The guy struggled to free himself until Carter applied more pressure to the arm, almost to the point where Carter expected to hear something snap. Finally the man ceased to resist and Carter leaned over and whispered into his ear. "Tell your boss I don't like being followed. And if you keep it up, it's going to be you who's disabled, not your car."

The man nodded in submission.

Carter hesitated a moment longer before pushing him away. The guy charged to retaliate, but Carter caught him with a straight left jab, followed with a crashing right hand, sending the guy to the pavement. Carter's eyes shifted to the two teenage boys slowly walking by, watching the whole thing.

When they realized Carter was looking at them, they hurried away, not bothering to look back.

Turning his attention back to his opponent lying on the blacktop, rolling side to side and groaning, Carter noticed a piece of paper in the man's shirt pocket. He reached down and retrieved it. When he unfolded it, he saw the addresses of the places he visited in South Bend. He stuck it in his pocket, shook his head in disgust, got back into his truck, and drove away.

EIGHTEEN

Jasper entered the security office of WLP&D early that evening after his regular employees left for the day. His "security" personnel were scattered around the room.

Sitting in a chair, leaning back against the wall with the front legs off the ground, sat Luke, sporting the fresh black eye Carter gave him in the parking lot. Luke's eyes drifted away from the disapproving glare of his boss.

"So let me get this straight," began Jasper, addressing the entire group, but primarily Luke. "You're supposed to be tailing this Mays guy, and somehow due to what I'm sure is your total ineptness, he catches you. So then you engage him, even though I instructed not to do anything of the sort."

Jasper's eyes shifted to Russell who Jasper had given the responsibility of overseeing things.

Russell conveyed his acknowledgement with a guilty nod.

"And I guess," continued Jasper, fixing his eyes back on Luke. "In the process of engaging this investigator, he kicked your sorry butt and left you stranded in a mall parking lot? On top of that, you lost the information you collected following him."

Luke kept his head turned away and let out a regretful sigh.

Jasper kicked the chair out from beneath the startled man, sending him to the floor. "Look at me when I'm talking to you."

Everyone in the room took a step back.

"What kind of an idiot are you?" Jasper yelled, as Luke stumbled to his feet.

Jasper spun around to face Russell. "Russell, did you tell him to keep a low profile?"

"I told him," confirmed Russell.

Jasper turned back to Luke and resumed yelling. "Luke, did you hear Russell tell you to lay low? Is there some type of medical problem that prevents you from hearing clear directions?"

"Yeah, yeah, he told me," admitted Luke, looking much more shaken than when the meeting began. "But then I saw him messing with my car and I guess I just lost it."

"You just lost it? Do I pay you to lose it or do I pay you to follow directions?"

"You pay me to follow directions."

"That's right. I pay you to follow directions, you moron. How incompetent can you be? The fact he saw you at all pisses me off, but then you go and pick a fight with him?"

"Hey Mick and Roy lost him, too," Luke offered.

"What?" Jasper asked.

Russell shot a nasty look in Luke's direction.

Jasper turned to Roy and Mick, who suddenly appeared uncomfortable. His eyes then returned to Russell. "What's this idiot talking about, Russell?"

Russell took a deep breath, then reluctantly explained. "They tailed Carter last night to your daughter's apartment."

"Yeah, and?"

"I guess Mays saw them, and next thing they know, a cop pulls up in a cruiser and starts questioning them while Mays and your daughter drove away. I guess he had an old buddy on the force running interference for him."

"The police? The police questioned them and you didn't feel the need to share that with me?"

"I was handling it," replied Russell.

Jasper placed his hand over the lower part of his face and closed his eyes, taking a deep breath. Walking over directly in front of Russell, Jasper placed his finger into Russell's chest. "You don't keep things like that from me. Do you hear me?"

Russell nodded in submission.

Jasper scanned the room, looking at each man. "I am not paying you losers to be incompetent. I'm paying you for results, and so far, I'm not getting any. Have I not been fair, even generous, toward you idiots? Haven't I taken good care of you while you've worked for me?"

Jasper's eyes caught the sight of Billy, sitting in the corner, his face still bruised and swollen from the interrogation. For a moment, Jasper's guilt flashed over him and he felt the regret of putting Billy through that.

Shaking it off, he continued to scold the men. "If you want to keep your position here, you better up your performance. I've got too much on my mind right now without worrying what kind of reckless and brainless actions you're committing. I will not tolerate any more screw ups."

Turning one last time to Luke, Jasper pointed his finger. "And you, you're fired."

Luke's eyes grew wide and panicked. "What? No, Mr. Bedford, please."

Jasper looked at Dan. "Dan, fire this worthless piece of crap."

Dan pulled out a pistol and a silencer, which he began attaching.

Luke swallowed hard. "Please, Mr. Bedford, I got it, message received," said Luke, with a nervous laugh. "You're kidding right?"

Luke yelled out one last time for Mr. Bedford before Dan fired off two quick rounds into his chest. The man dropped to the floor, motionless.

Everyone in the room quietly began to exit. Dan called out to Roy and Mick. "No, no, no; you two aren't leaving yet."

Both guys stopped, carefully watching the gun in Dan's hand.

Dan pointed with the gun at Luke's dead body, lying in an expanding pool of blood. "Clean up this mess. Make sure you do a thorough job."

As Jasper and Dan walked out the door, Mick and Roy commenced getting rid of their former co-worker.

NINETEEN

Confident nobody followed him for the moment, Carter stopped by his house to swap his truck out for his motorcycle. He left the truck parked closer to the road, hoping if any of Bedford's men showed up, they would see the familiar truck and assume he was home. And if by chance they did recognize him on the motorcycle, the bike would make it easier to lose them.

Carter passed Cindy's apartment, circling the building, watching for any suspicious eyes that may be waiting. A sharp-looking Cadillac parked down the street with an excellent view of the main entrance caught Carter's attention. Glancing in the window as he drove by, Carter recognized the driver from his initial meeting with Jasper Bedford. The driver didn't appear to pay him any attention as he passed.

On the other side of the block, Carter found the entrance to the parking garage reserved for residents only. He watched a woman in a sporty little BMW pull up to the gate to scan an access card, raising the gate and allowing her to enter. In a split second decision, Carter hit the throttle and zipped in behind her, ducking down as the gate lowered. After parking his bike in an out of the way corner, Carter entered the building and made his way to the elevator.

He knocked on Cindy's door and waited, shifting his eyes up and down the empty hallway.

She opened the door and stepped back, inviting him in but avoiding eye contact.

In an attempt to break the ice, he remained standing in the doorway and smirked. "What? No kiss hello?"

The comment caught Cindy off guard but did what it was intended to do. She shot him a dirty look and then laughed. "That's not even funny."

Carter let out a boisterous laugh and walked inside.

"I'm so embarrassed," commented Cindy as she closed the door.

Trying not to dwell on the subject, Carter asked, "So where's the file?"

Still shaking her head and smiling, Cindy walked over to her coffee table and picked up a manila folder. "Here it is."

Carter took the folder and sat on the sofa to peruse it.

Cindy sat next to him and peered over his shoulder.

He stopped and looked at her.

She backed off a little. "What? I'm just reading along."

"Like you haven't already read through this?"

"Yes, I did. But I may have missed something. Besides, what else am I going to do, sit here and watch you read?"

Carter resumed looking through the file and Cindy returned to her vantage point over his shoulder.

A moment passed in silence, as Carter reviewed each section.

"See anything yet?" Cindy asked.

Carter raised his eyebrows and replied, "Do you mind?"

"Sorry. How about if I get us something to drink, non-alcoholic of course?"

"That would be great," he replied, humored by the comment.

"I have coffee, diet soda, iced tea, and maybe some orange juice. Does any of that sound good?"

"Tea sounds good."

As Cindy went into the kitchen, Carter resumed reading the file once more. He came across something that held his attention and he called into the kitchen. "Hey, who is Tate Manning?"

"He's the Chief Financial Officer. He's worked for my dad since the beginning."

"So what is the status of your father right now? I assume he's a free man? Guys like him don't stay behind bars very long."

"What do you mean 'guys like him'?"

"Men with money," answered Carter.

"Oh," replied Cindy.

Carter stared at his client from across the room. "You know, for a moment you sounded defensive about your dad. I thought you already wrote him off."

Cindy stopped pouring the tea. "I guess I still don't like anyone else talking about him. And to answer your question, yes, he's out on bail."

"Have you talked to him?"

"No, I don't have any desire to right now, and I'd rather not talk about it."

"Okay."

Cindy returned with the tea and sat down next to Carter.

"So why are you asking me about Tate?"

"No reason. I just noticed that he hired Tyler."

"Yeah, so? Is that supposed to mean something?"

"No, I'm just trying to learn as much as I can," said Carter shaking his head nonchalantly as he continued to read. "Let's see, he started with the company straight out of college, and worked part-time delivering pizza while he was in school."

Pausing, Carter wrinkled his brow.

"What is it?" Cindy asked.

"I noticed he lived off campus in an apartment."

"Yeah?"

"If it's the same complex I'm thinking of, it was a nice place."

"It was a nice place. He showed me where he used to live."

"The only job he listed on the resume is the pizza delivery job, and he claimed to have worked about twenty hours a week. How does a guy with no family support who delivers pizza twenty hours a week afford that place?"

"Maybe he had roommates," suggested Cindy.

"Did he ever mention his roommates in college?"

"No, he didn't."

"How familiar are you with his finances?" Carter asked. "Was he paying back student loans?"

"We went over both of our finances to establish a budget. He never mentioned student loans. He was big on budgeting. He claimed he wanted to be completely self-sufficient, not depend on my family. Ha. What a joke that turned out to be."

Carter continued reading.

Suddenly, Cindy spoke. "Hey, maybe he sold drugs to afford living there. He does have a history."

"I don't know if I'd say he had a history. He had a minor possession offense. That's not the same as dealing."

After a few more minutes of reading, Carter tossed the file on the table and leaned back into the sofa.

"I don't see much here," he said.

"Now what?" Cindy inquired.

"I'm not sure. I'll have to think about it."

"Wow," replied Cindy. "I was hoping to hear something a little more confident."

Carter grinned and looked at his client. "You know," he began. "You're doing pretty well dealing with all of this."

"I'm not sure if I agree with that, but thanks. I think I've arrived at the place where I'm sort of glazed over. After the initial shock of finding out the last two years were just a big sham, and then everything going on with my dad, I'm on auto pilot. I'm still heartbroken and really pissed, but I don't have the energy to express it. This whole thing has sucked the life out of me."

Carter stood up, giving Cindy a light backhanded pat on the knee. "You'll survive this. Things will get better for you."

"When?"

"That I don't know," he said, walking toward the door. "But I'm sure your life will go on just fine without Tyler Moore or Steven Conway."

Cindy stood and followed him across the room. "Thanks for the encouragement."

Carter opened the door, turned and smiled. "Thanks for getting the file for me."

"I wish it had been more help."

"That's the way this stuff goes. Sometimes you hope for a home run and you get a strikeout. Other times, you're not expecting much and bam, you hit one out of the park. I'll talk to you tomorrow."

"See ya," said Cindy, closing the door.

Outside Cindy's building, Russell sat in his Cadillac with an ear piece in his ear. On a notepad he wrote the name Steven Conway.

TWENTY

Jasper Bedford and Tate Manning entered WLP&D just after ten that evening.

Russell and Dan waited for them in the main conference room. Nobody spoke as Jasper took his seat at the head of the table.

Tate sat in the chair beside him.

"Okay, first things first," said Jasper, looking at Dan. "Has the situation with Luke been taken care of?"

"Yes, sir," he replied. "Nobody will ever find him."

"You're sure?"

"Absolutely," promised Dan.

"Good," said Jasper leaning back. "Where are we on Tyler?"

Russell leaned forward, resting his forearms on the table. "We're still hitting a lot of dead ends."

Jasper shook his head in frustrated disapproval.

"However," said Russell, "I do have a new name."

"What?" Jasper inquired not expecting much.

"Steven Conway." The name initiated a quick jerk of the head from both Jasper and Tate.

"Conway?" Jasper asked.

Russell nodded and asked, "Does that mean something?"

Jasper and Tate glanced at one another. "Where did you get that name?" Jasper asked.

"The P.I. mentioned it at your daughter's place tonight," answered Russell.

"What did he say?"

"He told her that her life would go on just fine without Tyler Moore or Steven Conway."

Jasper looked at Tate. "Do you think there could be a connection?"

Tate shrugged. "I don't know, maybe."

"Who's Steven Conway?" Dan asked.

"I don't know for sure," replied Jasper.

Russell spoke. "It would also seem one of our employees pulled Tyler's file and gave it to your daughter."

Jasper rolled his eyes. "Let me guess, Daphne?"

Russell nodded to confirm.

"We'll fire her."

Dan raised his eyebrows upon hearing the instructions. "Do you mean...?"

"No," Jasper quickly replied. "I mean, just fire her from the job, not fire her the way you fired Luke. Geez, Dan."

"Oh, just making sure," said Dan.

Jasper rubbed his temples as he returned his focus to the name Conway.

"What do you think, Jasper?" Tate asked.

"I don't know. I'm trying to figure out if there could be some possible connection, and if there is, how does it relate back to her."

"That was a really long time ago," commented Tate. "And it's not like Conway is a rare name. I'm inclined to think it's just a coincidence."

"What else did the PI and my daughter talk about?" Jasper asked Russell.

"Nothing significant. It was a brief meeting."

"Where's the PI now?"

"We're not sure," answered Russell.

"What do you mean you're not sure? You were watching the building when he was there, right?"

"Yeah," said Russell, about to come up with an explanation.

"Did you fall asleep or step inside an alley to take a piss?"

"No, I kept an eye on the place the whole time."

"But you didn't see him leave, even though you heard him inside my daughter's apartment and knew when he was leaving?"

"No, sir."

"Where was he parked? How could he leave without you seeing him?"

"Actually, I never saw him arrive either," said Russell, bracing himself for a verbal assault. "I was told he was at home."

"Who told you that?" Jasper demanded.

Russell nodded his head toward Dan, who quickly threw out his defense. "His truck was in the driveway and there were lights on inside. He must have had another vehicle."

"Do you think so?" Jasper said with as much sarcasm as he could muster.

Dan looked down at the floor in front of him.

"So basically, he duped both of you? Great. You two are supposed to be my most competent guys and you can't even keep tabs on one guy."

"Sorry," said, Russell. "It won't happen again."

"You know, I'm starting to wonder if I shouldn't explore the market for better employees," said Jasper. "You can't find Tyler, even though he has no problem knowing everything you're doing. And now, you can't keep up with one two-bit investigator. Why am I paying you?"

Neither man spoke.

"My head is in a noose and I have to depend on complete idiots."

Jasper locked his hands together on top of his head and took a slow deep breath while looking up at the ceiling tiles. "Okay, here's what I need you to do," he said in a very condescending tone. "Find the PI. If you have to buy a horseshoe or a rabbit's foot to change your sorry luck, then do it. But find this guy and stick to him like your future depends on it, because it does."

"Yes, sir, Mr. Bedford," said Russell.

"I mean it. I don't want this guy anywhere where we don't have eyes on him. Right now, he's my best chance for finding Tyler.

Do whatever you have to do, but do not let him out of your sight. I don't care if he's driving his truck, taking a cab, walking, or swimming across Lake Michigan, I want someone behind him at all times. Anything this guy does, you report it back to me, whether it's what he eats for breakfast or what color his pee is when he goes to take a leak."

"Yes, sir," replied both men.

"Do you have his house and office bugged?"

"We'll have his office tonight," answered Russell. "His house is more challenging. He lives in a busy neighborhood and has a large, noisy, and uncooperative German shepherd. I sent one of the guys over there, but there's not a good way to access the house without doing something to the dog. And if we do anything to the dog, he's going to know something is up."

"I don't want to risk tipping our hand," said Jasper. "Plant someone outside and see what you can pick up with the portable."

"Yes, sir."

"And I swear if you screw this up again, I suggest you don't come back."

"Yes, sir, Mr. Bedford."

TWENTY-ONE

The sound of Booker's barking stirred Carter from his deep sleep. He rolled over to face his nightstand. The blurry numbers on the clock read 3:22 a.m. "Shh, Booker, what's your deal, dog?" Carter asked just before the strong smell of smoke assaulted his nostrils. He opened his eyes to see his bedroom filling up with smoke. Leaping out of bed, he ran toward the door and into the hallway where he moved to the top of the steps to see the intense glow pierce through the thick smoke.

After taking six steps down, Carter realized that there was no way he would be able to exit through the main floor. The heat was intense and he began coughing from the smoke.

He ran back to his room with Booker on his heels and still barking. He slammed the door shut to keep out the smoke and threw on the pair of jeans lying on the end of the bed. Grabbing the pistol from his nightstand, he tucked it into his waistband.

Running over to his open window he pushed out the screen. Grabbing everything he could, he began throwing it out onto the lawn, including some clothes, a few pictures, and a security box filled with important items like insurance policies and bank records. He felt the heat of the fire penetrating the floor beneath his bare feet. Carter heard someone shouting his name from below and looked out his window.

His next door neighbor, Dave, stood in his lawn looking up and yelling for him. "Carter, get out of there. The whole floor below is engulfed. It could go at any time."

Leaning out the window, Carter yelled, "Dave, you have to help me get Booker out of here. Go get a sheet and someone to help catch him."

While Dave ran back to his house, Carter grabbed more stuff. He could hear the sounds of his house shifting as the fire consumed more of the structure. He opened the door and was amazed by how much more smoke had filled the hallway. Quickly he slammed the door, but began coughing again from the smoke.

Booker looked panicked, running in circles, barking.

Carter went back to his window where he saw Dave and his teenage son, Alec, running from next door, past a crowd of neighbors drawn out by the commotion.

Dave and Alec stretched out a blanket just below the small section of roofing outside Carter's window.

"Carter," yelled Dave, "get your butt out of there now."

Carter grabbed Booker by the collar and led him to the window. Keeping his hand on the collar, Carter climbed out first and persuaded the reluctant dog to follow. Once they were both on the small section of roof, Carter picked up his dog and tossed him toward his neighbors waiting below. Booker landed dead center of the blanket and bounced right out onto the lawn, shaken, but okay. Dave and Alec repositioned the blanket for Carter.

Shaking his head, Carter said, "Guys, I don't think you're going to be able..."

Suddenly the entire second floor shifted, knocking Carter off balance. Barefoot on the steep shingles, Carter reached back toward the window to steady himself but was unable to latch onto anything, as he fell backwards off the roof, much to the surprise of Dave and his son.

When Carter regained consciousness, he was in a hospital room. A large portion of his body ached and his head throbbed with pain. He lifted his arm to see the clear tube traveling from the back of his hand to the I.V. bottle hanging beside his bed. He was alone.

Looking along the bedside, Carter looked for the call button to summon a nurse. He finally found it and pressed it twice.

A voice came over the little speaker in response. "Yes?"

"Where am I?" Carter asked, raising his head off the pillow.

"Mr. Mays?"

"That's right," he replied. "Where am I?"

"You're at County General Hospital," replied the mystery lady. "The nurse is on his way to your room."

"Thanks," said Carter, dropping back into the pillow.

Just seconds later, a black man in his mid-thirties wearing hospital scrubs entered the room.

"Hello, Mr. Mays. It's good to see you awake. My name is Luther and I'm your nurse. How are you feeling?"

"Crappy," replied Carter. "What happened? How long have I been here?"

"You fell off your roof," answered the nurse, writing something on Carter's chart. "You've been here about three hours now. You have a pretty good concussion."

"That explains the pick axe I feel in my brain."

The nurse chuckled. "I'll talk to the doctor and get something more for your pain."

"Anything broke?"

"No, all your bones are intact. You're a lucky man."

Dave walked into the room carrying a foam cup of coffee n one hand. His son Alec trailed in behind him with a can of apple juice from the cafeteria.

"He's awake," announced Dave. "How are you feeling?"

"Not good," answered Carter, attempting to sit up in bed.

"Hold on there," the nurse said. "You may not want to move around much yet."

Wincing and grunting from the pain shooting throughout his body, Carter found himself quickly agreeing with his caretaker.

"That was a nasty fall you took," said Dave.

"What happened?" Carter asked, a little fuzzy on the details of the morning.

"You were getting ready to jump down when the whole house shifted and threw you off the roof. Alec and I tried to catch you, but we only caught half of you."

"Your lower half," added Alec.

"Yeah, unfortunately we got the blanket under your legs, but your head hit the ground and knocked you out cold," said Dave.

"Sorry," said Alec.

"That's alright, you tried," whispered Carter. "Where's Booker?"

"We've got him in the backyard. He's fine. And I collected all the stuff you threw out into the yard and have it in my house."

"Thanks."

"I got your cell phone and called your folks," said Dave. "I hope you don't mind. I felt like I should let them know."

"They're on their way here, aren't they?" Carter asked, with a hint of regret in his voice.

"Yep, the first flight they can get."

"They don't need to come out here. Obviously I'm fine."

"Well, I don't know if you're fine," argued Dave. "Yeah, you're going to be fine, but for the moment you're homeless and you have a concussion. Besides, they're your parents. They want to be here."

"Is the house a complete loss?"

Dave apologetically nodded. "Yeah, I'd say so. Catherine called a few minutes ago and told me the fire department had it pretty well extinguished. She said one of the firemen told her that most of the second floor had collapsed."

Carter addressed his nurse. "How long will I be here?"

"I'll leave that to the doctor to answer," the man replied.

"Is he around?"

"She'll be in to see you in a little later," said the nurse, hanging the chart back on the end of the bed. "Do you need anything before I go, besides the pain medicine I promised?"

"No, thank you," responded Carter.

The nurse exited the room, freeing up space for Alec to walk over and lean against the window ledge.

"I'm really sorry about your house," offered Dave. "I know you've invested a lot of time and money into fixing it up."

"Yeah, but such is life. This is the second time I've had my home burn down."

"Really?"

"When I was about twelve, our house caught on fire. We weren't home at the time. My brother and I were at school. My folks were both at work. I remember getting off the bus and walking several feet before I even noticed the charred remains of my house."

"Wow, that would suck," commented Alec.

"Yeah, pretty much. They said it was caused by faulty wiring."

"Do you have a guess as to what may have caused this one?" Dave inquired.

"No. I'm hoping it wasn't something stupid that I did. Bad enough losing my home, but to find out I'm responsible will make it a lot worse."

Carter let out a prolonged yawn and Dave motioned to Alec that it was time to go. "Listen buddy," began Dave. "I know you need to get some rest, so we're going to bug out of here for now. Call me if you need anything. Okay?"

"Thanks, Dave. Thanks, Alec. You guys are good neighbors."

"Sorry again we didn't catch you very well in the blanket," said Alec as he walked by.

Carter smiled. "And here I thought you were a good ball player, Alec."

The kid smiled and shrugged. "I guess not."

"Of course, you've never had to catch a hundred-ninety-pound ball in a little blanket, huh? You probably saved me from getting hurt much worse."

"We'll talk to you later, Carter," said Dave, as he and his son left the room.

Lying there, staring at his sterile surroundings, Carter hoped his stay would be short-lived. He hated hospitals. His mind went through a list of all the projects he had completed in the house, some of his best craftsmanship. He had been really proud of it. Now it was gone, reduced to ashes. It was depressing. He tried to remember if he had done anything to cause the fire. That extension cord he had been using for his power tools had been around a while and had a few spots where he had wrapped it in electrical tape. Perhaps that had contributed to the fire. Of course, in the grand scheme of things, he wondered if it made any difference. He was still homeless.

Carter passed the time channel surfing between four different programs, none of which really interested him. Three men entered the room. Carter's friend, Bobby from Chicago PD led the way, followed by two guys wearing suits.

Carter hit the power button on the remote and sat up more.

"Hey, buddy," greeted Bobby.

"Hey, Bobby," said Carter. "How did you know I was here?"

"You haven't been gone from the department that long and word travels fast. Are you alright?"

"Yeah, pretty sore, but I'm okay. I have a concussion."

Bobby gestured toward the two guys with him. "This is Detective Frank Anderson and Detective Guy Nolin."

Frank Anderson, the older of the two stepped forward to greet Carter. He appeared to be in his late forties to early fifties, with a potbelly putting pressure on his shirt buttons and a tie that was too short. His neatly combed dark brown hair was obviously dyed, in sharp contrast to his white mustache. "Hello, Mr. Mays."

Guy Nolin was a much younger man, especially for a detective.

Carter figured him for one of the extremely ambitious go-getters who are able to take the fast track from the academy to the high ranks of the department.

His tailored and fashionable wardrobe seemed much more Esquire magazine than Chicago PD. He simply nodded his head and smiled, letting his counterpart take the lead.

"Mr. Mays," said Detective Anderson. "I'm sorry about your house. According to the Fire Marshall, it was definitely arson."

"Really?" Carter asked, his mind immediately fixating on Jasper Bedford and his so-called employees, particularly the one with a background in arson. Anger began to set in.

"Yes, sir. But that's not the only reason we're here."

"What's the other reason?"

"A man was found shot to death in the front seat of his car, parked on your street, just one house down from yours."

"Homicide or self-inflicted?" Carter inquired,

"Homicide. Shot from three feet or less."

"Wow."

Detective Nolin handed a large yellow envelope to his partner who removed photographs and handed them to Carter. "Do you know this man?"

Carter took the photographs and immediately recognized the victim slouched over in the blood-stained front seat of a car. It was Bedford's man, Dan Yielding, the arsonist.

"Yeah, I've seen this guy before," said Carter, looking at Bobby, but not disclosing anything about the files Bobby provided.

"Where have you seen him?"

"He was in my office a couple of days ago."

"May I ask why he was there?" Frank inquired.

"Actually, it was his boss who came to see me. This guy was just a background figure."

"His boss?" Detective Nolin spoke up for the first time.

"Yeah," confirmed Carter.

"Who is his boss?" Detective Anderson asked, taking back the lead from his younger partner.

"Jasper Bedford. He owns West Lake Properties & Development."

Detective Nolin perked up at the mention of Jasper's name and he tapped Anderson on the shoulder.

"Bedford? Isn't that the rich guy perv picked up for trying to meet a teenager this week?"

Anderson shrugged. "I don't know. I didn't hear about it."

"That's him," offered Carter.

"So what was your business with him? Is he a client?"

"No. He came to talk about his daughter who is a client."

"What about his daughter?"

"Well, just like I told him, I can't discuss that," said Carter.

"Of course not," replied Anderson, a little disgruntled that Carter wouldn't elaborate.

"Do you have any insight or theory as to how these two might be related?" Nolin asked.

"Not really."

"Do you know why this man would be parked on your street?" Anderson asked.

"Nope."

"Are you absolutely certain?" Nolin interjected. "Because I find it interesting that the man who was in your office a couple of days ago, and found shot to death on your street on the same day your house burned down, has a rap sheet that includes arson."

"Arson? Really?" Carter inquired as if he didn't already know, tilting his voice in surprise.

"Yeah, really," said Nolin. "With all those put together, I would think there's a connection somewhere."

"Yes, I would think so, too," agreed Carter. "But I don't know what that is. It doesn't make sense. You tell me the fire that burnt down my house was arson. Then you tell me that the dead guy has a history of arson. So are you implying that the dead guy set my house on fire, then ended up getting killed? Do you think I killed the guy in retaliation or something?"

"No," replied Anderson, resuming control over the questioning. "We're just trying to put the pieces together and were hoping you might help us."

"And I would if I knew what to tell you. But I don't know what to tell you. The guy was in my office with his boss. The only discussion I had with him directly is requesting that he not smoke in my office. I know, it's ironic."

"Look, in the event that you gain some insight to this mess, I would appreciate a phone call," said Anderson, reaching into his wallet for a business card. "Here's my number."

Carter took the card. "I'll keep that in mind."

"Until then," said Anderson, "I wish you a speedy recovery."

"Thank you," said Carter.

The three men exited the room, with Bobby being the last one out and motioning that he'd call later.

Carter sank back into his pillow to contemplate the new information. Was it Bedford's man who set the fire? If not, why was he there, and who else would have started the fire? Who shot him? This case seemed to produce more questions than answers.

TWENTY-TWO

Fatigued and frustrated, Jasper sat in his office not getting anything accomplished. It was his first official day back since Cindy's wedding fiasco. And now with this sexual importuning case hanging over his head, he had endured numerous stares and awkward hellos from his employees when he arrived that morning. He was sure everyone was wondering about the man who signed their checks, worried about how this was going to affect the business and their livelihoods.

A knock at his door stirred him from his thoughts and a visibly stressed Russell entered his office.

"What's wrong now?" Jasper asked.

"Dan's dead," came Russell's blunt reply.

"What?" Jasper stood and asked, "How? When?"

"The cops found him last night in his car parked on the investigator's street. He'd been shot in the head."

"The PI killed him?"

Russell shook his head. "I don't think so. Someone torched the investigator's house and he barely got out alive. He's at the hospital now."

"Who torched the house?" Jasper demanded an answer.

Holding out his hands and shrugging his shoulders, Russell answered, "I don't know."

"Was it Dan?"

"He had no reason. He was only there to keep tabs on Mays. We never discussed doing more than that."

"If he didn't, then who did?"

"I don't know," said Russell.

Jasper sat down again, turning his chair to face the window while he sorted things out. Russell waited patiently in silence. Finally, Jasper swung his chair around and picked up the phone from his desk, dialing a four digit extension. "Tate, get in here," said Jasper and hung up without waiting for a reply.

Within thirty seconds, Tate entered the office. "What's up?"

"We have a problem," said Jasper.

"What?"

"Dan's dead."

"When? How did it happen?"

"Somebody shot him last night," said Jasper.

Tate's eyes grew large and he sat down. "Who?"

"We don't know."

"Where did it happen?"

"Someone shot him in his car. He was parked on Carter Mays' street."

"The detective?"

Jasper nodded. "And someone also torched the detective's house."

"Was it Dan?" Tate asked.

"No, we don't think so," said Jasper.

Tate placed his hand over his mouth and stared at the floor. "So the detective is dead, too?"

"No, he got out."

"So, he's probably the one who shot Dan," suggested Tate.

"Not likely," said Russell. "He barely got out. From what I've learned, he fell out of his second floor window trying to escape the flames. They've got him in the hospital now."

"What are we going to do?"

"I don't know. But it's not going to take long for the cops to link Dan back to here and we need to be prepared. If we missed anything, they'll find it. You did get rid of all the records like we talked about, didn't you? I can't afford any more trouble right now."

"Yeah, yeah, yeah," assured Tate, still taking in the news. "I did everything just as you told me to. They won't find any links between WLP&D and our other business deals."

"You're sure?"

"Absolutely."

Jasper stood and began to pace behind his desk.

"I can't believe this," Jasper said in frustration. "All these years of smooth sailing and now everything is crumbling before my eyes, and in a week."

"We're not down for the count yet," offered Tate.

"You mean you're not down for the count," snapped Jasper. "I've still got this girl at the library to deal with."

"Hey, Dylan's got his best people working on that," said Tate.

"Oh yeah, good old Dylan is working on it. To be honest, I'm not so sure that cocky SOB wouldn't let me fry just so he could have a go at it with my wife."

Neither Tate, nor Russell, offered a comment on that one.

"And now," continued Jasper with his rant, "this PI probably thinks I burned down his house and will come after me with everything he's got."

"Do you think we should take him out?" Tate asked.

"What? And bring even more attention from the police than I already have? Are you a moron?"

"Sorry. I was just trying to help."

"Well, you're not helping," Jasper yelled.

The room grew quiet again, as Jasper paced back and forth like a caged animal.

Finally, Jasper stopped pacing and announced, "I'm going to have to hire him."

"What?" Tate asked.

"I'm going to have to hire him. At least then he'll be working for me."

"Hire him to do what?"

"To find Tyler. Tyler's the one behind this whole mess. If I find him, I can get it cleaned up."

"But Cindy already hired him to do that."

"There's no reason we both can't pay him to do the same thing. This way, I can better monitor what he's doing."

"Do you think he's going to work for you if he thinks you tried to incinerate him?" Tate asked.

"That's up to me to convince him that I had nothing to do with it."

"That's insane," argued Tate. "He's probably already gone to the police to claim it was you."

"Maybe so, but I'm running out of options here," said Jasper. Then he looked at Russell. "Come on, Russell. You're driving me to the hospital."

Dave sat on the window ledge watching Carter put on his shoes.

The doctor released Carter with strict orders to lay low for a few days, resting up and allowing his body to heal. His activity was to be minimal.

Without a home to go to, Dave offered Carter their guest bedroom for as many days as it took for the insurance company to provide Carter with temporary housing.

Jasper entered the room with Russell close behind him.

When Carter looked up to see his visitors, his demeanor indicated he was not pleased to see them.

"Hello, Mr. Mays," greeted Jasper.

Carter said nothing, but turned to address his neighbor. "Dave, can you give us a minute, please?"

"Sure thing," replied Dave. "I'll be out in the hall if you need anything," he said, offering a suspicious look to the men as he passed by them.

"Thanks, Dave."

Once Dave cleared the room, Carter stood up. "Did you come to finish me off?"

"I'm here for a couple of reasons," declared Jasper. "One is to assure you I had nothing to do with your house burning down."

"Word sure travels fast then," responded Carter.

"I found out because one of my employees was murdered."

"Yes, on my street, sitting outside my house, which is now a pile of charred rubble. If you had nothing to do with it, then why was your man there?"

"Look, I'll admit we were watching you to see if you might lead us to Tyler Moore."

"That's funny. I got the impression in our first meeting you didn't want him found."

"Actually, I didn't want you getting in the way of us finding him."

"That sounds like a pretty good motive for getting rid of me," said Carter.

"Yeah, I guess it would appear that way."

"And the fact that your man on my street has a history of setting fires doesn't bode well for you either."

"That's true, also. But it doesn't make sense that he would torch your house and then end up dead, unless you're the one who killed him. After all, what better motive for killing a guy than the fact you thought he burnt your house down with you inside."

"I've got a neighborhood of witnesses who watched me barely get out of that house alive."

"I'm not saying you're the one who killed him. I'm just saying that whoever killed him, is probably the same individual who set fire to your house."

"That still doesn't tell me why you're here."

"I want to hire you," replied Jasper.

Carter let out a laugh. "You want to hire me?"

Jasper nodded.

"To do what?" Carter inquired.

"To find Tyler Moore," said Jasper, in a calm tone.

"I've already been hired to do that."

"Just think of it as dual clientele. You won't do anything different. You'll just be getting two checks instead of one."

"And why the turn-a-bout?"

"Well, it's true what they say: you just can't beat a man at his own trade."

Carter snickered again. "You're unbelievable."

"And," continued Jasper, "as an extra incentive, I'll provide you with an apartment free of charge until you can get back into your house, up to, I don't know, let's say one year?"

"That could get expensive for you."

"I own a couple of complexes. It wouldn't be that much of a burden."

"My insurance will take care of the temporary housing."

"True, but you could stay in one of my units for free and pocket the insurance money."

"I don't think I'd be all that comfortable living in a place where you had that much control and access. You've already proven to be a huge invasion of privacy, with your guys following me and staking out my house."

Jasper smiled. "That's fair. I earned that."

"I am curious. Your employees, as you call them, I've noticed they don't have the most stellar of backgrounds," said Carter, looking directly at Russell. "I can't help but wonder why a 'legitimate' businessman like you would hire guys like that."

"Obviously, you've done some snooping of your own," Jasper said. "However, since you asked, in my business, I occasionally encounter unscrupulous and intimidating people, so as a matter of self-preservation, I've hired my own people who can be a little intimidating. It keeps people from trying to take advantage of me. And it gives guys like Russell here, the opportunity to go legit while still using some of the skill sets he's already comfortable with."

"Wow," said Carter. "You're doing a real public service; your own prisoner rehab."

Jasper allowed the sarcasm to go and returned to his proposition. "So are you interested in earning double pay for the same work?"

"It always comes down to money for you, doesn't it?"

"That is often how things get done in life," responded Jasper.

Carter knew the motive for Bedford wanting to hire him. What better way to keep tabs on everything? Most likely, Bedford also figured anything Carter found out about him during the investigation would be kept confidential due to the client-investigator relationship. And Carter was sure there was plenty to find out about Mr. Bedford's business dealings. As much as he wanted to explore that avenue, Carter knew his first priority was doing what Cindy hired him to do. Plus, he did feel that somebody was trying to keep him from finding Tyler, and he didn't believe it to be Bedford. It didn't make sense. That was one thing he and Jasper could agree upon.

"Well, what's it going to be?" Jasper asked.

Carter paused for a moment while he pondered his options. The old saying of 'keep your friends close, keep your enemies closer' kept popping into his mind. With that considered, he nodded. "Okay, but there are some stipulations."

"Name them."

"Cindy has to approve," Carter said, knowing Jasper wasn't on the best terms with his daughter.

A distraught look came over Jasper's face. He nodded in agreement.

"Whenever I have a new development on the case, you can be there, but Cindy is the primary client here. I won't discuss anything about the case with just you."

"Agreed," said Jasper.

"Thirdly, I don't want any shadows. Keep your boys away from me. I know they've been watching me and Cindy. That has to stop."

"You've got it," Jasper replied.

"My rate is $400 a day, plus expenses, but then I'm sure you already knew that. The first two days are up front."

Jasper pulled a wad of cash from his pocket and counted out eight hundred dollars, sticking what looked to be another three hundred back into his pocket.

"Do you want to talk to your daughter or should I?"

"You'd better do it. She doesn't want anything to do with me at the moment," answered Jasper.

"Oh yeah, the thing with the girl at the library," commented Carter.

"That was a set-up," Jasper adamantly insisted. "That was our boy, Tyler."

"What do mean?"

"Tyler walked me right into that mess."

"How?"

"By pretending he was going to meet me."

"Wait a minute, you've talked to Tyler?" Carter was shocked by the revelation. "Why didn't Cindy mention this to me?"

"She doesn't know. She won't give me a chance to explain."

"You're being up front with me?" Carter asked. "You talked with Tyler?"

"Yes, he's the reason I'm in this trouble. He called me asking to meet, so he could explain things. He gives me all these stupid instructions including approaching this young girl, and next thing I know, I'm cuffed and labeled a sex offender."

"That sounds very vindictive. Why would he do that?"

"I don't know why. He's been very vindictive. He used his company card to make huge donations to all these organizations he knows I would never support."

"And you have no idea why? I find that hard to believe."

"I swear to you, Mr. Mays, I don't have a clue. Up until the day of the wedding, I thought Tyler and I had a good relationship. I swear."

The years Carter had spent on the police force taught him to read people. He had developed a fairly reliable skill of knowing when someone was being truthful and when they were handing him a line. And he had sensed Jasper handing him more than one line during their brief encounters. However, his gut told him Bedford was genuinely stumped by the behavior of his almost son-in-law. Jasper's mannerisms reflected feelings of being violated. It was hard to explain, but Carter sensed Jasper had been caught completely off guard, and now even seemed a little hurt by the whole thing.

"What number did he call you from?" Carter asked, growing more intrigued by this latest development.

"It was a cell phone, but I didn't recognize it."

"Did you tell the police?"

"I did. They said it was from a phone reported stolen and they would look into it, but they seemed more intent on hanging me than finding out the actual truth."

"Is the number still on your phone?"

Jasper pulled his cell phone from his jacket pocket and searched through his incoming calls before handing the phone to Carter, who copied the number down on the back of the instructions the doctor gave him while he recovered from his concussion.

"What good is that number going to do you?" Russell broke his silence.

"Maybe none," replied Carter with much ambiguity. "But you never know."

Carter returned the phone to Jasper. "How many times did he call you?"

"Once to set up the meeting. As a matter of fact, I believe it was after we left your office the day you and I met. That's when we made arrangements to meet at the library. Then he called me again once I reached the library."

"So obviously, he was watching you from somewhere nearby."

"Obviously."

"And you've not heard from him since?"

"No, I haven't."

Carter pondered the new information and the best way to go with his investigation. Knowing Tyler was still around, and even making phone calls to entrap his former employer, put all the emphasis on Tyler as the guilty party here. One of the main questions to focus on now was the motive behind it. This brought up the matter of stolen money Cindy mentioned in their first meeting.

"One more question," began Carter. "The money Cindy claimed Tyler stole from you, but you denied, which is the truth?"

"I've already told you, it was a case of misunderstanding on her part," replied Jasper. Then he hesitated. "Well, let me correct myself. He did steal about thirty grand out of my home safe. Between that and the money I spent on a wedding that never happened, it adds up to a fair amount of money."

"Yes, it does," said Carter. "But not six million."

"No, that's a figure she got from me talking about the business we may lose in his absence."

Carter still didn't know what he could or couldn't believe coming from Bedford. "Okay, then, if you don't mind, I'm going to get out of here. I've seen enough of this room."

"Would you like me to make arrangements for you to see some of my apartments?"

"No, thank you. I'm still going to pass on that."

"Let me know if you change your mind," said Jasper.

Carter couldn't help but wonder if Jasper was trying to lure him in to future employment. "Yeah, I'll do that."

Carter picked up his few belongings and passed between the two men. When he exited the room, he saw Dave leaning up against the wall, waiting.

"Are you ready to go?" Carter asked.

"Yep," answered Dave. "Who were those guys?"

"New client," replied Carter.

"Really?"

"Yep."

The two men took a few steps down the hall before Dave spoke up. "I kind of got the impression they may not be the kind of people you would want to do business with."

Carter grinned and looked at his neighbor. "You're a perceptive guy, Dave."

"They didn't have anything to do with last night, did they?"

"If you are asking me if they are responsible for burning down my house, the answer is no, I don't think so. Is there an indirect connection? Possibly."

"I don't mean to pry, but why would you have anything to do with them?"

"For now it's a matter of necessity."

Dave's expression conveyed his questioning of Carter's judgment. "Just be careful."

"Don't worry, I am."

TWENTY-THREE

As Dave pulled into the driveway, Carter looked over the blackened rubble next door. Much of the second floor had collapsed, exposing the inner part of the home. He exited the vehicle and approached his house.

Dave quietly followed, not having anything of comfort to say to his neighbor other than the obvious. "I'm glad you made it out, man."

Carter simply nodded and continued to inspect the damage. Caution tape and warning signs made a perimeter around the structure. Ducking under it, Carter continued moving closer.

When Carter reached for the doorknob, Dave spoke up. "I don't think you should go in there, Carter. The firemen said it's pretty unstable."

Looking back at his neighbor, Carter spoke, "I'm just going to take a peek."

Black soot and water covered the entire area. A gaping hole in the ceiling revealed part of the upstairs. His furniture was barely recognizable. From his viewpoint on the porch looking in, Carter saw the remnants of the fireplace mantle he had been working on. He wanted to take a better look, but wisdom told him it was not a good idea. Some of the exposed second story floor joists appeared charred and cracked. Unsettling noises echoed throughout, sounding warnings to anyone who entered.

Backing out of the doorway, Carter moved around the side of the house to the back. Busted windows on the back door indicated how the firemen probably got in. Stepping just inside, the crunching sound of glass escaped from beneath Carter's feet. He scanned the room, looking at his melted kitchen appliances.

Eventually, Carter grew tired of the depressing sight and walked away, resisting the urge to see what he could salvage from his belongings.

"I'm really sorry, Carter," offered Dave. "I know this sucks."

"Yeah, well, like you said, I made it out."

From next door, Carter heard Booker barking. He smiled and picked up his pace to Dave's backyard. "And so did my dog."

The German shepherd went crazy with excitement, spinning around in circles at the sight of his owner. Before Carter reached the boundary, Booker jumped and leaned against the fence that separated them.

Reaching over, Carter vigorously rubbed and patted his appreciative dog. "Hey, boy, did you miss me?"

"Come on inside and I'll let him in so he can give you a proper greeting," suggested Dave.

Dave's wife, Catherine, greeted the men at the door with apologetic eyes and a warming smile. "Hi, Carter. I'm sorry about the house. I'm sure Dave told you already, but you're welcome to stay here as long as you need."

"Thanks, Catherine. I appreciate it, but I don't think I'll be here more than a night or two."

"How are you feeling?"

"Not bad, considering I fell off my roof. I'm sure I'd be feeling much worse if not for your husband and son."

Dave opened the back door to let Booker inside.

The dog charged directly at Carter, who knelt down to greet him. After a brief visit with Booker, Carter called Cindy and gave her an update on the latest happenings and asked to discuss her father. Rather than go into it over the phone, she agreed to meet him at his office.

As Carter prepared to leave, Dave voiced his concern. "Are you sure you shouldn't take the rest of the day off? You just got out of the hospital and you've got a concussion."

"I'll be alright," assured Carter. "Besides, there are some things I need to do as far as talking with my insurance company. I keep some relative information on my work computer as a backup."

"Don't push yourself too much," warned Catherine.

Carter smiled. "You two are like having an extra set of parents around." Then an annoyed look came over his face. "Crap. I meant to call my folks to tell them not to come. I completely forgot. I'll call them on my way."

"Do you want me to drive you?" Dave asked. "I'm not sure you should be driving."

"Dave, I'm fine," insisted Carter, heading for the door. "It's a concussion, not a brain tumor."

Carter was able to catch his mom and dad at the airport. They had yet to find flights that didn't require three or four different connections. After a long discussion with Carter answering all their concerns, he finally persuaded them a trip to Chicago would not be necessary. He suggested they visit after he settled with the insurance company and got a new house. The logic of it convinced his dad, who in turn helped sway his skeptical mother.

As he approached the entrance to his office, he noticed the clear piece of Scotch tape he placed in the corner of the door had pulled loose. Carefully, he opened the door and squatted down. He pulled up the corner of the rug inside the doorway to see the oyster crackers he put beneath the rug were smashed. Uninvited guests.

The sound of heels clicking on the tile down the hall caught his attention and he turned to see Cindy coming his way. His low position and her short skirt afforded him an eye level view of those amazing legs. Quickly he stood and placed his finger against his lips to signal to her. He gestured for her to stay there while he entered the office.

Carter scanned the room, hoping to see anything out of the ordinary. Everything looked undisturbed. These guys were getting better. He walked over to a locked cabinet and opened it, pulling out a hand-held electronic device.

Cindy maneuvered her way just inside the doorway, and once again, he motioned for her to remain silent.

Moving along the wall, Carter ran the device up and down, side to side, as he strolled along the perimeter of the office. With nothing registering, he stood on his desk and moved the instrument across the light fixture. A faint beep sounded and a green light illuminated on the device. Reaching his hand up inside the fixture, Carter removed a very small device.

Cindy's eyes grew bigger.

Carter left the bug on top of his desk while he scanned the rest of the office. When he was completely satisfied that was the only one, he left the scanner on the desk, picked up the bug and exited the office, with Cindy close behind.

Walking to the end of the hall, Carter opened the door marked as the utility room and located the trash shoot. He pulled open the silver door and tossed the device down the chute to the dumpster waiting at the bottom.

As soon as he closed the shoot door, Cindy began talking. "Was that a bug?"

"Yeah," replied Carter, exiting the utility room en route back to his office.

"Who is listening to you?"

"I'm guessing your dad."

"My dad?" Cindy repeated.

"Cindy, what do you know about your father?"

"What do you mean?" Cindy asked.

Carter stopped in the hall and turned to face his client. "Other than this recent thing with the girl at the library, has your father had any run-ins with the law?"

"No," replied Cindy. "Why do you keep asking me things like this? It's like when you asked me if I thought my dad would hurt Tyler. What are you trying to say?"

"I think your dad is a crook."

The accusation caught Cindy off guard and her expression showed a mix of hurt and anger.

"Cindy, those men who work for your dad are some really unsavory characters. They all have a rather impressive criminal resume. I'm talking everything from extortion to felony assault to arson. Speaking of which, someone burned down my house last night with me inside it."

Cindy gasped. "What? Your house burned down?"

"Yeah," replied Carter

"And you think my dad is responsible?"

"When I first learned it was arson, I did. That Dan Yielding who worked for your father seems to have specialized in arson. His background included two or three convictions for arson."

"Why are you speaking in the past tense?"

"Because he's dead."

Cindy gasped again. "What?"

"They found him shot to death in his car. Oh yeah, and he was parked on my street."

Carter resumed his path into his office with Cindy trailing behind him. "That's the only reason I doubt your father's involvement. But I'll be honest with you, I haven't completely ruled it out."

Moving behind the desk, Carter reclined in his chair and motioned for Cindy to take a seat. "Look, Cindy, I've dealt with shady crooked guys in my time, and I'm sorry to tell you this, but your dad is one of them. I don't know what he's in to, but it's illegal. And I'm not talking about the library thing. As a matter of fact, I don't think he's actually guilty of anything there."

"They caught him red-handed. They've got emails he's exchanged with her."

"I think he was set up."

"What? One second you're telling me my dad is a crook and the next you're telling me he's innocent?"

"I said I think he may be innocent of the thing with the girl. I didn't say he was innocent."

"Well, then, Mr. Mays, what is he guilty of?" Cindy asked.

"I told you, I don't know."

"But you're ready to throw him in jail without a trial."

"Yeah, and so were you," said Carter, reminding her she had already declared her father guilty without even talking to him about the library incident.

Her eyes narrowed, but she didn't argue Carter's point. "So who set him up with the girl?"

"Tyler."

"Tyler? How do you figure? Nobody knows where Tyler is."

"He called your dad," said Carter.

The look of disbelief was back. "He did what?"

"Tyler called your dad and asked to meet him somewhere so he could explain. It turns out he was playing your dad, walking him right into a police bust."

"Why didn't my dad tell me this?"

"He said you won't even talk to him," answered Carter.

"When did you talk to him?"

"Today. He came to see me at the hospital."

"Why were you at the hospital?"

"I fell off my roof trying to get out of my flame-engulfed house. I have bruises and a slight concussion." Carter pulled up the sleeve on his t-shirt to reveal a nasty bruise that covered his shoulder. "It continues on around to my back and neck," he added.

Cindy's countenance softened. "You have a concussion?"

Carter nodded.

"Are you okay?"

"For the most part," he answered.

"Why did my dad come to see you at the hospital?"

"Two reasons. First he wanted to assure me he had nothing to do with burning down my house. The second reason is something we need to talk about. He wants to hire me."

"Hire you?" Cindy exclaimed. "To do what?"

"To find Tyler."

"That's what I hired you to do. Why would he do that?"

"His argument was that he's realized I'm better qualified to find Tyler. But I'd say the main reason it to keep tabs on me. He's had his men following me, watching us, and as you just saw, listening in on us. He probably figures it would be easier and more productive just to hire me."

"Did you tell him to shove it?"

"No."

"You didn't say yes, did you?"

"I told him that you would have to agree and you were the primary client. I told him there could be no conversations about my progress without you. You have to be present before I share any information."

"Why would I agree to that?"

"Because it may help find Tyler. Neither one of us knew about Tyler's call to your father."

"He might be making that up in some lame attempt to explain the thing with the underage girl."

"I don't think so."

"So you think my dad's a crook, but you don't think he's capable of being a pervert?"

"Right," agreed Carter.

Cindy stood and paced back and forth with her arms folded across her chest.

Carter could see her agonizing over the thought of her father being involved. "Do you still want to find Tyler?" Carter asked. "I would understand if you didn't."

"I still want answers. I want to confront him face to face. I want to know if I ever meant anything to him this whole time or if he just played me like a fool."

"Then it may help having your father involved. If Tyler contacted him before, he may do it again. Obviously, he's not a big fan of your dad. If I could figure out why, that may help clear things up."

"Plus, you'll be getting paid double for the same amount of work," commented Cindy.

"Yes, I will. But if that's the only reason, then I'll not charge you. I'll just charge your dad, but you'll still be the primary client."

"You would do that?"

"You're kind of like your dad. You think everyone is motivated solely by money."

"That's not true. And I'm going to pay you. I don't care if you're getting triple the money."

"So you're okay with your dad coming on board?"

"I guess, if you think it may help in the long run."

Cindy returned to her chair. She gazed at the floor and shook her head. "I don't know how all this happened. Last week I was happy, engaged to the man I love, and a real daddy's girl. Now, I've been dumped, used, lied to, and found out surprising things about my father, with whom I'm not on speaking terms."

Carter watched Cindy wipe at her eyes and try to control her emotions. He felt sorry for her. It had to be extremely disheartening to go through everything she experienced in recent days. He stood and walked around to the front of his desk and knelt down beside her, placing his hand on her shoulder.

Her teary eyes locked in on his and for a moment they just stared without saying anything. Carter found himself thinking back to the night she kissed him. And now, being this close and looking into her beautiful face, he found himself hoping she would kiss him again. He wasn't sure he would resist this time. For that matter, he thought about initiating it.

He felt transparent, as if she could see what he was thinking. Quickly he stood up and backed against his desk.

Cindy sniffed and Carter was quick to hand her a box of tissues from his desk.

She took two and thanked him.

"So now what? What's your next move?"

"I need to figure out why Tyler is so pissed at your dad."

"I honestly have no idea on that one. I swear they got along great. And they spent a fair amount of time together, even without me around."

"Well, there's got to be some reason."

"My dad didn't have any insight?"

"No. He seemed genuinely hurt by it when we talked. As a matter of fact, it's the only time I didn't have the feeling he was giving me a load of crap."

Cindy stared at Carter. "You know, I realize my dad and I aren't on the best of terms at the moment, but I still don't like hearing you rip on him so much. I understand you don't like him, but could you be less vocal about it when you're around me? He's still my dad."

"I'm sorry," offered Carter.

Cindy sat quietly while Carter formulated his next move. He scribbled on a notepad and moved his lips as he thought to himself. Finally, he spoke. "I think I'll start with West Lake Properties. That is where your dad and Tyler spent the most time together."

"What can I do?" Cindy asked.

"For now, go home. I'll stop by later. I want to sweep your place for bugs."

"Bugs?" Cindy repeated. "You think my father would bug his own daughter's apartment?"

"It's a possibility," replied Carter.

Cindy began to argue, but instead let out a long defeated sigh. "Fine, whatever."

"For now, I suggest you don't say anything you wouldn't want someone else to hear."

Cindy rolled her eyes.

He knew that in spite of everything that had happened, she still didn't believe her father wouldn't stoop that low.

"By the way," said Carter. "I'd prefer you not mention anything to your father concerning what I said about him being a crook."

"I guess you wouldn't want me to say anything. Besides, we're not doing much talking lately. But it seems a little unfair not giving him an opportunity to defend himself, don't you think?"

"Again, you haven't given him any chances to explain the library thing. What's with the double standard?"

"He's my dad," replied Cindy.

"Look, after we get this Tyler thing resolved, you can tell him anything you want. I don't care. But for now, I'd rather not give him any more reasons to not trust me or cooperate."

"Fine," she responded with another eye-roll.

"Thank you," he said. "I'll call you later."

Once Cindy left, Carter took care to put everything in its place before exiting the office. After locking the door, he placed a new piece of Scotch tape in the corner. Perhaps he should get an alarm, he thought, as he walked down the hallway.

TWENTY-FOUR

Driving to WLP&D, Carter painfully decided to call Carina. Given his current state of homelessness, his extremely limited wardrobe, the concussion, and the long list of things he needed to do with both the Moore case and his insurance claim, he felt it best to postpone his date. Carina was pleasant, understanding, and very sympathetic regarding Carter's loss of his house.

Carter parked in a visitor's space of the WLP&D parking lot and walked inside. He took the elevator up to the fifth floor. The doors opened and he stepped inside the large expanse of WLP&D.

An attractive girl in her mid-twenties greeted him with a smile from her place at the receptionist's desk. According to the nameplate on her desk, her name was Jillian. "Hello, sir. May I help you?"

"Hi, Jillian. Is Mr. Bedford in?"

"No he isn't. Did you have an appointment with him today?"

"No. Actually, I already met with him this morning. He's hired me to look into the disappearance of Tyler Moore. My name is Carter Mays. I'm a private investigator." Carter handed the young lady a business card.

"Oh," she replied. "I'm not certain when he will be in today, if at all. He has a lot going on lately. Would you like me to take a message?"

"No thank you," answered Carter. "I would like to talk to a few people around the office though."

"Talk to a few people? Like who?"

"Anyone who may have worked closely with Tyler. I was hoping maybe you could point me in the right direction," said Carter with a smile. "I know Mr. Bedford would really like to get this resolved as quickly as possible."

Jillian rose to her feet and instructed Carter to follow her. She led him back through the maze of cubicles, stopping at the entrance of one that belonged to Todd Glick. "Todd," she interrupted. "This is Mr. Mays. Mr. Bedford hired him to find Tyler."

Todd, a small-framed young man with extremely light blonde hair, looked up from his computer monitor.

"Todd works in the same group that Tyler did," informed Jillian. "He probably worked as closely with Tyler as anyone."

"Thank you, Jillian," said Carter as Jillian returned to her post.

The young man wrinkled his brow, stood and invited Carter to sit.

Carter lowered himself into the guest chair in front of Todd's desk, watching Todd sit down and take a long sip from a can of soda, his eyes darting around the cubicle.

Todd swallowed hard and tugged at his buttoned up collar.

Carter said nothing at first. He just stared, studying the man's behavior.

Todd grew fidgety and he spoke up. "What questions do you have?"

"How well did you know Tyler?"

"We worked together here. That's about the extent of it. I can't really say we were friends."

"Did you have a lot of contact with him here?"

"Yes," replied Todd, taking time to swallow hard again. "We worked on a lot of projects together."

"Are you okay? You seem upset," said Carter.

"I don't like confrontations. I get really nervous," admitted Todd.

"Confrontations? Do you feel like this is a confrontation?"

"A little bit."

"All I'm doing is asking you some questions."

"I know. I'm just weird that way. I'm not really a people person."

Carter's first thought was that perhaps Todd knew something that nobody else knew. His behavior certainly indicated he had something to hide. "Todd, is there something you should tell me?"

"No. Not at all. I just don't like getting involved in things that aren't my business."

"Okay, calm down."

"Especially when it's Mr. Bedford's business," added Todd.

The comment sparked Carter's curiosity. "Oh yeah? Why's that?"

"Huh?" Todd asked.

"Does Mr. Bedford make you nervous?"

"I really need to get back to work," he stuttered.

Scooting to the edge of his chair and leaning forward, Carter lowered his voice. "Todd, it's okay. Talk to me. Does he make you nervous?"

Todd folded his arms across his chest and perched his head up to see if anyone was standing near the cubicle. "A little bit, sometimes," he whispered.

"Why is that?"

"I don't know," said Todd, continuing to whisper. "He just sort of intimidates me."

"Have you had any confrontations with him?"

"Absolutely not. I keep to myself and do my job."

"Would you say that Mr. Bedford is a hard man to deal with?"

"I thought you were working for Mr. Bedford to find Tyler?"

"I am."

"Then why all the questions about Mr. Bedford?"

"I'm trying to get a handle on what kind of relationship the two of them had. Would you say they got along well?"

"Yes, they got along fine," answered Todd.

"Did you ever hear them argue?"

"No."

"Did Tyler ever say anything to you about being upset with Mr. Bedford?"

"No," said Todd. "I told you they got along just fine. Tyler was even allowed back in the inner sanctum," he said with a certain amount of sarcasm.

"The inner sanctum? Where's that?"

Todd stood up prompting Carter to do so as well. Nodding his head, Todd directed Carter toward the glass doors on the back wall of the room. "Over there," he said.

"Why do you call that the inner sanctum?"

"Because most of us aren't allowed to be back there. There are only a handful of people that have access."

"Really?"

"Yeah, really," confirmed Todd. "I've worked here for seven years and I've never been past those doors."

"But Tyler was allowed?" Carter inquired.

"Yes, only occasionally, but often enough I'd say he was on good terms with Mr. Bedford."

"Who else is allowed back there?"

"Tate Manning and most everyone from our corporate security. Mr. Manning's office is back there next to Mr. Bedford's."

"That's it?"

Todd nodded.

"Now this Tate Manning, he's the CFO, right?"

"Yeah."

"What kind of man is he?" Carter asked.

"What do you mean?"

"Is he a nice guy? Is he a jerk? What kind of guy is he?"

"He's a nice enough guy."

"Is he here today?"

"Yeah, I think so," answered Todd.

"Did Tyler have much interaction with Manning?"

"Some, I guess."

"Maybe I should go talk to him for a while," said Carter.

Appearing relieved, Todd agreed. "Yeah, maybe you should."

Carter stood to leave and Todd suddenly blurted out, "But don't tell him I said you should talk to him."

"Why? What's the big deal?"

"I told you, I don't like to get involved in things that aren't my business or drag other people into it either."

"Don't worry," assured Carter. "I'll keep your name out of it."

Carter walked across the expanse of the office toward the glass doors leading to the inner sanctum. A secretary in her late forties sat at the desk outside the doors. "Hello, Ann," greeted Carter reading her nameplate. "I'd like a moment of Mr. Manning's time."

"Do you have an appointment?" Ann asked.

"No, I don't. Mr. Bedford hired me this morning to investigate the disappearance of Tyler Moore. I would like to ask Mr. Manning a couple of questions."

"Let me see if he is available."

Ann picked up the phone and dialed the extension. After a few seconds, she hung up. "He'll be right out," she said.

"Thank you," replied Carter.

Carter watched Tate Manning walk through the glass doors and approach him, producing what Carter strongly sensed was an artificial smile.

Tate extended his hand. "Hello Mr. Mays. Jasper mentioned that he was going to hire a private investigator. How may I help you?"

"I wanted to ask you a question or two about Tyler Moore."

"Okay."

"Would you prefer to go somewhere more private," asked Carter, glancing toward Ann and hoping he could get a look at the so-called inner sanctum.

Tate shook his head. "No, this is fine. I doubt I can help you much anyway."

"Why is that?"

"Well, I just didn't have much interaction with Tyler outside of work."

"Still, I would think that you would get to know someone fairly well, working with them for three years."

"Perhaps," replied Tate, his facial expression communicating his lack of enthusiasm.

"What kind of person was Tyler? Did he get along with most people?"

"Yeah, he seemed to get along okay."

"How would you describe him as an employee?"

"He was quite capable; very bright young man."

"Were you surprised by his sudden departure?"

"Of course, everyone was surprised."

"How much money did he steal from the company?"

The secretary, Ann, looked up following Carter's blunt question and then shifted her eyes to Tate.

Tate replied, "Money? What money?"

"I was under the impression that Tyler embezzled some funds from the company," said Carter, fishing for some type of reaction from Tate.

Shaking his head, Tate answered, "No, I'm not aware that any money was stolen. We may have lost some future business because of his absence."

Carter nodded. "Oh, my misunderstanding."

"Mr. Mays, I don't mean to be rude, but I have a great deal of work to do and I really don't believe that I have any insight to any of this that is worth your time and effort to invest in me."

"Okay," said Carter. "Just one more question and then I'll let you go."

Tate let out an impatient sigh. "What is it?"

"Does the name Conway mean anything to you?"

"Conway?" Tate repeated. "Well, let's see, there was a country singer a few years back. I believe he went by the name Conway Twitty, if I remember correctly. I was never much of a country music fan, but my first wife loved the stuff."

"No, this would be as a last name," said Carter, not amused by Tate's reply.

"I can't say that it means anything to me then," said Tate. "Will that be all?"

Nodding, Carter extended his hand. "Well, thank you Mr. Manning. I'm sorry for bothering you."

"Not a problem," replied Tate.

Carter watched the man scan his keycard across the security scanner to gain access through the glass doors and disappear inside his office. As Carter turned away, he heard the secretary speak up.

"Excuse me," said Ann, softly. "Obviously with me right here, I couldn't help but hear your conversation."

"Yes," said Carter. "Is there something you'd like to tell me?"

"Well, when you mentioned the name Conway, it reminded me that there used to be a woman here and I'm pretty sure her name was Conway."

Ann now had Carter's undivided attention. "Really?"

"Yes. I never worked with her. I believe she had this job before I started. The only reason I remember that is for the first several months after I started, I kept seeing her name on various documents."

"Do you remember her first name?"

Ann stared off into the distance. "Hmm, what was her name?"

Carter resisted the urge to offer any help, just to make sure whatever the woman remembered was based on her actual memory and not the power of his suggestion. He watched her moving her lips as she thought.

She glanced at Carter and grinned. "Sometimes when I'm trying to remember a name, it helps me to go through the alphabet."

"Take your time," he said smiling.

He could see her working her way through each letter, J, K, L. Suddenly she snapped her fingers. "Louise. That was her name. Louise Conway."

Carter was now blown away. Was it really possible that the mother of one Steven Conway, aka, Tyler Moore, actually worked for WLP&D?

"Does that help?" Ann asked.

Hiding his excitement, Carter offered a nonchalant nod. "Yeah, it might."

"I hope so," she said.

"Is there anyone who has been here long enough to remember Louise Conway?"

"You mean other than Mr. Manning?"

"Yeah," said Carter. "Someone who's not quite as busy."

Ann raised her head high and looked past Carter. "You might want to speak with Gerald. He's an engineer. I'm pretty sure he's been here the longest behind Mr. Bedford and Mr. Manning."

Ann pointed Carter in the general direction and he thanked her for her help before making his way over to Gerald's office.

The door was open and Carter saw a heavy-set man close to retirement age sitting hunched over at his desk. His bright white hair was neatly groomed and his head was tilted back allowing him to see the computer monitor through his bifocals. Carter knocked to get the man's attention.

Dragging his gaze away from the monitor to Carter, the man eventually made eye contact. "Yes?"

"Hi," began Carter. "You're Gerald, aren't you?"

"Yes, I am."

Pointing back across the large office space Carter stepped inside the door. "Ann suggested that I speak with you. My name is Carter Mays."

Gerald removed his bifocals and stood up. Walking around the desk he stuck out his hand. "Hello, Carter Mays. What can I do for you?"

"Do you remember working with Louise Conway?"

The man's brow wrinkled as he folded his arms across his barrel chest. "What is the nature of your business, Mr. Mays?"

"I'm a private investigator. Mr. Bedford hired me."

"For what?"

"To find Tyler Moore."

"Hmm ... the wedding skipper. Yes, I would imagine there are a few people who would like to find that young man. What does that have to do with someone who hasn't worked here in decades?"

"Maybe nothing," answered Carter. "But Ann mentioned her and thought you might remember her."

"Oh, I remember her. She was quite a looker."

"An attractive woman, huh?"

"Absolutely. Having her around the office made it hard to stay focused on your job. She was a stunning lady."

"What happened to her?"

"She quit. The best I remember, she didn't even give notice. She just up and left one day."

"Did she take another job or something?"

"I don't know. There were a couple of rumors flying around, primarily due to her sudden departure. Some people said she came into money. Some folks said she got knocked up. Then some people thought maybe she ran off with some fella."

"Which one did you believe?"

"Ah, I didn't give it a whole lot of thought. All I knew was that it was going to be easier for me to focus on my work."

"Did anyone ever have any follow up contact with her? Did she have any friends in the office; perhaps another woman she confided in?"

Gerald scoffed. "Not in this office, especially in those days. We had a catty bunch of women working here back then. Most of the women didn't like each other, especially Louise."

"Really?"

"Oh yeah. Well, you know how women can get. See at the time, the women we had working here were older, married with kids, about five sizes bigger than they used to be. So when this young attractive single girl starts working and getting all the attention from the men in the office, that's when you start seeing the ugly, jealous, bitter sides of these women emerge."

"How long did she work here?"

"Hmm," thought Gerald out loud. "Let me think. I'd say she hung around for about a year or two."

"And you don't know what prompted her to leave?"

"Nope. I can't say I do."

Before leaving, Carter reached into his pocket and retrieved a business card. "If you think of anything else, anything, please call me," he said, handing it to Gerald.

"Yeah, sure," replied Gerald.

Walking out of the office and riding down the elevator, Carter couldn't believe that revelation he had just experienced. This information brought a whole new set of questions. Obviously, Tyler Moore seeking employment here was no accident. But how was it connected? What was his motive? Something had to have happened in the past.

When the elevator doors opened, Carter stepped off and came face to face with Jasper Bedford and Russell. Bedford appeared a little unsettled by Carter's presence. "Hello, Mr. Mays. What brings you here?"

"I'm doing the investigative work you hired me to do," replied Carter.

"Here?"

"Well, yeah. Tyler Moore spent a lot of time here and with these people. So it makes sense I would want to check it out."

"Yes, I suppose it does," said Jasper.

"Is there a problem with me being here?"

"Oh no, but I'm pretty sure my guys exhausted any potential leads here already. But that's my fault for not bringing you up to speed on the areas we have already explored. I don't suppose you found out anything significant, did you?"

Carter shook his head, reluctant to disclose much at this point to his untrustworthy client.

Jasper stroked his goatee. "I really should have you and Russell sit down and compare notes so you're not spinning your wheels. No reason we can't work together."

"That's not necessary. I kind of have my own way of doing things. But thanks anyway."

Carter could tell that Jasper didn't like the response.

Jasper chewed on the inside of his cheek for a moment before responding. "I assume by your presence here that my daughter is okay with my involvement?"

Carter simply nodded.

Changing the subject, Jasper pointed toward Carter's head and asked, "So how's the head feeling?"

"It's okay. I'm down to a dull ache at the moment."

"Well make sure you don't over-do it," said Jasper.

"I'll be fine," said Carter, fully aware that Jasper genuinely didn't give a crap. "Thanks."

"So where are you off to now?" Jasper asked.

"I'm off to follow up on some things," answered Carter.

"You will keep me updated, right?" Jasper asked.

"Of course."

"Okay," said Jasper. "Well, good luck. I guess I'll hear from you soon."

"Yeah, I'll get back to you." Carter turned and walked away.

Jasper and Russell watched Carter exit the building. Russell glanced over at his boss. "I don't trust him."

"Neither do I," said Jasper. "He seems like he might be holding out on me. I don't like it."

"Do you want me to follow him?"

"You haven't proven to be very proficient at that, so no, I don't. How about if you take on something you can handle and go wash my car. It's filthy."

Russell frowned and walked away.

Proceeding up the elevator, Jasper made his way to his office. Again, he was greeted by a few awkward hellos from people who were no doubt wondering about his guilt in the library incident. Most people just avoided eye contact.

As he passed Tate Manning's office, he heard Tate call him.

Jasper stopped and took a step back putting him directly in front of Tate's office. "What?"

"Do you have a second?"

"What's on your mind, Tate?"

"That detective was just up here snooping around. Are you sure it was a good idea for you to hire him?"

"Yes, Tate, I know he was here. I ran into him in the lobby."

"I don't like him poking his nose around here. I'm worried he might uncover things he shouldn't."

"You moved all the files, right?"

"Yeah," answered Tate.

"Who did he talk to?"

"I saw him talking to Gerald after he talked with me. I don't know who he spoke to before that."

"He talked to you?"

"Yes."

"What did he say?" Jasper inquired.

"He asked me about Tyler. Wanted to know what kind of employee he was and things of that nature. To be honest, I didn't give him a lot of time to ask me too much. It makes me nervous having him around. We have too many skeletons in our closets."

"Did you say something you shouldn't have?"

"No. Not at all," replied Tate.

"Well, unless you let something slip, I don't think we have anything to worry about. None of those people know anything about our other dealings."

"Maybe we should postpone our next deal," suggested Tate.

"Look, nobody is in hotter water than me right now, but I think it's a little premature to call off anything. We're still several weeks out. I'd rather wait to see how all this unfolds before I jump the gun. Besides, after the hit we took from Tyler, we could use the revenue."

Tate reached into his pocket for the ever-present antacids and popped one into his mouth.

"Listen," said Jasper. "All I have to do is find Tyler and all of this goes away. In fact, it may go away without finding him. I got some good news on the way over here. Dylan called me and he is sure he'll be able to get the laptop thrown out as evidence. They don't have my prints on the thing. There's no purchase history that links it to me. And best of all, they cross-checked the emails in the sent box with my schedule the last two months and there is a conflict with several of them. Two of them occurred during the exact time I was getting a colonoscopy last month. Then there were several that happened while I was in business meetings and we have numerous witnesses who can attest to that, including you. Once we are able to prove that the laptop was a bogus setup, it shouldn't be far-fetched to convince a jury the whole thing was an attempt to slander my name and reputation."

Tate still appeared anxious, but offered a half smile. "That's great. It sounds promising."

"Yeah that arrogant jerk Fitch is actually earning his money," said Jasper. "And as far as Mays is concerned, you let me worry about him."

"I hope you're not making a mistake."

"Like it or not, our best chance of finding Tyler and getting our money back is that investigator. When he's served his purpose, I'll make sure he doesn't cause us any problems."

TWENTY-FIVE

Carter lightly tapped on the door and waited. After a moment without any response, he tapped a little louder, but still much softer than one would normally knock. Eventually, Cindy answered the door and Carter greeted her with his index finger pressed against his lips.

She rolled her eyes and stepped back to allow him to enter.

He passed by her and placed a small duffle bag on the sofa and unzipped it to remove the same instrument had used at his office. With Cindy following him, he ran the scanner over every possible surface in her apartment. It wasn't but a moment when the scanner beeped as Carter passed it beneath a cold air return vent at the top of her wall.

Immediately he made eye contact with her.

This time there was no rolling of the eyes with her. Instead, her mouth fell open in complete disbelief.

Carter pulled a screwdriver from his bag and stood on a kitchen chair to help him reach the vent cover. After removing the cover, he reached inside and removed a tiny transmitter. Gently he placed it in a cloth napkin from Cindy's table, rolled it up, and tucked it into the depths of his bag.

As soon as he had pulled his hand from the bag, Cindy began to speak. "I can't believe..."

Immediately Carter placed his finger against Cindy's lips and shook his head.

Cindy stopped talking.

Moving throughout the entire apartment, Carter continued to thoroughly scan each room. He located two more devices, one in Cindy's kitchen and one in her bedroom. After he was finished, Carter packed away each one, closed up the bag. Then moving to the bathroom, Carter placed the bag on the tile floor, turned on the exhaust fan and closed the door to ensure there was no chance they could be heard.

Cindy followed Carter down the hall and into the living room where he turned to face her. "Hi," he said, nonchalantly.

"Is that all of them?" Cindy asked softly.

Carter nodded.

"I can't believe my own father could stoop so low. None of those were cameras were they?"

"No," assured Carter.

"You're positive?"

Carter simply nodded.

"Why would he do that?" Cindy asked.

Carter didn't answer.

"That really creeps me out to think someone was in here and I never even knew it."

Knowing he couldn't say much to console his client, Carter remained silent.

Cindy grabbed her phone from the coffee table and started dialing.

"Who are you calling?" Carter asked.

"My dad," replied Cindy. "I have some things to say to him."

Taking the phone from Cindy's hand, Carter shook his head. "No, you can't do that."

"Why not?" Cindy snapped.

"Look, if you're angry with your dad, there's a better way to retaliate."

"How?"

"He invaded your privacy, so you help me invade his."

"What do you mean?"

"I need to get inside your dad's office."

"His office?"

"Yes, the inner sanctum as some folks would call it."

"The inner sanctum? What are you talking about?"

"Have you ever been in your dad's office?"

"Of course I have," replied Cindy.

"From what I've learned, you're part of a select group. Most of the people at your father's company have never been inside those glass doors that lead to his office."

"Why do you want in there?"

"I think your dad is hiding something. I think he has some skeletons in his closet and Tyler knew about them."

"How would Tyler know and I don't?"

"Because Tyler's mom used to work for your dad's company."

"What?" Cindy practically yelled.

"Tyler's mom worked as a secretary at West Lake Properties years ago. I think somehow she found out about some shady things going on in the company. Eventually, she disappeared and that information was passed on to Tyler, who I guess decided to capitalize on it. I'm also guessing your father may have done something to hurt Tyler's mom, causing him to seek revenge."

Cindy stared off into the distance. "That's why he changed his name?"

Carter nodded.

"What do you mean you think my dad may have hurt Tyler's mom?" Cindy asked. "What kind of shady things?"

"I don't know," said Carter. "But if I can get into those offices, maybe I'll find something."

"So what do you want me to do? Write you a hall pass from the boss' daughter? They have a key card security system."

"Yeah, I know. I watched people going in and out today."

"If you're thinking I have an access card, I don't."

"I know. But your father does," said Carter.

Cindy stared at Carter, squinting her eyes. "You want me to steal my father's key card?"

"More like borrow it," answered Carter.

"How am I supposed to do that? One, I think he keeps it in his wallet. And two, I'm not talking to him at the moment."

"I have a plan. You go over to your parents' house tonight."

"I just told you I'm not speaking to my dad."

"Well, you may have to," insisted Carter.

Cindy expelled a loud huff in protest.

Carter ignored her and continued talking. "Anyway, I want you to go to your folks' house. Tell your mom you wanted to hang out with her or something. I would imagine that you do that from time to time, don't you?"

Cindy crossed her arms. "Yes, I guess so."

"Good. So you hang out over at Mom's for the evening and stay late enough that you decide to spend the night because you're too tired to drive home."

"I have to spend the night?" Cindy questioned in protest again.

"Just part of the night," replied Carter. "At least long enough to let them go to sleep. What time do they usually go to bed?"

"I don't know, it varies, but usually around eleven to eleven-thirty."

"What does your dad do with his wallet when he's home? Does he leave it on the counter top in the kitchen or perhaps in a desk somewhere?"

"No, I'm pretty sure he keeps it on the dresser in his room."

"Okay, then, after they've had enough time to go to sleep, say maybe an hour, you'll sneak in and get his key card."

"It's not that easy, Carter," claimed Cindy. "My dad is a light sleeper. I'm afraid he'll hear me and wake up. Then what am I supposed to say when he catches me going through his wallet?"

Carter let out a sigh while he thought. "How would you feel about slipping your dad a little sleep aid?"

"What?" Cindy exclaimed. "You want me to drug my own father?"

"Yes, I do. And keep in mind the three bugs I just found, compliments of your father."

Carter's reply was quick and effective in gaining Cindy's compliance. In a way, he felt bad for the girl. Up until recently, she had a positive image of her dad, completely unaware of what kind of man he truly was. And now, thanks to Carter, this former daddy's girl had caught a glimpse of the real Jasper Bedford. Carter was certain that image would be totally destroyed as more things were to be uncovered.

"What am I supposed to give him?"

"I'll take care of that," answered Carter.

"It's not something that will kill him, is it? I know I'm really pissed off at him right now, but I don't want to hurt him."

"No, it won't kill or hurt him. It will just put him in a deep sleep."

"How am I supposed to get him to take it?"

"Pour him a drink after dinner and slip it to him then."

"How long does it take to kick in?"

"I don't know, ten to fifteen minutes I think."

"How long will he be out?"

"Around six hours," answered Carter.

"What about my mom? Won't she be a little suspicious if my dad suddenly passes out?"

Carter hesitated for a brief moment before responding. "Slip some to your mom, too."

Cindy's mouth gaped open. "I'm not going to drug my mom."

Carter shrugged his shoulders and looked disappointed.

"No. I refuse to do that to my mother. She hasn't done anything to me to deserve that."

"Then come up with a good excuse for when your dad slips off to dream land," suggested Carter.

Cindy moved around in a small circle with her hands on her hips while she pondered what she might say. Finally she stopped and stared at Carter. "You're sure it won't hurt them?"

Fighting the desire to smile over Cindy's change of mind, Carter nodded. "I promise you they'll be fine. They'll probably get the best sleep they've had in a while."

"I can't believe you're making me drug my parents," said Cindy, sitting down on the sofa to rest her elbows on her thighs and bury her face into her hands. "This is so wrong."

Carter sat next to her on the sofa and gently placed his hand on her shoulder. "Listen. I'm not making you do anything. If you're not completely comfortable doing this, then we won't." Although Carter was genuine in his statement, he felt confident that Cindy wouldn't back out.

Cindy glanced up at him and shook her head. "My life sucks so bad right now."

"Look, we're getting close to the end of this whole thing. If I can figure out what your dad is hiding, then maybe I can uncover why Tyler did what he did."

"Does it even matter anymore?" Cindy asked.

"That's up to you," replied Carter. "If you don't want to pursue this any further, I can stop right now."

Cindy's teary eyes made contact with Carter while she considered the option of quitting. "I don't know what to do. Part of me is so bewildered with hurt over being manipulated and humiliated that I want to keep going, if for nothing else to have the chance to make him look me in the eye while I tell him what a horrible human being he is for using me like he did. The other part of me is so done with all of this. I just want to move on with my life. But now I have these new revelations about my dad, so it's not like I can go back to the way things were before Tyler."

Carter said nothing. He merely listened as Cindy sorted her thoughts out loud. With his hand still on her shoulder, Cindy leaned in and rested against Carter. He wrapped his arm completely around her as the two of them sat there in silence. He could feel her tears soaking into the fabric of his shirt. He wished he had something profound to say to make her feel better, but nothing came to mind. So he just held her, caressing her shoulder and brushing the hair from her flushed face.

Cindy's hand moved up and pressed against Carter's chest; soon her fingers began to move in a small circle.

Carter's gaze wandered toward his client who raised her head to look at him. Even in her anguish, he couldn't help but think how beautiful she was. He wanted to kiss her. Her wounded and fragile emotions begged to be kissed, but she wasn't advancing like the night she'd been drinking. She was waiting. Slowly, he moved closer, stopping just short of their lips touching. Her eyes remained locked on his and she wet her lips with her tongue. Carter closed the distance and kissed her.

Conflicting thoughts waged in Carter's brain as he gradually pulled away and their lips separated. This was his client. This was supposed to be business, but he had allowed himself to become emotionally attached. It wasn't just because she was drop dead gorgeous. He genuinely had feelings for her. The spoiled rich daddy's girl who had first showed up at his office days earlier had transformed into a sweet, vulnerable woman who was hurting. Never before, had Carter felt so much sympathy for a client, and he had witnessed many folks who were dealing with a lousy situation that was not their fault. Why was this different? He didn't know.

"So what do you want to do?" Carter asked trying to re-capture some sort of professional perspective.

Cindy revealed a half smile. She pulled away to put some space between them. She noticed where her tears had soaked through his shirt. She brushed at the spot with her finger and apologized. "Sorry, I dripped on you a little."

Carter looked down at the area and shrugged. "It'll dry."

Cindy sighed. "I want to see this through."

"Yeah?" Carter asked.

"Yeah."

"Okay."

"So after I drug my parents, then what?"

"We'll pick a place to meet and you can give me the key card. From there I'll go take a tour of the office to see if I can find anything."

"I want to go with you," said Cindy.

Shaking his head, Carter replied, "No, that's not a good idea."

"Why not?"

"Because this isn't exactly legal and normally I don't cross that line, but I feel like it's necessary this time. And if something happens, you don't need to be anywhere around."

"I disagree," claimed Cindy with a hint of sassiness.

"Oh you do, huh?"

"If you get caught, I think it would be advantageous for you to have the owner's daughter with you."

Temporarily tempted by Cindy's argument, Carter shook his head again in disagreement. "Thanks, but I'll be fine. Nothing's going to happen."

"But you just indicated that something could happen."

"Yes, but it's not likely."

"So there's no reason I can't go with you," replied Cindy.

Carter let out a frustrated sigh. "No, I still don't think that's a good idea."

"What am I supposed to do while you're lurking around my dad's office?"

"Go have a cup of coffee somewhere. I'll call you when I'm finished and we can meet. I'll give you the key card back and you can return it to your dad's wallet before he wakes up."

"Okay, how about this?" Cindy began. "I'll go with you, but I'll wait in the car while you're inside the building."

Carter leaned back on the sofa and stared up at the ceiling while he contemplated the idea.

"Oh, come on Carter," said Cindy. "If I'm willing to drug my own innocent mother, you should let me go with you."

"Alright, but you stay in the car."

Cindy's bright perfect smile indicated her feelings toward the decision. "Thanks, Carter."

"Remember, you're staying in the car," he repeated emphatically.

"I will," agreed Cindy. "What time are we doing this?"

"I've got to run out to pick up the sleep aid. I'll come back here and drop it off. After that, it's up to you when you go to your folks' place. Just call me when you're on your way, and again whenever they check out for the evening. I'll be in the immediate area. We'll meet up and go from there."

Carter stood, retrieved his bag from the bathroom, and headed for the door with Cindy following behind him. He turned around and she smiled. "I'll be back in a little while," he said.

"By the way, Carter," said Cindy. "Thanks for the kiss. It was really nice."

He nodded. "Yeah, I thought so, too. But we'll talk about all that when this thing is over. Okay?"

"Okay," agreed Cindy.

"I'll see you later," he said.

"I'll be here."

TWENTY-SIX

Cindy arrived at her parents' house a little after eight o'clock that evening. In her purse were two small vials Carter gave her earlier. He told her the name of the substance, but she didn't remember what he said. The important thing to her was that it wouldn't harm her mom or dad.

She walked up to the front door and took a deep breath to prepare her for the face-to-face encounter with her father. She was not looking forward to it for a number of reasons. The fact he had been busted trying to pick up an underage girl was bad enough. But the real sense of betrayal came from the invasion of privacy he initiated by the listening devices planted in her apartment. Suddenly, Cindy was slammed with another thought that added to her anxiety. What kind of questions or thoughts might her father have, now that he's not able to hear what's going on in her apartment any longer? He had to realize that something was wrong. That, along with her impulsive visit might make him suspicious, perhaps too suspicious for her to successfully slip him the sedative. She thought about turning around and abandoning the whole idea. Taking another deep breath she tried to recapture some sense of calmness and slow down her racing heartbeat. All she was doing was dropping by to see her folks, like countless times before. Although this was the first time she would be secretly drugging them.

After a brief moment to collect her thoughts, Cindy knocked on the door and entered the house. "Hello," she called out.

Darlene Bedford rounded the corner and met her daughter in the foyer. "Hi, Honey. I'm so happy you came by."

Cindy hugged her mom with one hand, while she held a bakery cake in the other. "Hi, Mom."

"I have to admit, with the way things have been the last couple of days between you and your father, I was a little surprised to hear from you."

Cindy shrugged and attempted to smile.

"Sweetheart, I know I was devastated when your father was arrested. I was ready to file for divorce and take him for everything he has. But, now that I've had time to listen and examine the facts, the more I'm convinced that he's innocent."

"That's why I'm here," Cindy lied. "I thought I should hear his side of the story."

"I think that's a wonderful idea," said Darlene.

"Where is Dad?" Cindy asked.

"He's in his office on the phone. He'll be out in a moment."

For the first time, Darlene took notice of the box in Cindy's hand. "What did you bring?"

"Dessert," answered Cindy. "I thought we could have dessert and coffee if you want. It's a dark chocolate torte."

"Yummy," said Darlene. "That's sounds fantastic. Let's go into the kitchen. I'll put on a pot of coffee to go with it."

Cindy followed her mother to the kitchen, dreading the thought that her father would appear any moment.

"Can I get you something to drink, dear?" Darlene asked, after getting the coffee brewer going.

"Sure," answered Cindy, sitting on one of the stools that surrounded the kitchen island. "I'll have a diet."

Watching as her mom poured a glass of diet soda, Cindy questioned if she even go through with her plan? Drugging her innocent mother seemed so detestable. She struggled to think of a way to get around it.

Darlene brought the glass of soda and sat down on the granite top in front of Cindy. "There you go, Babe."

"Thanks, Mom," said Cindy.

Darlene poured a glass of wine for herself, to begin her nightly ritual of alcohol consumption. Cindy had first noticed the increased frequency of seeing her mother with a drink in her hand about five years ago. Time and time again she had wondered if her mother was an alcoholic, but never mustered the courage to say anything. If her mom was an alcoholic, she was a functioning one.

Darlene took a long sip of wine followed by a relaxed sigh. "So how are you holding up, honey?"

"I'm fine," replied Cindy.

"Fine? Really? I find that hard to believe."

"What do you mean?" Cindy inquired.

"Betrayed by the man you fell in love with and planned to marry, and you say you're fine?"

"Of course I'm hurt over it. But I'm not going to curl up in a fetal position and quit living my life."

"That's my girl," whispered Darlene, patting her daughter on the hand. "That's the attitude to have."

Cindy took a drink of her soda, knowing her mom had more to say.

Darlene rested her surgically sculpted cheek in her hand while her other hand swirled the wine in her glass. "So are you still determined to find him?"

"Yes."

"Why?"

"You don't think I should?"

Darlene downed another swig. "It's not up to me."

"True, but you have an opinion."

"I guess I'm afraid that you're inviting more hurt to come your way and I think you've suffered enough."

"What do you mean?"

"I think you want to know that at least some of what you and Tyler had was real; that it wasn't all just an elaborate fabrication. I think you want him to tell you that what he did was difficult for him to do, because he did have real feelings for you."

"So you think that none of it was authentic? You think he was using me from the beginning?"

Darlene shook her head. "Babe, I don't know. And I don't know how it could have been like that. I've spent the last three years seeing you two together and I don't believe anyone could fake that. But at the same time, I don't see the point of pushing the issue. I think it would be better to put it behind you and move on with your life."

"Maybe so, but I don't want to let him off that easy. I want him to have to answer for what he did."

Darlene simply nodded her concession and took another drink.

The two women sat there quietly. Cindy's mind eventually circled back to her present task and she started to grieve again over the thought of drugging her loving supportive mother. Maybe her mother would drink enough to pass out on her own and spare Cindy the guilt.

The silence was broken by the familiar voice of her father. "Hello, Cindy."

The moment she was dreading was here. She turned to see her dad standing in the doorway. "Hi, Dad."

"I'm glad you came by tonight," he said, softly.

Cindy responded with a brief nod and took a sip of soda.

"Look, Jasper, Cindy brought us dessert," Darlene said, pointing toward the torte. "It's a dark chocolate torte."

"Sounds good," replied Jasper with little enthusiasm.

"Honey, would you like a drink?" Darlene asked Jasper.

"No, I'm fine."

Cindy could sense her father being somewhat guarded around her, dialing back the level of authority in his tone with her. That wasn't his personality.

"I think I need to top off my glass," said Darlene

"What a surprise," remarked Jasper.

Cindy didn't appreciate her father's sarcasm and rolled her eyes in disapproval.

"Why don't we move into the family room where it's more comfortable?" Darlene suggested.

Without saying anything, Cindy stood and led the way, ensuring she could have her choice of seating. She elected to sit in the recliner, guaranteeing a comfortable distance from her dad. She was mad at him and was not ready to make nice. As a matter of fact, she entertained the idea of going ahead and slipping him the drugs now to avoid having to talk to him. Knowing that he went behind her back to persuade Carter to drop her case started the downward spiral of her respect for him. Then discovering what kind of people he employed only added to the decline. The final straw of course came in knowing he actually had her apartment bugged to eavesdrop. With the recent revelations, she found it difficult to even look at him.

Jasper sat on the end of the sofa.

Darlene positioned herself beside him and even snuggled up close, placing her hand on his thigh.

His body language and facial expression communicated he was annoyed by her close proximity. He crossed his arms across his chest and slightly turned away from her.

For the first time, Cindy realized she had seen her father treat her mother in a dismissive manner numerous times before. Why had she never been offended by it up until now?

Had she been so wrapped up in being daddy's spoiled little girl, that she had completely blocked it from her mind? She felt guilty and sad for her mother.

No wonder the woman drank constantly.

"Cindy," began Jasper. "I know you've been hurt and embarrassed by this thing that happened in the library, but I swear to you that it's not what you think."

"Then what is it?" Cindy asked.

"I was set up," claimed Jasper. "Tyler set me up."

"That's what I was told," she replied.

"Did Mr. Mays tell you?"

"He mentioned it."

"It's the truth," said Jasper. "I swear to you I never even knew that girl existed before."

Cindy decided to do a little digging on her own. "Why would Tyler do that?"

Jasper expelled a long breath. "I don't know."

"I mean, that sounds terribly vindictive," said Cindy. "There would have to be some reason to go to such drastic means to harm you."

"Honestly, I don't know why. I really don't."

Cindy stared intently at her father trying to tell if he was hiding something.

"Honey, your father has explained everything to me and I have to say I believe him," said Darlene.

"So is this whole set up thing you're claiming the reason you went to Carter for help?"

"I guess desperate times call for desperate measures," conceded Jasper.

Cindy wanted to confront her dad with other reasons he may have for hiring Carter. However, she couldn't afford to tip her hand. For a moment, the two of them sat in silence, their eyes drifting around the room but never looking at one another. Cindy sensed her mother getting restless and ready to play the role of mediator again.

Now was Cindy's opportunity to act. She quickly stood up. "I could use some dessert now," she said.

Darlene began to stand, but Cindy stopped her. "Stay where you are, Mom. I'll get us all some. Would you like another glass of wine or maybe some coffee?" Cindy asked, noticing that Darlene was nearing the end of her second glass.

"I'll have more wine, please," said Darlene, draining what she had left and handing the glass to her daughter.

"Dad," said Cindy. "What would you like to drink with your torte? Coffee? Milk? Something else?"

Jasper answered, "I'll have some coffee."

"I'll be right back," she said.

"Are you sure you don't need a hand carrying all that in here?"

"That's what they make trays for, Mom."

Cindy made her way into the kitchen, retrieved some small plates from the cabinet and cut three pieces from the torte. After getting three forks and locating a tray to carry everything, she poured two cups of coffee and refilled her mother's wine glass. Reaching into her pocket, Cindy removed two vials of the fine white powdery substance Carter gave her. He assured her that it would completely dissolve and be unnoticeable, with no dangerous side effects.

She emptied the first vial into her mother's wine and worked the glass in a circular motion to mix it in well. Just before she poured the second vial into one of the two identical coffee mugs, Cindy became concerned that by the time she returned to the family room, she may forget which coffee mug belonged to her and which one went to her father. The last thing she needed was to accidently sedate herself.

After stressing over the situation for a brief moment, Cindy opted to drink water instead and remove any chance she'd screw this up. Quickly she dumped her coffee back into the pot and replaced it with a bottle of water. Now she could empty the second vial without the worry.

The powder quickly disappeared into the coffee and Cindy did a thorough visual check to make sure there wasn't anything visible around the rim or on the handle. It all looked okay. With the vial still in her hand, she held it up to her nose to see if she detected a smell.

"What's that?" Darlene asked from directly behind Cindy.

The sound of her mother's voice startled Cindy to the point where she almost dropped the vial.

Immediately her heartbeat began to race like it had been injected with adrenalin. How long had her mother been there? What did she see? Cindy took a deep breath before turning to face her mom. "What?"

Darlene pointed to the vial in Cindy's hand. "What's that?"

"Oh this? This is some migraine medicine I got from a friend of mine. She gets them all the time and said it really helps."

"You have a migraine, dear? You don't usually get those do you?"

Cindy shook her head and fought to remain calm. "No, not usually. But since the wedding, I've had a couple of bad ones. I think it's the stress I've been under."

"Does it help? How does it work?"

"Oh yeah, it works great. She pre-measures them into these little containers and you just put it on your tongue to let it dissolve into your blood stream," lied Cindy, praying that her mom didn't see her actually pour it into her father's mug.

"You poor dear," said Darlene. "I hate to see you feel bad."

"I'll be okay," replied Cindy, desperately wanting to move on from the conversation and hoping Mom didn't say anything to Dad about it.

"Well, since I'm here, can I help you carry anything?"

"Sure," answered Cindy

Darlene took the tray with the torte servings and led the way back into the family room, as Cindy followed with the drinks. Their entrance into the room disrupted Jasper's blank stare at the floor in front of him.

"Here you go, Sweetie," said Darlene. "Doesn't that look good?"

"Yeah, it does," came his mediocre reply.

Cindy followed directly behind and handed her father the mug of coffee. "Here you go, Dad."

"Thanks, dear," he answered, bringing the cup up close so he could breathe in the aroma.

Cindy could feel her body tensing up, fearful that her father would see or taste the substance. For a moment she froze, too nervous to move.

Jasper took a sip of coffee and then looked up at his daughter and scowled.

Cindy swallowed hard, sure that her father could taste the drug. "What?" Cindy asked, trying to hide her guilt.

"What's wrong with you?" Jasper asked. "Why are you standing there staring at me?"

Cindy did her best to play off her guilt. "I was just waiting to see if the coffee tasted okay."

"It's fine," replied Jasper. "You can sit down."

Moving back to her chair, Cindy sat down and attempted to regain some form of inner calm. Her stomach violently churned and she so wanted this to be over.

She wondered how much of the coffee her dad would have to drink for the drug to take effect. Looking at her mother, half of the wine glass was already gone. Truth be told, she probably wouldn't have had to slip anything in her mother's drink. Darlene was quite capable of self-sedation.

"So," began Jasper. "What do you think of this detective?"

"What do you mean?" Cindy inquired.

"Do you think he's worth the money he's getting?" Jasper asked.

"Yeah. Why?"

"I'm just not that sure I would have gone out and hired the first guy I saw to find Tyler."

"I didn't hire the first guy I saw," defended Cindy. "A friend of mine referred him to me."

"Oh," said Jasper. "I guess that counts for something."

"If you don't like him, why did you hire him?"

"Now, wait a minute," answered Jasper. "I didn't say I didn't like him. I just don't know much about him."

"I know he's made a lot more progress than those guys working for you," snapped Cindy.

"You seem awfully defensive of him, considering you haven't had time to really get to know him."

She rolled her eyes and took a bite of her torte.

"I noticed he's a fairly good looking man, isn't he?"

"What does that have to do with anything?" Cindy asked.

"Nothing," claimed Jasper. "I was just making an observation."

Cindy turned her gaze away from her father and stared at the wall.

"He strikes me as the kind of guy who takes a special interest in young attractive women like yourself."

"What?" Cindy asked. "What are you talking about?"

"I just think you should be extra careful around this guy. You're kind of in a vulnerable state right now, and I know this Mays character is the type of guy who would take advantage of that. I hope you're keeping your guard up when you're around him."

Her father's comment reeked of arrogance and unjustified judgment. Cindy immediately thought about that night she had thrown herself at Carter. Her dad couldn't be more wrong. Then she began to think about the listening devices Carter found.

How long had they been there? What conversations had taken place between she and Carter that perhaps her father had overheard?

Jasper took another sip of his coffee.

"Keep drinking," thought Cindy, anxious for her dad to slip off to dreamland.

"So? Are you?" Jasper asked.

"Am I what?"

"Are you keeping your relationship with this man strictly business?"

The audacity of the question ate at her. At that moment she wanted to unload on her father for everything she had learned. "That's really none of your business, is it?"

"Yes, it is my business," insisted Jasper. "You're my daughter and I want you to make good decisions."

"If I recall, you thought Tyler was a good decision. For that matter, a great one."

Jasper paused, grimacing. "Tyler fooled me. I'll admit that. But I'm right about this guy. He's an opportunist. He'll try to get everything he can out of you, financially and whatever else."

Darlene interrupted. "Cindy this torte is absolutely delicious. Where did you get it?"

Completely ignoring her mother, Cindy glared at her father. "Whatever else he can get? What is that supposed to mean?"

"You know what it means," said Jasper.

"Maybe I'm not paying him with money," snapped Cindy. "Maybe I'm offering him special favors in exchange for his services."

Jasper shot his daughter a mean look. "Hey, how about if you quit talking like a whore?"

Darlene quickly stood up and suddenly she stooped over and placed her hands on her knees. "Oh, my."

"Mom, what's the matter?" Cindy asked, rushing to her mother's side.

"What do you think is the matter?" Jasper barked. "She's drunk like every other night."

Darlene kept her head facedown but still managed to communicate to her husband with the aid of her middle finger before backing down into her seat again to avoid falling over.

"I'm going to bed," said Jasper. "I don't need this right now," he said, leaving the room with his coffee mug in hand.

As she was tending to her mother, Cindy wondered if the two sips of coffee her dad had taken would be enough. She hoped he would drink more before going to bed. If all he had were the two sips she saw him take, it may not be enough to really knock him out. Without knowing, she ran the risk of waking him when she went for the key card.

"Are you okay, mom?" Cindy asked.

"I just stood up too soon," said Darlene. "I'm light-headed."

"Why don't you stretch out on the sofa for a few minutes and regain your bearings?"

"Yeah, that's a good idea," agreed a disoriented Darlene.

Cindy placed a pillow under her mother's head and covered her with a blanket.

"How's that?" Cindy asked. "Are you comfortable?"

"Yeah, thanks."

"Just chill out here for a while," suggested Cindy, knowing that the drug was taking effect.

"Your father can be such a jerk sometimes. However, I still hate seeing the two of you not getting along like you have this last week."

"It'll be alright, Mom," assured Cindy, not really believing what she was saying.

Darlene's eyes began to take long sleepy blinks as she faded out. She was still talking, but it was soft, low, and mumbled. Cindy kissed her mother's forehead and made her way to the kitchen. On the counter she saw her father's coffee mug.

Walking over to inspect it, it appeared that perhaps her dad had taken another drink or two before abandoning it. Was it enough to do the job?

She walked to the entrance of the kitchen and looked down the hall. With nobody in sight, she pulled her cell phone from her pocket and dialed Carter.

"Hello," he answered. "Are they out already?

"My mom is," whispered Cindy. "But I'm not sure about my dad. I slipped it into his coffee, but he only drank about half of it before he went to bed."

"Did he go to bed because he was getting tired?" Carter asked.

Cindy expelled a long sigh. "I'm not sure. He may have been just trying to get away from me. We kind of got into it."

"You got into it? Over what?"

"It doesn't matter," answered Cindy, not wanting to explain.

"Did anything happen that would keep me from getting into the office?"

"No, nothing like that. I'm just not certain he drank enough to really knock him out. I don't want him to wake up while I'm going through his wallet."

"What about your mom?"

"She's already out."

"I think your dad probably got enough in his system that you should be okay, but give him about twenty minutes before you try to get the key card."

"Twenty minutes? What am I going to do here for twenty minutes?"

"Cindy, it's your parents' home. It shouldn't be that big a deal to kill twenty minutes."

"I know," said Cindy. "I'm just feeling a little on edge right now. I want to get this over with."

"You're doing fine. Relax and call me when you're on your way."

"Okay."

Cindy hung up and took another look at the coffee mug. She wished she had kept her cool longer to give her father time to drink all of it. But no, instead she allowed herself to be pulled into an argument, thus prolonging her night.

After eighteen minutes, Cindy grew too anxious and bored to stay a minute longer. She exited the kitchen and walked up the steps to her parent's bedroom. There was no light coming out from beneath the door. She placed her ear against the door and listened. Nothing. Reaching for the doorknob, she hesitated. What if he woke up? What if he caught her? She needed a story, something to tell him.

The best thing she could come up with was to offer him an apology. That would totally suck to have to fake an apology to him, but it was by far her best angle.

Taking a deep breath, she slowly turned the knob and pushed open the door just enough to peek inside. The room was too dark to focus on much of anything.

She pushed it open more and stepped inside. The light from the hallway fell across the bed and she saw her father's form lying still in the darkness.

Her first few steps were toward the bed. She watched Jasper's torso expand with deep relaxed breaths.

"Dad," she whispered.

There was no stirring. She whispered again, but this time a little louder. "Daddy?"

After one more call, Cindy felt confident that the drug had taken effect. Not wanting to take any chances, Cindy remained as quiet as possible as she back peddled toward the dresser where she knew he was prone to emptying his pockets at night. Nothing was there. Her eyes moved to the nightstand next to the bed, but again, nothing.

Near the wall, opposite the bed, Cindy saw her father's slacks draped across the chair. She eased the pants off the chair and slipped her hand into the back left pocket to retrieve his wallet. A loud exhale from her father sent her heart into high speed. Her eyes focused on the mirror in front of her and she strained to see his reflection. His body remained motionless and she attempted to calm down. "Get a grip, Cindy," she muttered beneath her nervous breath.

With the wallet in her hand, she located the key card, returned the wallet and pants to their previous spots and quickly exited the room, easing the door closed behind her.

Walking out of the house and to her car, Cindy dialed Carter. He answered immediately.

"You got it?"

"Yes, and I'm a nervous wreck."

"Why, what happened?"

"Nothing happened, but I'm still a wreck. I'm going to need a dose of that stuff to sleep tonight."

"You did good. Relax," assured Carter.

"Where are you?"

"I'm at the coffee shop about three miles from your parents' house."

"Okay, I'll meet you there in a few minutes."

TWENTY-SEVEN

The parking lot of West Lake Properties & Development was brightly illuminated when Carter and Cindy arrived, far brighter than Carter would have preferred. He worried that a lone pick-up truck parked in front of the building late at night might catch the eye of a patrol officer. Carter elected to park near the side where it was darker and further away from the front door.

He shut off the engine and looked at his passenger. "Okay, you stay here. I'm not sure how long I'll be in there."

Cindy looked around the vacant lot and frowned. "Can I come with you? This is sort of creepy out here alone."

"No," replied Carter adamantly. "That's why I wanted you to stay behind. And you agreed, remember?"

"I know, but I didn't think about it being so scary here."

"Look. I'll leave the keys in it and you can slide over behind the wheel. If you get too scared, take a drive and I'll call you to pick me up."

"You're sure I can't go with you?"

"Absolutely not."

"Okay," agreed Cindy. "But I'm not leaving you here by yourself, so hurry."

Carter exited the truck and Cindy slid over into the driver's seat and locked the doors.

Carter, dressed in dark jeans and hoodie, approached the entrance with his hood up.

He swiped the key card and disappeared inside.

Making his way to the elevator, Carter kept his covered head tilted down and his hands in the pockets of his hoodie as he passed the security cameras recording his movement. Hopefully, by using the key card, nothing would spook whoever may be monitoring. Inside the elevator, he continued to look down. When the doors opened he was back inside the offices of WLP&D.

Moving quickly, Carter crossed the floor to the heavy glass doors that separated the rest of the office from the so-called inner sanctum.

With another scan of the card, he was inside. He didn't think there would be any cameras in this part of the office, but he kept his hood up and his posture low key just to be cautious.

The first office on the right was Tate Manning's. The second door on the right led him into Jasper's office. To keep from attracting any unwanted attention, Carter left the lights off and used a small flashlight to guide him.

His first move was to check the computer. With his gloved hand, he switched it on and waited. Just as he had figured, a password screen appeared.

Knowing his chances were slim, Carter typed in a few obvious choices for a password, including Cindy and Darlene. From time to time, he had run across people who had used no imagination or wisdom in selecting a password. He was amazed how predictable some folks could be. However, he did not anticipate Jasper being that foolish. As expected, Carter was unsuccessful.

Having tried the most obvious source of information, Carter searched the desk drawers. As he inspected each one, his mind produced a mental image of Jasper's men doing the same thing to his office.

After finding absolutely nothing of interest in Jasper's desk, Carter scanned the office for more places to check out. He saw a set of file drawers against the wall. Before moving onto them, he tried a few more password choices that came to him. They proved to be as ineffective as the other ones.

Unfortunately, a search of the file cabinets proved unproductive. Frustrated, Carter paused for a moment while his eyes moved around the office. Was there something he was missing?

Looking at his watch, Carter was sixteen minutes into his fruitless search. He didn't want to spend a long time there. The longer he was there, the more likely something could go wrong. He decided to move on.

Tate Manning was not the primary interest here, but given his position in the company, Carter felt it was worthwhile to give his office a look over as well. As with Jasper's computer, Tate's computer files weren't accessible either. Carter wished he were much more adept at hacking. However, the reality was this was not one of his best talents.

The rotary address organizer on the corner of Tate's desk captured Carter's attention. He pulled it over in front of him, placed the flashlight between his teeth to hold and began to flip through the numbers. Many of the names in the rotary appeared to be vendors and contractors, including building supply places, electricians, plumbers, and so forth.

Toward the end, an index card captured Carter's attention. The name and location of the company was Tainan Cement in China. Beneath the name and contact information were the words, "Bagged Cement."

Carter ran his fingers up and down his scruffy jaw line while he pondered why a company who develops property on the scale that WLP&D did, would possibly need bagged cement, particularly at a volume to justify shipping from China. Immediately something popped into his mind and he quickly returned to Jasper's office to confirm what he thought he remembered seeing.

Flipping through the pages of the desk calendar on Jasper's desk, Carter located the date where he had remembered seeing the word "cement," August 14th. It was the only thing written on the entire calendar. The whole thing seemed odd enough to look into, so to ensure he didn't forget it, Carter returned to Tate's office one more time to copy down the name of the Chinese cement company, before exiting the inner sanctum.

As he passed through the office, he noticed a small sign suspended from the ceiling tile to the left. It read "Accounts Payable." Carter decided to look through the file cabinets for some record of the cement company.

He located the set of drawers labeled "Suppliers" and opened it. The vendors were kept in alphabetical order, but he did not find any files for Tainan Cement.

With time quickly passing, Carter decided he should leave. He had already been inside longer than he planned and he figured Cindy was getting restless.

Carter exited the building and hurried to the truck. He tapped on the window and Cindy slid across the seat to the passenger side.

As soon as Carter was positioned behind the wheel, Cindy started talking. "What took you so long? You were in there forever."

"It wasn't that long, but sorry."

"It seemed like a long time to me," she argued. "Did you find anything?"

Carter paused, exhaled and shrugged. "Maybe, maybe not."

Cindy fell back into her seat and sighed.

Then Carter said, "Your dad's company buys bagged cement."

"Well, it is a construction company," reasoned Cindy.

"Yeah, but given the scale that his company develops property, bagged cement doesn't seem practical or cost effective."

Cindy shrugged her shoulders. "I don't know."

"I wonder where they keep that kind of stuff."

"My dad owns a big warehouse where he keeps most of his equipment."

"How far is it from here?"

"Half hour," answered Cindy. "Why? Are you going to visit?"

"I thought I'd take a look," Carter said. "Do you know what kind of security they have?"

"No. Sorry. But we can check it out. And this time I'm going in with you. I'm not waiting in the truck again."

Carter shook his head. "No, that's not a good idea."

"I didn't ask."

"No," repeated Carter.

"Then I'm not telling you where it is," replied Cindy.

"That's childish."

"Whatever."

"You know I could find out on my own where it is, don't you?"

"Not in time for you to go tonight," replied Cindy, smugly. "And I'm willing to bet you don't want to wait."

Carter stared at her, trying to devise an argument.

"Don't waste your time arguing. You know I'm right."

"Fine," conceded Carter. "You win. Now where are we going?"

Cindy flashed a victorious evil grin. "Turn right out of here," she said.

Carter drove as Cindy directed him. With the low volume of traffic during the late hour, they arrived in only twenty-two minutes. The large steel building sat on a three-acre lot surrounded by an eight-foot chain link fence with only one gate.

A heavy chain and pad lock held the gates securely closed. Carter parked his pick-up next to the fence and exited the truck, followed by Cindy.

Standing near the fence, Carter scanned the moderately lit property.

Cindy stood next to him. "So how are we getting in?" she asked.

"I was hoping they would have the same key card entry system that the office has. Unfortunately, they don't."

"Now what?"

"We improvise," answered Carter.

With his truck parallel to the fence, Carter hopped up in the bed, stepped up on the side, reached up to grab hold of the fence and pulled himself up and over, climbing down a little before dropping to the pavement.

Once he was on the other side, he stopped to look at Cindy. "Since we can't use the gate, you may want to just wait in the truck."

Cindy tilted her head to the side and narrowed her eyes. "Why? You don't think I can scale a fence?"

"I just wouldn't want you to get hurt," replied Carter.

Cindy leaped into the bed of the truck and with little effort was soon standing beside Carter. "Just because I'm a girl doesn't mean I can't hop a fence."

Carter grinned, genuinely impressed by Cindy's display of athleticism. "Guess it doesn't."

"Eight years of gymnastics," bragged Cindy as she walked past Carter on her way toward the building.

"So," said Carter, walking behind her and trying not to stare. "Any other talents you'd like to share?"

"What fun would it be if I told you everything at once?"

They stopped at the set of double doors on the front of the building, locked of course. Carter scanned up and down, side to side, looking for some point of access. He continued walking around the corner, circling the perimeter of the building. Around the back, he located a row of windows positioned high on the building. Perhaps one of them might grant him access if he could somehow get up there.

Turning around to view the surrounding area, Carter noticed a small, yet sizeable dumpster on wheels. With the stiff, noisy wheels grinding across the pavement, he maneuvered the dumpster beneath one of the windows.

The height of the dumpster was about eye level, still several feet short of his target. He looked around the grounds and noticed a pile of wood skids. Working quickly, Carter began to stack the skids on top of the dumpster.

Cindy jumped in and began dragging them over to him as he threw one on top of another.

After stacking six skids, Carter climbed up on the dumpster and placed the seventh and final skid on its end, leaning it against the wall of the building to use as a make-shift ladder.

"That doesn't look very stable," commented Cindy.

"That's because it isn't," replied Carter.

"But you're going to climb on it anyway?"

"Yep."

"Don't fall," said Cindy. "I can climb that fence to get in, but there's no way I could get your butt over on the other side if you came up lame. Not to mention you already have a concussion."

"Oh yeah," said Carter. "That would explain this dizzy feeling I've got going on"

"It's not funny to joke about that."

"Who's joking?"

Carter climb the precarious platform. By standing on the very top of the heap, he could see into the window. He pushed on it, and to his surprise, it opened.

"No way," said Cindy.

Out of curiosity, Carter reached out and pushed against the adjacent window, but it didn't budge. Neither did the window on the other side. "Hmm, that was pure luck."

"Can you get inside?" Cindy asked.

"Yeah, I can get inside, but there's not much for me to use to get to the ground level, except for gravity. I'd rather not break my leg."

Poking his head in further, Carter saw something that encouraged him. "Wait, there's a set of shelves just to the side of this window. I think I can land on those and then climb down."

"Are you sure? Don't take any unnecessary risks."

"Yeah, I think it's doable," replied Carter.

"Be careful, Carter," pleaded Cindy.

Carter pulled himself up and halfway into the window. The force of his foot pushing him off the top skid sent the shaky wooded foundation tumbling from the dumpster. The ruckus of falling skids caused Carter to turn his head, trying to see if Cindy had been crushed behind him while he did his best not to lose his grip. He called out, "Cindy?"

"I'm fine," she replied. "Are you okay up there?"

As his legs dangled from the window, he answered. "Yeah, I'm okay. I'm going in now."

Carter maneuvered his legs up and over the window ledge. He hung there momentarily while he assessed what he needed to do to swing his body to the side and onto the shelf below. Taking a deep breath, he lunged toward his target, hitting it perfectly.

However, during his decent, Carter lost his balance and his body scraped along the shelf and wall before landing on the concrete floor.

He dusted himself off and continued to the front door to let in Cindy. A brief moment of panic hit him when he opened the door and saw no one waiting on the other side.

Jogging around the building, Carter followed Cindy's voice and saw her in the same spot he left her, staring up at the windows.

"Why didn't you meet me at the front door?" Carter asked, startling Cindy.

"What happened to you? I heard this thunderous crashing noise and then you wouldn't answer me."

"Sorry, I didn't hear you. I kind of fell the last few feet."

"I thought you were hurt."

"If it makes you feel any better, I scraped a big chunk of skin out of my arm."

Cindy looked down at the small stream of crimson fluid running down from Carter's elbow. "Let's just get inside and then get out of here," she said.

Carter led the way around to the front entrance of the building. When they were both inside, he closed the door behind them and locked it.

Producing a small flashlight from his back pocket, Carter began his tour of the equipment building. Large pieces of excavating equipment sat parked throughout the space. Various tools and attachments for the machines were spread about in no particular order, including different sized buckets for the backhoes and loaders.

Following slightly back and to the right side, Cindy tagged along. Moonlight shined through the high windows, providing a fair amount of light, except when the occasional cloud passed overhead.

The building was separated into three main sections. The center section, where you entered by the main doors, housed all the large, heavy-duty driving pieces of equipment. To the right, they discovered a machine shop, probably used to do repairs to the equipment.

On the opposite side was a room that collected everything else, including smaller miscellaneous tools, like shovels, wheelbarrows, chainsaws, and an assortment of other odds and ends. At the far end of the room, near a large garage door, Carter noticed a big, sturdy skid with a few torn empty bags around it.

As he approached, he saw an 8"x11" piece of paper on the ground next to the skid. It read, *Tainan Cement* and included some Chinese writing as well.

"What is it?" Cindy asked.

"It's a cement company your father uses"

"Yeah, so?"

Carter ignored his tag-along and continued walking and looking at the ground.

He picked up one of the bags. It appeared that it had been punctured in the middle and pulled apart. As he studied the floor surrounding the skid, he noticed a significant amount of powdered cement, like the bags were opened there on the spot. Nobody would be mixing cement there to use elsewhere.

"Why are we looking at empty cement bags?" Cindy asked.

Without answering, Carter tossed the bag aside and picked up the 8"x11" paper. It had a date stamped on it from February. He folded it up and tucked it into his back pocket.

Cindy tapped Carter on the shoulder. "Have you completely quit answering my questions or have you gone deaf from the fall?"

"Oh, sorry," said Carter. "What did you say?"

"Forget it."

"Are you ready to get out of here?" Carter asked.

"Yes," replied Cindy. "Unless you want to inspect those long orange sticks over there."

Carter glanced in the direction Cindy had been looking. "That's rebar, and no, I don't need to inspect those."

Off in the distance, a lone approaching siren sounded through the night air. Immediately, Carter shined his flashlight throughout the building, following a path that ran from corner to corner and passed by all the doors. Carter's light beam stopped on a small plastic box with a lens covering it. "Motion detectors," he announced. "I never even saw them."

"An alarm?" Cindy inquired.

"Yep," he answered with a hint of panic in his voice.

Flipping off his flashlight, Carter's path out was illuminated by the light filtering through the windows. "We've got to scoot," he said, grabbing Cindy by the arm and running toward the exit.

Once they were outside, the siren grew much louder. Carter slammed the door closed behind them as they both scurried across the lot. After another impressive display of athleticism by Cindy, Carter followed her over the fence and they were in the truck, keeping the headlights off and racing away in the opposite direction of the approaching police car.

By the time they reached the house, Cindy's anxiety was growing by leaps and bounds. Besides nearly getting caught by the police, Cindy still had to return the proxy card. Knowing her father hadn't finished the entire cup of coffee left her worrying his sleep may not last as long as it should.

Carter dropped her off at the end of the drive and disappeared down the street with instructions to send him a text to confirm when the key card had been successfully returned.

Entering the house, Cindy made her way upstairs, slowing her pace as she drew nearer to her parent's bedroom. Pushing the door slightly open, she peered inside to check on her father's status. His back was to her. When several moments of her dad's peaceful, motionless sleep had passed, Cindy tiptoed her way inside the room and returned the card to its place in Jasper's wallet. Mission accomplished.

Just as she reached for the door on her way out of the room, she heard footsteps approaching from down the hall. She knew those steps were her mother's. How in the world had that woman managed to regain consciousness after the wine and sleep aid?

Cindy stepped behind the door and crouched down.

Darlene staggered her way past Cindy and slipped into her side of the bed.

Jasper turned over when his wife disturbed his restful state with her entry.

Cindy held her breath and froze in place. Although she could tell her dad was now facing her direction, she couldn't tell if his eyes were open or not. She immediately began to concoct a story in the unfortunate event he caught her. Never had she been that still and that nervous at the same time.

Soon after she heard the soft rumble of her father snoring and she knew her window of opportunity to leave had opened. Quietly, but quickly she exited the bedroom and disappeared into her room.

Standing in the darkness of her childhood haven, Cindy struggled to slow the pace of her heart. It had been a stressful evening of firsts for her. Never before had she drugged her parents, snuck anything from her father's wallet, or participated in breaking and entering. She was mentally and emotionally drained. She sent a text to Carter that simply said, mission accomplished.

Finding an old t-shirt that she kept there to sleep in, Cindy changed clothes and climbed into her bed. After a long battle with a mind full of thoughts and distractions, Cindy's body eventually overcame her brain and she drifted off to sleep.

TWENTY-EIGHT

Carter elected to spend the remainder of the night sleeping on the love seat at his office as opposed to creeping into his neighbors' and waking Dave and Catherine. He managed to get in two solid hours of sleep before two of his fellow tenants in the building woke him with their entry and loud, in-depth discussion of who was supposed to pick up donuts on their way into work. Apparently, nobody in their office would get breakfast that morning.

After some time in the bathroom washing the sleep from his eyes, Carter settled in at his desk and began to search out information on the web for Tainan Cement. He soon discovered the company had absolutely no web presence whatsoever, strengthening his suspicions.

Checking the time, Carter decided to call a friend of his at the FBI, Shawna Feingold. The two of them dated briefly, before Carter realized Shawna was too busy to be in a relationship. The girl was a workaholic bent on rising through the ranks of the Bureau.

Shawna had willingly relocated from city to city whenever the FBI asked her. She started in Cincinnati before transferring to Houston. From there it was a three year stint in San Diego before coming to Chicago.

Carter figured she was about ready to move again at any time. During her ambitious twelve-year career, she had built up quite a network of contacts throughout various government and law enforcement agencies. Perhaps she might be able to find some information on Tainan Cement.

Shawna answered on the first ring. "Agent Feingold."

"So how many hours have you been at work already?" Carter asked.

"Hello, Carter Mays," she replied. "You know how it is for us girls trying to get ahead in this boys club. We have to burn the candle at both ends."

"Shawna, I have no doubt you'll be running that boys club in the near future."

"Thanks for the vote of confidence, hun. So to what do I owe the pleasure of hearing your voice this morning?"

"I need some information," answered Carter. "I know a girl with your connections will be able to get it."

"I'm listening."

"I'm trying to find out about a cement company in China; Tainan Cement. Anything that you could come up with, like U.S. customers, shipping history, et cetera, would be greatly appreciated. I'm pretty sure a shipment of theirs passed through customs around February of this year."

"Wow," she replied. "That's the most obscure thing you've ever asked me for. I may need a little time."

"Yeah, I figured you would."

"I'll do what I can, but we've been swamped here. It may take a day or two."

"Thanks, Shawna. I owe you one."

"How about buying me dinner?"

"Do you mean like a date?" Carter asked.

"No, not a date. It'll be just two old friends catching up. But hey, if we happen to reignite a spark or two, who knows?"

"I thought all that was history."

"What can I say? I still have a soft spot for you."

"Well, I'll tell you what. We'll plan on dinner regardless of what you're able to find out. But it will depend on the quality of information you provide to determine if it's steak or a hot dog."

Shawna snickered. "I'll certainly do my best then to make it steak. I'll call you when I find something."

"Thanks, Shawna. I can always count on you."

Carter hung up and stared off into the distance at nothing for a moment. The thought of seeing Shawna again made him smile. They always seem to connect, more so than the other girls he had dated. If she wasn't so ambitious, he could see something more serious happening between them.

Then his mind wandered over to Cindy. Of course that whole situation was bad news on a couple of levels. Yes, she was one of the best looking girls he had ever encountered. Yes, there was definitely some chemistry between them. However, the baggage that came with her made it highly improbable it would really lead to anything lasting. First of all, she was fresh off the rebound of a seriously screwed up relationship based on a big lie. Secondly, there was the whole thing with her father. In spite of the fact that a part of him wanted to explore the possibilities with Cindy, Carter knew it would probably end up a train wreck.

Finally, thoughts of Carina surfaced. Here was something brand new. He knew very little about the girl. Maybe she was the one. Or perhaps she was a psychotic stalker, although he doubted it. It might be fun to find out.

The two hours of sleep on the small office love seat did not leave Carter feeling his best. A dull ache was forming in the depths of his brain, most likely due to the combination of sleep deprivation and his recent head injury.

In order to recharge his batteries, Carter went back to his neighbor's house to get more sleep. Dave and Catherine would be at work, and Carter was certain their son, Alec, usually stayed at a friend's house during the summer days, leaving Carter to catch up on sleep in a quiet house.

As he drove along the highway, fighting fatigue, Carter's cell phone rang. "Hello," he answered.

"Hello, Mr. Mays. This is Jasper Bedford."

"Oh," replied Carter, wondering if something had happened to tip off Bedford concerning the previous night's activities. "Hello, Mr. Bedford. What can I do for you?"

"To be honest, I'm calling because I'm a little disappointed in the lack of communication from you concerning your progress in finding Tyler. I've hardly heard a word from you since I paid you your advance."

"I apologize for that, Mr. Bedford. I'm afraid I don't have a great deal to report as of yet."

"So you've found out nothing?"

Carter couldn't tell if Jasper was being up front with him or trying to fish for information. Was there a chance the man knew more about Carter's actions than he was letting on? He'd been certain nobody had been following him, and Cindy's text after he dropped her off indicated all was well. However, there was always that chance he underestimated Jasper. Plus there was the alarm tripping at the warehouse. Carter had scanned the property for security cameras, but didn't see any. No doubt Jasper knew the alarm had been tripped, but it was unlikely he had any evidence to know who was involved. Carter decided to stick with the same old story line and assume Jasper had no credible information that would incriminate Carter. "Nothing of any significance."

A pause at the other end of the phone made Carter a little uneasy.

Finally, Jasper spoke. "I'd like to meet with you just the same and compare your notes with ours. Maybe we can help each other out."

"Okay, we can do that," Carter agreed. "How about tomorrow evening?" He asked trying to put it off as long as possible.

"Actually, I was thinking today."

"Today?"

"Yes. Is that a problem?" Jasper asked.

"No. Can we make it this evening?"

"What time?"

"We could make it around seven?"

"That will be fine," responded Jasper.

"You do remember that according to our agreement, Cindy has to be present?"

Jasper expelled a deep sigh. "Oh yes, of course. I'll leave that to you to call her."

"I can do that," agreed Carter, hoping that Cindy wouldn't be available and he could delay the meeting. "Where would you like to meet?"

"We'll do it over dinner," said Jasper. "Are you familiar with Shay's?"

"Yeah, I know the place."

"Then we'll meet there tonight at seven."

"I'll call Cindy and make sure she can make it," said Carter.

"Fair enough."

Carter ended the call and immediately dialed Cindy. He asked her about the scheduled dinner meeting and questioned her about her father's behavior that morning.

She agreed to the meeting and indicated that for the very brief time she'd seen him before leaving her parent's house, he didn't act like he suspected anything.

Then Cindy began to wonder aloud over the phone if her father discovered their actions by some other means after he left the house, perhaps by some surveillance video or someone had seen them.

Carter could hear her level of anxiety climbing. He sought to assure his client everything was okay and she had no reason to panic, although he wasn't completely certain of that himself.

TWENTY-NINE

Jasper was on his way to Shay's to meet with the investigator. As usual, Russell was accompanying him.

Ten minutes from the restaurant, Russell received a call, which he promptly answered.

At first, Jasper paid little attention to anything Russell was discussing. However, the tone of Russell's voice and a few key words of conversation stirred up Jasper's interest in what was being discussed.

"Okay, we'll meet you there," said Russell, before hanging up the phone.

"Who was that?" Jasper asked.

"That was Billy. He's got Tyler."

Jaspers' jaw dropped open. "What?"

"Billy has Tyler," replied Russell.

"What do you mean, he 'has' him?"

"He caught him."

"Billy? How?"

"He said Tyler called him wanting to meet alone. He said Tyler wanted to explain everything to him. So Billy agreed to meet him. Somehow, Billy managed to coax him into his car where he tased him."

"Where are they now?" Jasper inquired.

"He's holding him on the top floor of the Timber Hills job site. I told him we'd meet him there."

"Timber Hills?"

"Yeah, Billy figured since production has been delayed on that job and given its remote location, it would offer the necessary privacy to deal with this."

Jasper stared at the dashboard in front of him, biting his nails.

"What's wrong?" Russell asked.

"Something doesn't feel right about this. Billy and Tyler were too tight for us to walk in there unprepared."

"You think Billy is trying to set us up?"

"Think about it for a minute, Russell. Billy and Tyler were best of friends. Then of course, you and Dan more or less torture him for information about Tyler. Even if he wasn't in on it from the beginning, we may have pushed him to the point where he wants revenge."

"I suppose you may be right."

"I would think that would be an obvious consideration to the guy who is supposed to be my head of security. Sometimes I think you're actually getting more incompetent."

Russell looked away from his boss, keeping his eyes on the road in front of him.

"Okay, here's what we're going to do," said Jasper. "Call Mick and Roy and tell them to meet us there."

Russell nodded as he began to make the phone call. While waiting for his associates to answer, he asked his boss, "What about your meeting with the PI?"

"Screw him. Apparently, I don't need him anymore. We'll figure out what we're going to do about him later."

Carter sat patiently at the table sipping water and waiting. At 7:19 he tried to call Cindy to see if she was on the way. The fact neither she nor her father had shown up yet made him a little uneasy. It would be different if they were riding there together and were late. However, in light of the strained father/daughter relationship, Carter was certain they would not arrive together.

Calls to Jasper Bedford's phone went unanswered as well. Why would Bedford request the meeting and then not show up? Carter's suspicions dominated his mind creating a host of unpleasant speculations. Did Jasper want him here to keep him out of the way for some reason? Or perhaps it was an attempt to set him up for something. Maybe Bedford did know about Carter's nighttime tours of the office and equipment property.

After another fifteen minutes of waiting, Carter gave up and left the restaurant. As he walked to his vehicle, Carter dialed Cindy's cell once more but again, no one answered. As he reached his truck, he heard something behind him and turned around, but not in time to avoid the impact of a gun to the back of his head.

Russell rolled the car up and parked about thirty yards from the Timber Hills job site. The building was six stories of office space a pharmaceutical company had hired WLP&D to build. A little more than halfway through the building process, the company ran into some serious financial troubles and the building came to an abrupt halt. Seven months had passed without any progress or resolutions. Up until Tyler's disappearance and the subsequent false importuning charges concerning the girl in the library, this project had been Jasper's thorn in the flesh. He longed for the day when this was his biggest headache.

Russell shut off the engine and the two of them stared ahead at the building.

From a little patch of nearby trees, Mick appeared and approached the passenger side of the vehicle.

Jasper rolled down his window.

"What's up, Boss?" Mick said, squatting beside the car.

"Where's Roy?" Jasper asked.

"He's parked on the other side of the building, waiting."

Jasper looked at his watch and then at Mick. "I want you to go over to where Roy is and the two of you to enter the building from that side. Billy is supposed to be holding Tyler on the top floor. You two should stay close, but stay quiet and out of sight unless I need you. I'll give you a few minutes to meet up with Roy and get into position inside the building. Go."

Mick's portly frame disappeared into the trees and the two men sat in silence. Jasper hoped Billy wouldn't try to double-cross him. But if he did, it wouldn't fair well for him.

When an adequate amount of time passed, Jasper gave the command and Russell started the car and drove onto the property next to the building. The two of them exited and Jasper led the way inside.

Since the building was under construction, there was no working elevator yet, forcing them to climb the stairs to the sixth floor.

"I'm getting too old for this taking the stairs crap," complained Jasper, looking back at Russell. "You should have told him to bring him down to at least the second or third floor."

"Sorry," said Russell. "I didn't even think about it."

Once they arrived on the top floor, Jasper nodded at Russell to be prepared and then proceeded to call out to Billy. "Billy? Are you up here?"

"Back here," came the faint reply.

Jasper remembered the last time he entered a building under construction he saw Billy being worked over by Dan and Russell. The image made him all the more leery about this meeting. He continued following the voice until he finally saw Billy coming down the corridor to meet him.

"Where is he?" Jasper asked.

Billy motioned with his head. "He's back this way."

"Lead the way," he commanded, not allowing Billy to get behind him.

Upon entering the large unfinished room, Jasper saw his almost son-in-law and now number one enemy sitting in a chair with his hands behind him.

Tyler sat with his head down, wearing jeans and a Notre Dame shirt.

"Well, well, well," said Jasper, keeping a distrustful awareness of where Billy was in the room.

Tyler looked up and stared at Jasper, void of any emotion.

For a moment Jasper said nothing. He fixed his eyes on his now defeated adversary and remained silent. Then turning his attention toward Billy, Jasper nodded his approval. "Good work, Billy. I'm going to take good care of you for this one. You've definitely earned a promotion."

Billy nodded and grinned. "Thank you, sir."

"So, here we are," resumed Jasper to Tyler. "What am I going to do with you?"

Tyler turned his head to the side.

"Whatever I do," said Jasper, "it's not going to be very pleasant for you. I'll guarantee you that."

Tyler casually spit on the ground.

Arching his eyebrows at the insult, Jasper eventually snickered and revealed a humored grin. "I've got to know," he said, pacing back and forth in front of the chair. "Before I start making life a pain-filled living hell for you, I've got to know why. Why did you do it? I mean, I guess I understand the money thing, but why would you go out of your way to come after me in an attempt to destroy my life, especially when you already had the money? What did I do to piss you off so bad?"

"You're just reaping what you sowed," replied Tyler in a calm voice.

The reply caught Jasper off guard. "What?"

"You can't use people and then dispose of them without repercussions," said Tyler with a little more boldness in his voice. "You can't just ruin their life and go on living your own like nothing happened. It's called payback."

Bedford squinted and held his hands out to the side. "What are you talking about?"

"Do you remember Louise Conway?"

Jasper stopped walking and cast a disgruntled gaze at Tyler. "What about her?"

"She was my mother," answered Tyler.

Jasper repeated. "Your mother?"

"Yes, my mother. Do you remember? The little fling you had, taking advantage of her, using your position as her boss to manipulate her? But then she became pregnant and you decided that wasn't convenient for you so wrote her a check, insisting that she have an abortion. But she couldn't go through with that, could she? And even though she told you she didn't want anything from you, that she'd just walk away and you'd never hear from her again, that wasn't good enough for you. So what did you do? You lost your temper and pushed her down a flight of stairs; you selfish, cowardly bastard."

Jasper averted his eyes. "It was an accident," he claimed.

"Yeah, right. After her fall down the stairs, she told you that she lost the baby," continued Tyler. "But she lied."

The thought that Jasper was staring at his own son weighed heavy on him. Several thoughts went through his head, one of which was the whole relationship between Tyler and Cindy. Had Tyler knowingly hooked up with his blood sister to position himself for some type of revenge? Jasper sought to maintain a hardness he felt slipping away. "How is your mom these days?"

"She's dead," answered Tyler.

"Really? That's too bad," replied Jasper with little conviction.

"Several years ago," replied Tyler. "That tumble down the stairs didn't leave her unscarred. The impact of the fall had lasting effects in the form of brain seizures for the rest of her life. As far back as I can remember she would get these horrendous headaches, so bad she'd just lay in bed and cry. But they weren't nearly as bad as the seizures that hit her with no warning. She'd zone out and get this blank expression on her face. It would last for a few seconds up to a few minutes. Do you know how scary that is to a little kid to see your mom like that, completely unresponsive? Eventually, they became more and more frequent, lasting longer. We ended up having to move. She couldn't drive. Toward the end, I couldn't leave her by herself more than a few minutes at a time; worried she'd have a seizure and burn herself while cooking or fall again. Then one day, she got tired of it all and ended it. I walked into her room to discover she'd hung herself."

Trying not to dwell on the implications that this was indeed his biological son, Jasper responded. "Well I guess you're destined for a tragic life? You both would have been better off if she had just had the abortion like I told her to do."

Tyler said nothing.

"Now I have to finish what I failed to do back then and get rid of you. Of course first things first," said Jasper. "First you're going to tell me where my money is."

"I doubt that," replied Tyler.

"Oh you're going to tell me," assured Jasper. "I'll guarantee that. But I'll make you a deal. You tell me where it is, and I'll have them kill you quickly. However, if you're going to be stubborn, then this whole ugly situation will drag out for days, and maybe weeks. And to be honest with you, part of me would be willing to sacrifice the money just to see the latter come to pass."

Tyler leaned back and smiled. "I'm not telling you anything."

Jasper scoffed and shook his head with disappointment. "Tyler ole' boy, you're going to regret this decision."

"I don't think so," replied Tyler. "And by the way, my name is Steven Conway."

"Well I'll be sure they get that right on your headstone. Now I'm going to give you one more chance."

"Screw you," he whispered.

Looking at Russell, Jasper nodded in Tyler's direction. "Do your thing."

Russell didn't move.

Annoyed by Russell's failure to respond, Jasper addressed his number one man. "Hey Russell, how about you wake up and follow directions instead of standing there dumbfounded not paying attention?"

Russell looked at his boss. Casually he reached inside his jacket, pulled out his gun and pointed it at Jasper.

Russell's action sent a shockwave over Jasper and he stepped back. "What the hell?"

Standing there with the gun still pointed at his boss, Russell looked at his employer and shrugged.

Jasper yelled, "What are you doing? Have you completely lost your mind?"

"He doesn't work for you any longer," said Tyler, standing up and allowing the ropes to fall loose to the ground.

Jasper's eyes followed the ropes to the floor. Then he looked over at Billy, who was staring un-phased by the turn of events.

"So you guys working for him now?" Jasper asked, glaring at Tyler who was in the process of circling around him.

"No," replied a familiar voice. "They're working for me."

Looking over his shoulder toward the voice from behind, Jasper saw Tate Manning enter the room. "Tate? What is this?"

"This is a changing of the guard, so to speak," replied Tate, his walk and posture much bolder than usual.

Jasper began to scan the room for a quick exit.

Tate offered a word of caution. "I know what you're thinking, Jasper, and I would highly advise against it. As a matter of fact, why don't you sit down in Steven's seat, now that he's not using it?"

Jasper looked at Russell. "You don't want to do this, Russell."

Russell motioned with the gun. "Sit down, Jasper."

Jasper moved toward the folding chair and sat down. He wondered where Mick and Roy were and if they were dead or perhaps they had betrayed him as well.

After allowing the situation to fully sink in, Jasper sought to regain the attitude of confidence and authority. "So what is this, gentlemen, some sort of mutiny? Am I being forced out?"

"Yes, something like that," replied Tate.

"By the way, Tate, have you had the chance to meet my son, Tyler or Steven, whatever his name is?"

"Actually, Jasper, he's not your son," said Tate. "He's mine."

Jasper cocked his head. "Do you want to say that again?"

"Steven is not your son. He's my son."

Jasper turned to look at Tyler. "Well, Tyler, I have to say I'm a little confused at the moment. Is this true?"

"It's true," replied Tyler.

"Then shouldn't Tate be the one you're trying to destroy?"

Tate nodded at Russell who approached his former boss and patted him down, removing his cell phone from Jasper's inside jacket pocket. Once he had possession of the phone, he walked it over and handed it to Tate.

Tate turned his back and began to dial. Seconds later, Tate tossed it back to Russell who returned it to Jasper's pocket.

Jasper folded his arms across his chest. "Would someone like to fill me in on what this is all about?"

"This is about making things right," answered Tate. "This is about correcting past wrongs."

"Well that all sounds very noble, but I still don't have a clue what this is about."

"Before you became involved with Louise Conway, she and I were seeing each other."

"Really?" Jasper questioned. "I find that surprising. I would have thought she was a bit out of your league."

"Before you forced your way into her personal life, the two of us were developing a good relationship."

"Forced my way? As I recall, there was no force necessary. She seemed quite eager to start up a relationship with me. Maybe her perception of your relationship wasn't quite as positive as yours."

"Oh, you definitely forced your way. That's the only way you know how to do anything. You've always thrived on your ability to intimidate and bully people into doing whatever you want. You've bullied me for nearly thirty years and quite frankly, I'm done with it."

"I've bullied you? That's what this is about? You think I've bullied you?"

"You pushed your way in and took away the woman I loved. Then when she got pregnant, you tried to bully her into having an abortion," accused Tate. "Then when she dared challenge your wishes, you shoved her down a flight of stairs."

"It was an accident. I didn't mean for her to fall."

"After they released her from the hospital, I gave her some money and set her up in a little house in Indiana, far from you but close enough to where I could see her."

"If you loved her so much, why didn't you go with her?"

"That was my plan. I just needed a little time to sort some things out here. Louise didn't understand that and she ended it with me. I went to see her several times trying, but she would just shut me out. Eventually, she asked me to not come back. So I honored her wishes."

Jasper nodded toward Tyler. "So you say he's your son?"

"That's right."

Jasper laughed. "You're pathetic."

Tate's eyes honed in on Jasper again. "I know I've made mistakes and I've had to live with them all these years."

Jasper looked at Tyler. "Are you listening to this? I don't know why you're taking this out on me. He's the one that abandoned you."

"He knows everything. I confessed my sins to him a long time ago," said Tate. "I've apologized time and time again for allowing you to rob me of the woman I loved and my son. I've paid dearly for it, too."

"How so?" Jasper replied. "You seemed to have lived a rather comfortable life and gained a lot while working for me all these years."

"Oh yeah, things have been great. I've endured two nasty divorces which are still costing me sixty percent of my income. And because you refuse to give up the secret part of our business and fully go legit, I'm constantly facing the possibility of going to jail."

"I guess you think if I hadn't interfered with whatever it was you thought you had with Louise, your life would have turned out rosy, huh?"

Tate nodded. "That's right, it would've. I firmly believe that."

"And I can't believe you're still harping on the business thing. We've been doing this for years, Tate, and not once have we ever come close to having any problems. Plus it's not like we're doing deals all the time. It's maybe two or three deals a year now."

"It only takes once, Jasper."

Jasper chuckled and looked at Tyler again. "Well, Tyler or Steven or whatever, we've established two things this evening. Your dad is a cowardly, weak, and pitiful excuse for a man. And apparently your mom was a whore willing to screw anyone in the office."

Tyler charged toward Jasper and struck him across the face with his fist, knocking him off the chair. Tyler unleashed a barrage of obscenities trying to get in another swing while Russell and Billy pulled him off Jasper.

"Let me go." Tyler demanded.

Tate quickly moved over to confront Tyler.

"Don't let him taunt you like that," Tate said. "We must keep our eyes on the big picture here."

"Now, Tate," said Jasper, holding his cheek and staring up from the floor. "Is that any way to talk to your boy?"

"Shut up," Tate commanded.

"Whoa, Tate. Don't tell me you've finally grown a pair after all these years."

With Tyler calming down, Tate said to Russell, "Get him back in the chair."

Russell moved over and grabbed Jasper by the back of his collar, lifting him off the ground and plunging him back into the folding chair.

"You're making a grave mistake here, Russell. I can't believe you let this pathetic excuse for a leader persuade you into this. Do you really think you're going to have it better with him running things? You'll be out of work in a year."

"Russell and Billy both know a good opportunity when they see it. Plus they're tired of putting up with your abusiveness."

"What about Roy and Mick?" Jasper asked Russell. "Have they been duped like you?"

"As a matter of fact," interrupted Tate. "Roy and Mick are on board with us."

Still rubbing his face, Jasper spoke to Russell. "What's the matter, Russell? Aren't you allowed to answer any questions? At least I let you speak for yourself."

Russell said nothing in response.

"I've got to hand it to you, Russell, the other day when you told me Dan had been killed, I never would have guessed you were involved. That was a nice piece of acting."

"He wasn't involved yet," said Tate. "I did that."

"You? You killed Dan?"

Tate nodded. "He never saw it coming."

"So I guess you're going to kill me now?" Jasper inquired.

"No," replied Tate. "You're going to do it."

"Oh, you think so?" Jasper asked, sneering at the thought.

"You see what was originally supposed to happen was that we would set you up for that whole thing at the library and you would be shamed, lose your family and be sent to prison for a very long time. And once you were in prison, I was already making arrangements to have you violently killed. But now, upon hearing that you may actually have a chance of beating this thing, I can't allow that to happen. For whatever reason, you are one of the luckiest S.O.B.'s I've ever had the sorry pleasure of knowing. It doesn't matter how much crap you manage to fall into, you somehow always come out smelling like roses."

"I guess it's just my good clean living," commented Jasper.

"Fortunately, your luck is about to run out."

"I'm still curious why I would kill myself," said Jasper.

"You're going to write a note confessing your guilt. You're going to admit that you like and pursue young girls on the Internet. Then you're going to hang yourself, just like Louise did."

Jasper watched as Billy pulled a new rope out of a bag, tied a noose, and threw it over one of the exposed steel beams above.

Tate continued. "Then, of course, your shamed, distraught wife will be devastated. Fortunately, I will be there to be a close, and I do mean close, friend to Darlene. As a matter of fact, I can see something lasting developing between the two of us. After that, it won't be long until I'm controlling the whole company."

"That's a great plan you've got there, Tate, except for one important thing. I'm not going to write a note and I'm not going to hang myself. And if you try to force me, you'll end up having to beat the crap out of me and tie me up first, which will ruin any chances of making the police believe it was a suicide. That's obviously why you quickly stopped Tyler from doing any more damage, isn't it?"

"Oh, you're going to hang yourself," promised Tate. "You're going to be begging me to let you hang yourself."

Jasper snickered again. "You're cracking me up, Tate. If you boys think I'm going to beg you for anything, you can all burn in hell."

"You always have to be so hardnosed about things, don't you?" Tate said.

Jasper shrugged. "What can I say? I'm not a beggar."

"I figured that would be your attitude," replied Tate. "Jasper Bedford, the hardest man alive. Fortunately, I know just the thing to soften you up."

Tate whistled loudly, signaling Mick and Roy.

Carter entered the room, trailed by Roy who kept a gun pointed at his back. At Roy's command, Carter knelt down, keeping his fingers locked together on top of his bleeding head.

Tate looked at Carter and addressed Roy. "Why did you bring him in here? You should have left him in the trunk."

"I thought we were going to, you know."

"Not here," replied Tate.

Mick came in followed with his hand firmly gripped around the arm of Cindy.

Jasper stood up to go to her but was quickly knocked down by Russell.

Cindy cried out.

Tyler took two steps toward Tate. "What is she doing here? This wasn't what we agreed to."

"Relax, Tyler. Her presence is necessary," said Tate.

"We talked about this," he said emphatically. "She has no involvement here."

Cindy spoke out. "Are you going to at least acknowledge me personally, Tyler? You stand there like we're strangers or something, talking about me like I can't hear you. We were engaged for crying out loud. The least you could do is talk to me."

Tyler turned his attention to his former fiancé. "This wasn't supposed to happen this way, Cindy. I'm sorry."

"You're sorry? That's all you can say is that you're sorry?"

Tyler offered no response.

"You used me you lying bastard."

"That's enough," interrupted Tate.

"Don't talk to my daughter," Jasper insisted.

Tate held up his hands. "Everybody calm down. There's no need for all of this hostility."

Carter's eyes shifted back and forth, assessing his bleak situation.

"Now let's see, where were we?" Tate asked. "Oh yes, Jasper was just about to hang himself."

"What?" Cindy exclaimed.

Russell prompted Jasper to get up off the floor and return to the chair.

"It's okay, sweetheart," said Jasper.

"Daddy, what's going on?"

"Your dad is paying for past sins, Cindy. You're here to ensure it," said Tate. Then he looked at Billy. "Give him the pen and paper."

Billy approached Jasper and handed him a single sheet of plain paper, a pen, and a scrap piece of drywall to put under the paper while he wrote.

Reluctantly, Jasper accepted. "I'll do what you want, Tate," said Jasper. "Just let her go now."

"Hmm..." said Tate. "I wish I could believe you, Jasper. I really do. But I know you tend to have some problems telling the truth. As a matter of fact, this might be a good time to come clean with your daughter."

Jasper's head sort of fell down to the side.

Tate continued. "Come on, Jasper. Tell your daughter how you manage to keep her living at the level of comfort she's grown accustomed to all these years."

Carter glanced around to see Cindy until Roy kicked him between the shoulder blades. Carter absorbed most of the impact with his forearms.

"Keep your eyes forward," commanded Roy.

"Okay then," said Tate. "I'll tell her. Not only is your dad a successful businessman, but he's also a drug dealer, killer, and an all-around nasty human being."

"Daddy? What's he talking about?" Cindy asked.

Tate smiled. "It's okay, Jasper. I'll tell her. You see, Cindy, for pretty much your entire life, your dad has been smuggling drugs into this country for a very sizable profit. And I'm not talking just a few pounds of marijuana either. I'm talking heroin by the boatload. Isn't that right, Jasper?"

Jasper sneered as Tate exposed him.

Cindy asked, "Is that what you're doing with all that bagged cement?"

Carter dropped his head, fearful that Cindy just made matters worse. His eyes shifted over to see how Tate would respond.

Tate's smile quickly faded. He walked up directly in front of her and asked, "How did you know about the bags of cement?"

Cindy ignored him.

"Answer my question," commanded Tate.

Cindy glanced at him and looked away.

He asked again, getting more forceful. "How do you know about the bags of cement?"

The room fell quiet waiting for a response.

"Do you mean the cement from China?" Cindy asked.

Tate grabbed her by the arm and snapped, "Yes, those bags. Now tell me how you know about them."

"Get your hands off of her," Jasper yelled.

Tate glanced at Jasper, then slapped Cindy hard across the face.

Jasper lunged at Tate but was subdued by Russell and Mick.

Tyler rushed over and stood between Cindy and Tate. "What do you think you're doing?" Tyler yelled. "This isn't happening."

"Did you not hear her?" Tate replied. "The fact that she knows this could put us all in great jeopardy."

Carter watched, as the situation grew volatile. Needing a strategy, he decided on a divide and conquer approach. "He's going to kill her, Tyler."

"Shut up," demanded Tate, looking at Roy, who threw another foot into Carter's back, plunging him face down on the floor.

"Leave him alone," yelled Cindy.

Tate repeated his question. "Who else knows about the bagged cement?"

"Hold on a second," Tyler persuaded Tate, then turned his former fiancé. "Cindy, sweetheart..."

"Sweetheart? How dare you call me 'sweetheart.'"

"I'm trying to help you here," defended Tyler. "Just tell me everything you know about the cement bags and who else may know about it."

"Are you okay, Carter?" Cindy asked.

With his face on the floor, Carter watched Tate approached him and point the gun at his head.

Cindy screamed out, "Don't."

Tate's thick fingers grabbed hold of Carter's hair, jerking his head back, and pressed the gun into Carter's temple. "I swear, Cindy, if you don't start telling me what I want to know right now, I'm going to splatter his brains all over the floor."

"Okay, I'll tell you," relented Cindy.

Tyler stepped back, opening up the line of sight between Cindy and Tate.

"Start talking," Tate commanded.

"Carter and I saw the bags in the equipment building last night."

Tate released his grip on Carter's hair and called to Mick. "Get over here and help Roy get this guy to his knees."

Carter soon felt two sets of hands lifting him off the floor. The rough treatment wasn't helping with his aching head.

"Who else?" Tate barked at Cindy.

"Nobody," she replied.

"Nobody?"

"No one," confirmed Cindy.

Gradually, Tate's breathing slowed to normal and he approached Carter. "Did you tell anyone?"

"I may have mentioned it," replied Carter, hoping he could scare Tate out of doing whatever he was planning to do.

"To who?"

"A friend...at the FBI."

"The FBI?" Tate huffed, biting down on his lower lip and shaking his head.

"I'm sorry," offered Carter. "Was I not supposed to tell anyone?"

Carter could see the anxiety building. Tate was pissed and struggling to keep it together. Tate closed his eyelids, squeezing the bridge of his nose. Then he held up a finger directly in front of Carter's face. "I'll deal with you in a moment. First things first."

Tate pointed at Jasper and crossed the floor, coming to a stop beside Cindy.

Grabbing her from behind, he wrapped his arm around her throat and drew his pistol once again. "Now start writing what I tell you to write, Jasper."

"I don't agree with this," Tyler said. "She has nothing to do with this. This is only about him."

"You don't have to agree. But this is the way it has to be," answered Tate.

Tyler turned away and began pacing.

Billy gathered up the paper and pen that had been scattered during the struggle and handed it to Jasper.

Jasper took possession and looked at Tate, waiting for instructions.

Tate smiled. He began to speak while Jasper wrote.

> *Dear Darlene,*
> *I'm sorry. I can't live this way any longer. I'm ashamed of the man I've become. I can't go on victimizing young girls anymore. I don't deserve to live. Please tell Cindy I'm sorry.*

Jasper handed the note to Billy, who read it back to Tate.

"Okay," said Tate. "Now move over to the chair and put that rope around your neck."

"Not until you've let her go," replied Jasper

"Do it," Tate answered, pressing the gun against Cindy's head. Cindy screamed and closed her eyes.

"No, not until you let her go. If you let her go, I'll do whatever you want."

"Once you get that rope around your neck, I'll let her go."

Jasper hesitated, but then ventured over and stepped up on the chair, but didn't put the rope around his neck.

"The rope," insisted Tate.

"I'm not that stupid, Tate. You have no intentions of letting her go. But you're going to have to in order to get my cooperation. Otherwise you'll be answering a lot of questions about this staged suicide."

Tate stared down his adversary. "You're right, Jasper. I'm not going to let her go. But here's the way it's going down. You see, a little while ago, a call was made from your phone to hers." He held out his hand.

Mick handed him Cindy's phone.

Tate continued. "The police are going to think you called to say goodbye before you killed yourself. Of course, Cindy, being the loving daughter she is, rushes here to stop you. Sadly, she's too late and finds the note and your lifeless body. Being so distraught by the tragic suicidal death of her father, she throws herself out of one of these windows and plummets to her own death." Tate stuffed the phone into Cindy's back pocket.

Jasper stepped down from the chair. "Then why would I do what you want?"

"Why? Because if you do what you're supposed to, I promise she'll die quickly. She's going to die anyway. A couple of seconds of falling and it will all be over. But if you don't, she's going to suffer greatly. Cindy is a beautiful girl and I'm sure the guys would greatly appreciate an opportunity to enjoy her for a while. And I'll make you watch the whole thing."

Tate continued threatening Jasper. "Just imagine, seeing them all pawing at her the way you did Louise, over and over and over. What a horrible image for one to bear in the final hours of life. Seeing your little girl used and abused until she's praying for death to overcome her. Do you really want to be responsible for putting her through that? It doesn't have to be that way. You have a choice. Either way, you're both dead. I'm going to get what I want. There's no way out of this for you."

"Have you lost your mind?" Tyler exclaimed. "I won't allow you to do that. This was only supposed to be about him."

"Quiet," Tate snapped. "This isn't your call."

Cindy cried out to her ex-fiancé. "Please don't let him do this to me, Tyler."

"It is my call," Tyler yelled, getting up in Tate's face and pushing the gun away from Cindy.

Tate grabbed Cindy by the hair and pulled her away from Tyler. "She's a liability. If we let her go, we're all finished."

Tate looked at Mick, motioning for him to intervene.

Mick moved in to subdue Tyler.

"This is the only option we have," said Tate. "Do you think I'm going to turn loose another threat to our success? It has to be this way, the only thing that will work."

With most everyone focused on the standoff between Tate and Tyler, Carter prepared to make a desperate attempt to do something to free Cindy.

Suddenly, a loud commotion captured everyone's attention.

Carter looked over to see Russell lying on the ground, struck with the chair in Jasper's hands.

Blood flowed from Russell's face.

Jasper pounded down on Russell's head once more.

Carter turned his attention toward Cindy, only to feel the barrel of Roy's gun press against his head.

Billy stood motionless, still holding the suicide note.

"Do something," Tate yelled.

Billy charged toward Jasper, driving him to the ground next to Russell.

Tyler broke loose long enough to grab the gun from Mick's shoulder holster.

A gunshot rang out through the building and Mick dropped to his knees, bleeding from the abdomen.

Carter felt the Roy's barrel leave his temple, at which point he spun around on his knees and grabbed Roy's gun hand, and using his other hand to punch Roy in the groin, dropping the man to his knees, but still struggling to maintain his hold on his weapon.

While struggling with Roy, Carter's peripheral vision took in the chaos unfolding around him. On the other side of the room, he saw Jasper lying on his back holding Billy in a chokehold.

Between him and the door, Carter glanced over to see Cindy bite down on Tate's gun hand, causing him to yell out in excruciating pain.

The gun fell and Cindy released his hand from her teeth, followed by a stomp to Tate's foot and a violent backwards head butt that crushed Tate's nose.

Tate's stocky body tumbled to the floor.

With Roy's offensive breath in his face, Carter punched and clawed to get possession of the gun. An exchange of gunfire sounded and voices yelled out in agony.

From his back, Carter peered over Roy and yelled for Cindy to get out.

Tyler and Jasper yelled out the same instructions.

Cindy fled from the room, with Tate swiping at her ankles to stop her.

Blood poured from Tate's nose as he crawled toward his gun, swearing and gasping for breath.

Tyler stumbled out after Cindy.

Carter successfully knocked the gun from his opponent's hand, only to feel Roy counter with a crashing elbow to Carter's jaw, leaving him momentarily stunned.

By the time Carter regained his bearings, he saw Roy had retrieved the gun and was pointing it at him.

"I'll take care of the detective," yelled Tate. "You get Cindy before she gets away."

When Roy turned his back, Carter jumped up and ran past the lumbering Tate, tackling Roy from behind, knocking him out into the hall and sending them both tumbling down the stairs.

Carter landed hard on the bottom with the dead weight of Roy on top of him. Was he dead or unconscious?

Another exchange of gunfire from the floor above prompted Carter to get out from beneath Roy and locate the gun.

Putting his hand at his side to push off the floor, his fingers felt the steel barrel. The sound of footsteps from the top of the stairs drew Carter's attention and he looked up to see Tate pointing the gun in his direction and take a step down. Carter's arm slung out beneath the pile and fired a shot up the stairwell, sending Tate scrambling down the hall.

Outside the building Cindy was running for her life, with Tyler behind her giving chase, but telling her to keep running. Cindy looked back to see him tumbling and she slowed her pace.

He struggled to get back to his feet, but fell again, letting out a pained grunt.

Cindy stopped and placed her hands on her hips while she tried to catch her breath. She bent over at the waist in response to cramping in her side. Her eyes scanned the surroundings and she contemplated what to do. The thought of her father still inside with the men who wanted him dead weighed heavy on her mind. Guilt quickly consumed her for abandoning him.

Then there was the sight of the man who had broken her heart but also just saved her life. The fact that he stood up for her and even put himself in harm's way told her that maybe he did have some feelings for her.

She moved toward his fallen body writhing around on the ground. As Cindy grew closer, she could see his hand clinging to his side, covered in blood. She hurried to him and knelt on the ground beside him.

"You have to get out of here," he said.

"You're bleeding," Cindy replied. "Is that a gunshot?"

"I'll be fine," assured Tyler. "Now get lost."

Ignoring his plea, Cindy pulled the handkerchief that she knew Tyler always carried in his back pocket and pressed it against the wound.

He jerked in pain.

Dusk was settling in and light was fading out. Off in the distance they heard the sound of Tate yelling for Tyler. Immediately Cindy thought the worst and assumed her father had been killed. She began weeping.

Tyler shushed her, staggered to his feet, grabbed Cindy by the hand, leading her off into the surrounding wooded area.

THIRTY

On the top floor, Jasper Bedford fought to stand up. When he finally did, most of his body weight had to be supported on one side due to a gunshot wound to his hip. He limped two steps toward the door, before hearing Russell's weakened voice mumbling in distress. Jasper stopped, walked over and hovered over him. A bullet to the stomach had Russell bleeding out quickly. Blood flowed from his thigh as well. Russell labored to get oxygen.

He looked up and attempted to apologize. "I'm sorry, Mr. Bedford. Please help me."

The apology fell on deaf ears as Jasper stared down at his wounded captor. Jasper placed the toe of his shoe against the bullet hole in Russell's abdomen.

Russell cried out in pain almost to the point it looked as if he might pass out.

Exhausted and angered, Jasper pointed the gun directly into Russell's face and spoke. "Russell, you're fired."

Russell closed his eyes in defeat.

Jasper unloaded a single shot into the downed man, extinguishing what little sign of life that remained.

Billy began to stir as he regained consciousness.

Jasper glanced over at Mick who wasn't moving at all, before he proceeded to approach a waking Billy.

When Billy saw the gun pointed at him, he braced himself and frowned.

"How long?" Jasper asked.

"How long, what?" Billy replied.

"How long have you been playing me?"

"Since yesterday," answered Billy. "Mr. Manning approached me yesterday. He already had the other guys. I didn't feel like I had much choice. I'm sorry. I never should have gone along with it. I swear I didn't know they were going to do anything to your daughter. I never would have gone along with that."

Jasper noticed Billy's face, still showing signs from the beating he received upon Jasper's orders. Jasper lowered his pistol. "I suggest you leave town," said Jasper. "Move away from here. If I ever see you again, I'll kill you."

Jasper turned his back and limped out of the room.

Having traveled as far as they could, Cindy and Tyler stopped behind a large oak tree so Tyler could catch his breath. He grimaced as Cindy helped him sit down on the ground and lean against the tree. Most of the daylight had disappeared, providing additional cover for them. Cindy's phone began to ring and she rushed to remove the phone from her pocket and pressed the call button. Not recognizing the number, she hesitated, holding it up to her ear, but said nothing.

"Hello?" Carter spoke. "Hello?"

"Carter, is that you?" She whispered. "Thank God. I almost didn't answer it."

"I took a phone off Roy."

"Are you okay, Carter?"

"I'm fine," he replied.

"What about my dad?"

"I don't know for sure. He was still alive the last time I saw him. Where are you?" Carter asked.

"I'm with Tyler and he's been shot."

"Tyler?"

"Yes," she replied.

"Are you still in the building?"

"No, we're outside in the woods."

"Stay put. I've called the police."

"No. No police," Tyler insisted.

"Was that Tyler?" Carter asked.

"Yes."

Carter lowered his voice. "Are you safe with him?"

Cindy looked Tyler up and down. "I'm a lot safer with him than he is with me right now."

Tyler turned away.

"Where in the woods are you?" Carter asked.

Cindy gave Carter the best description she could as to her location, considering it was getting dark.

"Stay there. I'll find you," he promised.

Cindy ended the call and silenced her phone.

Tyler's eyes were closed tight as he clutched his side and groaned.

Cindy poked her head out to look around. There was no sign of anyone. "We need stay here until Carter shows up," she said.

"No, I can't. He's already called the cops."

"Tyler, you're bleeding. You've been shot. You need medical attention."

"I'll be fine until I can get it checked out," claimed Tyler.

"Where are you going to get it checked out? You know all the hospitals have to report any gunshot wound."

"I'll think of something," he said.

The sound of Tate's voice caused both Cindy and Tyler to immediately stop talking. The two of them stared at one another in motionless silence while they listened to Tate call out for Steven.

After a brief moment, Tate's voice faded off into the opposite direction.

Tyler expelled a short breath of relief.

When the voice was barely audible, Cindy whispered. "So your real name is, Steven, huh?"

Tyler glanced up and then quickly dropped his gaze. "Yeah."

"Why did you lie? Was it always about the money?"

Tyler labored to breath. "No. The money was secondary."

"I don't understand," replied Cindy.

"It was all about getting revenge on your father."

"Revenge? For what?"

Tyler paused, before sharing about the relationship between his mom and Jasper.

The more Cindy learned of her father, the more disconnected she felt from him. "When did this happen?" she asked.

"Right before I was born," replied Tyler.

Cindy sucked in a large breath. "Are you telling me that you're my brother?"

"No," answered Tyler. "I'm not your brother. You see, at the same time your dad was having an affair with my mother, she was already secretly seeing Tate. Tate is actually my father."

"Are you certain?" Cindy asked.

"We had a blood test to prove it."

Cindy stared down toward the ground, absorbing the information. "So I guess I still don't fully understand what happened."

Tyler repeated the history that had served as his motivation for revenge.

"How did you find out about all this?" Cindy asked.

"My mom told me that she had fallen and that's why she had the health issues, but she never mentioned anything about your dad or being pushed. Several years ago, after she passed away, Tate showed up and told me everything. He broke down crying, begging me to forgive him. Of course I was really pissed off at first. He told me he tried to get involved in my life and had actually seen me a few times as a baby. But eventually my mom told him he lost the right to be involved and to leave her alone. He sent her checks, but she quit cashing them. He'd call and ask to see me, but she wouldn't let him. So when she died, he showed up for the arrangements, took care of all the financial obligations of the funeral, set up a bank account for me, and agreed to pay for my college. Then he told me about your father and I really got angry. That's when we started talking about getting back at him."

"Why did you have to involve me? Was that your plan from the beginning?"

"It was Tate's idea. I never should have gone along with it. I'm sorry."

"Three years," Cindy said. "You took away three years of my life that I'll never get back. And all you can keep telling me is your sorry. I hate you."

Tyler shifted and winced.

"Ah, did that hurt for you to move like that?" Cindy asked. "Good. I hope that pain lingers for a long, long, time."

"You know," said Tyler. "Even after your dad was under the impression that I was his son, it still didn't matter to him. He was ready to torture and kill me over the money. And he didn't bat an eye when I told him about the hell he put my mom through."

Cindy could see tears welling up in Tyler's eyes.

"I don't know why I'm surprised," he said. "If he didn't want me then, why would he care if I lived or died now?"

"I don't know what to say, Tyler, I'm sorry," offered Cindy.

"I've got to keep moving," said Tyler, dragging his sleeve across his eyes and struggling to his feet. "I can't be here when the police show up. Yes, I'm sorry for what I've done to you and I don't want you to get hurt, but I also don't want to go to jail. So stay put until help arrives."

"You need to see a doctor," insisted Cindy. "I might hate you, but I don't want to see you bleed to death either."

"I'll be fine."

Cindy watched Tyler disappear into the night. The darkness around her seemed much heavier now that she was alone. She wondered if Carter would be able to find her in her current hiding place and hoped Tate or his thugs wouldn't do so first. She thought about her father and pondered his fate. Was he dead? Her mind told her he was almost certainly dead.

Every little noise Cindy heard kept her on edge. Time dragged by while she waited for help. She wondered if Carter was okay or if he ran into trouble. She remembered her kidnappers brought her car along so the police would think she drove herself to the site. The car was parked on the opposite side of the building. Perhaps she could make it to her car, where Cindy was certain the keys would still be in it. Then she would have a way out for her and Carter. God only knew how long the police would take.

Poking her head out from around the tree, Cindy scanned the darkness as best as she could, before making a cautioned break for it. Keeping low, she moved from tree to tree until she reached the fifty yards of clearing that separated the tree line from the building. Crossing the open field seemed far too vulnerable. Cindy elected to follow the tree line around as far as she could go.

Carter entered the woods, keeping his gun pointed out in front of him. The debilitating pain in his head, along with the injuries he endured in his battle with Roy, had impeded his speed in getting to Cindy's location. He was certain he was in the right area based on the information she provided. He wondered if Tyler had done something to her. Perhaps someone else had gotten to her. Maybe something spooked her and she had to move. Continuously scanning the surroundings, Carter strained his eyes to see around the darkened woods. Frustrated, he kept cautiously moving deeper into the trees, cursing himself for not getting there faster.

Stepping lightly through the woods, Cindy moved as quietly as her feet and the debris-covered ground would allow. Every twig that snapped below her feet resulted in a momentary halt, followed by a wary scan before she continued walking. Eventually she ran out of trees. Standing five feet inside the cover of the woods, Cindy saw her car parked about forty yards away. There appeared to be at least a dozen spots where her captors could be waiting to ambush. She backed up against a tree, closed her eyes and took a deep breath. Then as fast as she could, Cindy ran toward her car, constantly looking all around her for danger. Closer and closer she approached; forty feet, thirty feet, twenty, and then ten. Her momentum carried into the front fender, absorbing most of the impact in her arms. Cindy flung open the door and jumped in behind the wheel.

In the rear view mirror, she saw Tate's reflection and screamed.

Tate grabbed her by the hair and yanked her back against the headrest. "I was beginning to wonder if you were ever going to show up," he whispered.

"What did you do to my dad?" Cindy cried out.

"Shut up," commanded Tate.

"How can you do this, Tate? You've known me my entire life. Why are you treating me like this?"

"Yes, I've known you your entire spoiled life. I've watched you grow up with your father giving you everything you ever wanted. Of course this was after he ruined any chance of me having the same opportunity to enjoy my own son."

"Let her go, Tate," Jasper yelled from across the parking lot.

Cindy looked through the driver's side window and saw her dad standing with Tyler directly in front him, pointing a pistol at Tyler's head.

Tate's reaction included a hate-filled rant of vulgarity. He slid to the passenger side of the backseat, pulling Cindy by the hair to the same side. He demanded that Cindy open her car door and wait for him to get out.

She complied with his demand.

Opening his door, Tate continued to hold Cindy by the hair, switching his hands around as he exited the car. Once they were clear of the vehicle, Tate forcefully positioned Cindy in front of him, using the clump of hair as a set of reins to control her movement.

"Let her go," repeated Jasper.

"How's that hip feeling, Jasper?" Tate asked. "If it's hurting I can put you out of your misery."

"Tate, this is between you and me. She has nothing to do with it. Let her go and we'll settle this."

"That's pretty funny coming from a man who has a gun pointed at my son's head."

"Hey, I believe it was your son that started all this. My daughter is innocent."

"Maybe so, but she's also leverage."

"Tate, let her go now!"

"Do you think because you yell louder that I'm just going to give in? That may have worked for you in the past, but this is a different game my friend."

Tyler leaned forward more, succumbing to the pain.

Placing his hand on Tyler's shoulder, Jasper pulled back on him to straighten him up.

Tyler shouted out in agony.

Tate jerked Cindy's head back in retaliation and she screamed.

The sound of police sirens could be heard in the distance, and Cindy grew hopeful for a rescue.

Tate backed up to the car, pulling Cindy along with him.

Fumbling for the door handle, Tate finally opened the passenger side door. He got in first, keeping his firm grip on Cindy. Then he scooted across the seat and behind the wheel, pulling her onto the passenger seat. "Close the door," he snapped.

Cindy complied and Tate started the car.

Jasper watched helplessly as Tate drove away with Cindy. With the sirens drawing closer, Jasper labored to choose a course of action. Cindy's car disappeared to the south as the police cruiser lights approached from the north.

Tyler's body began to go limp.

Having only seconds before the police were close enough to see him, Jasper quickly flung Tyler around and pulled him down on top of himself, firing one round into the young man's abdomen as they fell to the ground. They hit the pavement hard and Jasper absorbed all the force of both their body weight on his shoulder. Lying on the ground with Tyler on top of him, Jasper positioned the gun directly in front of Tyler's heart and fired once more, before letting the pistol fall beside him.

Upon hearing the gunfire, Carter turned around and rushed out of the woods as quickly as the limited visibility and his throbbing headache would let him. When he reached the clearing, visibility improved considerably, not having the blanket of the trees blocking out the moonlight. He paused, debating which direction to go. Police sirens sounded to the left, but off to the right he heard a car engine racing away, so he ran in that direction.

As he rounded the corner of the building, Carter caught a glimpse of what he thought looked like Cindy's car racing away. Something had gone wrong. He turned and hurried back to the car that Roy used to transport him in the trunk. He pulled open the door, but there were no keys in the ignition. He dropped down and positioned his torso across the driver's seat with his feet remaining on the gravel lot, while he used his fingers to find what he needed. Jerking wires down out of the steering column, he frantically worked. Time was ticking and he felt like his window of opportunity was rapidly closing. Eventually, a spark flew from the wires and the engine started. Carter sat up behind the wheel, threw the car in gear and raced off in pursuit of Cindy's car.

The police cruisers stopped with their headlights on the two bodies lying stacked on the pavement. Officer's exited their vehicles with guns drawn and encircled the bodies, yelling for Jasper to show his hands.

From beneath Tyler's lifeless body, Jasper extended his arms. One officer approached and kicked the gun away. Immediately, three more policemen were trying to separate the entangled men. Jasper yelled out in agony, creating the role as a scared victim. "Help me. Help me. I've been attacked. They shot me."

An older policeman pulled a clean white handkerchief from his pocket and handed it to Jasper. "Here, put some pressure on that wound."

Jasper took the handkerchief and pressed against his hip.

The only female officer on the scene squatted down beside him. "It's okay, sir, the paramedics are on their way. Who shot you? Can you tell me what happened?"

A male officer knelt by Tyler and felt for a pulse. "This one's dead," he said.

The lady cop attempted to calm Jasper who was playing his part like a Broadway actor. "Who shot you, Sir? Is there someone besides this guy?"

"Inside," replied Jasper. "There are more inside."

"How many?"

"I don't know. It all happened so fast. There was a lot of shooting."

Instantly, the officer was calling for backup.

"They took my daughter."

"What did you say?" the lady asked.

"He has my daughter. He just drove off with her moments ago, heading south."

"Who has her?"

"His name is Tate Manning. He works for me. He was the mastermind behind a kidnapping attempt."

"What's your name, Sir?"

"My name is Jasper Bedford. I own West Lake Properties and Development. Tate Manning and some of my other employees plotted to kidnap me for ransom. This is one of our properties. Tate called me here to discuss the project. I believe his plan was to kidnap me then. However, my daughter was with me because she and I were supposed to have dinner tonight. When she showed up with me, I guess it spoiled their plan and they started arguing over how to handle it. Next thing I know, all hell is breaking loose and bullets were flying."

"What kind of car are they in?" she asked.

"It's a 2011 silver BMW, 6 Series."

The officer used her radio to alert other officers and relay the information that Jasper had provided.

As much as Jasper hoped the police would get his daughter back, he hoped that she would be able to go along with his story. He also prayed Tate would resist and give the police plenty of reason to blow him away.

THIRTY-ONE

Tate Manning sweated profusely while he sped along the road, quickly changing direction the moment he got out of site and headed west. His nervous eyes kept jumping between the road, his rear view mirror, and Cindy. He steered with one hand, while keeping his gun pointed at her. The man was clearly on the edge and Cindy feared for her life.

Realizing that she still had her cell phone in her pocket, Cindy had to figure out a way to use it without Tate knowing. The phone was in her right front pocket. However, her jeans were tight enough that it would be extremely difficult to retrieve the phone without Tate seeing her. After a moment of thought, she came up with a plan.

Letting her head drop back against the headrest, Cindy did her best to appear distraught to the point of illness. Gradually, she began to make subtle little noises to get Tate's attention. Out of the corner of her eye, Cindy saw Tate's head turn her way and she convulsed and puffed out her cheeks like she was on the verge of vomiting.

Tate flinched back. "What's wrong with you?"

"I think I'm going to be sick."

"What?"

"I'm getting car sick," she answered.

Cindy acted like another wave of nausea was sweeping through her, adding a gurgling noise as she slightly heaved.

"Stop it," Tate demanded. "Don't you dare throw up in here."

"I can't help it," replied Cindy weakly.

"Get in the back then."

Tate's response was perfect; exactly what she needed. "Fine," she said.

"Lie down and put your head at that end so you don't puke on the back of my head and I can see you," instructed Tate.

Cindy complied and lied down in the back seat.

For the first few seconds, Tate kept looking back to check on her.

Cindy kept up the act that she was nauseated.

Eventually, Tate lost interest in Cindy and kept his attention on the road.

Moving with great caution, Cindy slid her hand into her pocket, pulled out the phone and dialed the most recent number in her call history. Holding the phone closer to her head, but not where Tate could see it, Cindy listened for Carter to answer. As soon as she did, she lowered the phone to the floor and began talking to Tate. "Where are you taking me, Tate?"

"Shut up and stay quiet," Tate snapped.

"Can we at least get on the highway so I don't get so sick? There's a ramp to get on I-294 just pass the ball fields coming up on the right. These back streets are going to make me puke."

"I said shut up. I'm not getting on the highway to keep you from throwing up."

On the other end of the phone call, Carter listened to his clever client drop subtle hints to her location. He turned the car around and headed west. Normally, he would call the police to help locate and close in on the vehicle. However, Carter didn't want to risk losing contact with Cindy.

Driving sixty-eight in a thirty-five mile an hour zone, Carter sped his way through the light traffic, following the route he felt certain would lead him to Cindy. A few minutes into his pursuit, Carter saw the ball fields on the right. A moment later, Carter heard

Cindy whispering one word every few seconds. "Sinclair. Talbert. Rutledge."

Carter recognized them as names of roads. Realizing he was on the right path, Carter sped up. His guess was that Tate and Cindy were no more than a mile in front of him now. The light at the intersection ahead of him turned yellow, so he sped up to make the light, which changed to red twenty feet in front of him.

A passing car sounded its horn in protest as Carter zipped through the intersection.

"Locust," Cindy whispered.

Suddenly, Carter heard Tate's voice yelling in the background. "What did you say?" What are you doing back there? Who are you talking to?" Tate screamed.

The rage in Tate's voice caused Carter to floor the accelerator pushing the car to nearly eighty miles an hour past the everyday traffic, blowing his horn and weaving wherever he needed to in order to avoid a collision.

Tate reached back, violently swapping at Cindy's arms to gain possession of the phone. He cursed and yelled, all the while still driving, but now much more recklessly. "Hang up now or so help me…"

Cindy tossed the phone over into front passenger floorboard.

Tate slammed on the breaks long enough for him to reach for the phone. The forceful stop threw Cindy forward into the floor.

With the car nearly at a complete stop, Cindy flung open the back door and jump out of the vehicle, taking off down the road.

She looked back to see Tate open his door, however, in his haste he forgot to take the car out of gear and it moved forward, causing yet another angry outburst of cursing.

Cindy ran with every ounce of energy she had left. A shot rang out and she turned to see Tate chasing after her and fire another round.

Beyond Tate she saw the speeding car coming toward them and watched as Tate turned and fired several more shots, hitting the car's windshield and causing it to swerve out of control, and off to the left.

The car hit the roadside ditch and went into a roll. The image horrified Cindy. Recognizing that it was Carter, she ran toward the rolling wreckage.

The grinding, crunching metal and shattering glass echoed through the night air. Clouds of dust and debris scattered along the streetlight-illuminated path of Carter's car. The vehicle finally came to a halt, resting upside down on its smashed top.

Cindy watched for any kind of movement as she drew closer. She dreaded what she might see when she reached the wreckage.

Within twenty–five feet of the car, Cindy saw movement.

Carter's hand extended from the busted window, pointing a gun in Cindy's direction.

Two shots fired off in rapid succession and Cindy fell to the ground in fear. Why would he shoot at her?

When she glanced behind her, Cindy saw Tate, dropped to his knees with a pistol on the ground beside him. His chest bore the crimson evidence that Carter's aim had been true. With an incoherent look in his eyes, Tate fell forward face down on the ground, motionless.

Leaping to her feet, Cindy ran to the car and dropped down on all fours to see inside the tangled mess. Carter's gun lay on the ground.

He was still buckled in but barely conscious and nonresponsive to her voice.

She was surprised that he had been able to fire off a shot, let alone hit anything. Beside his head, she saw a cell phone. Lying flat on the ground and stretching her arm inside, Cindy reached for the phone and dialed 911.

The dispatcher promised help was on the way and cautioned her to not attempt to remove Carter from the vehicle unless there was imminent danger from remaining inside.

Cindy hung up and quietly began to pray. Occasionally, Carter distracted her with low, pained grunting noises.

Though he was unresponsive to her questions, Cindy continued to talk, reassuring him that everything would be fine.

Within minutes, sirens sounded from nearby. Two police cars, a fire truck, and an ambulance arrived. Initial attempts to remove Carter from the demolished car were unsuccessful.

Two of the officers tried to question Cindy about the events of the evening, including an explanation of Tate's dead body.

However, Cindy was far too distracted watching the firemen cut their way to Carter and remove him from the vehicle.

Her answers were often extremely brief and vague or she simply asked them to repeat the question because she wasn't paying attention.

As soon as the rescue workers had Carter free from the wreckage, Cindy abandoned the officers in mid-sentence to be by his side.

She lingered with him until the ambulance door closed her out and the paramedics drove away.

As the police were preparing to resume questioning Cindy, a third squad car arrived escorting a second ambulance.

An older officer exited from behind the wheel and approached Cindy and his fellow officers. "Her father's in the back and is insisting he get to see her. The EMTs said his wounds weren't life threatening and since we're on the way to the hospital, I figured I'd give them a minute. I know I'd be the same way if it was my daughter."

Cindy didn't wait for a response before hurrying to the ambulance.

The back door of the ambulance was already opened by the time Cindy made it to the vehicle. Inside, she saw her father lying on a stretcher with an oxygen mask and his hip packed with bandages.

The attending paramedic removed the oxygen mask from Jasper's face, informed him that his daughter was there, and then stepped down to give them some time together.

Cindy stepped up into the back and sat beside her father.

Jasper grabbed her hand. "Are you okay, honey?"

"Yes, Daddy, I'm fine. How are you?"

"I'm fine, but I need you to listen to me very closely," answered Jasper. "Come closer."

Cindy leaned in and Jasper began to whisper. "Have you talked to the police yet?"

"Sort of, but not really."

"What have you told them so far?"

"All I've told them so far is that Tate forced me into my car and kidnapped me."

"What happened to Tate?"

"Carter shot him. He's dead."

Jasper sighed in relief. "Good. The bastard should be dead."

"Carter's hurt though. He wrecked his car really bad."

"That's too bad," said Jasper, half-heartedly. "Okay, listen closely. You have to be very, very cautious what you tell the police. I told them Tate and the other guys lured me to the property in a plot to kidnap me under the guise Tate needed to meet with me. But you were with me because we were going out to dinner afterwards. Then when they realized you were with me, they got into an argument over how to handle the situation and everything became chaotic. You and I tried to flee in the process, but Tate grabbed you and that's all you know."

Cindy said nothing; she just stared at her father.

Squeezing her hand, Jasper asked, "Are you with me, Sweetheart? This is very important. You can't tell them anything else. Not about Tyler's disappearance, not about the cement bags, absolutely nothing else. If you do that, we can get out of this. Okay?"

"What about Tyler?" Cindy said. "He knows everything."

Jasper paused and bit down on his lower lip. "Tyler's dead."

"What? He's dead?" Her whisper got louder.

"As soon as you and Tate drove away, Tyler tried to overpower me and the gun went off. It was in self-defense."

Tears welled up in Cindy's eyes and her head dropped.

"Are you okay, Cindy? I need you to take care of this."

Wiping at her eyes, Cindy maintained a whisper, but the anxiety of the situation was loud and clear in her reply. "You want me to lie to the police?"

Jasper shushed his daughter, looking toward the back door. "No. I just don't want you to tell them everything. You need to calm down and get a grip on yourself."

"Get a grip on myself? Are you kidding me? What do you expect? I just found out you're a drug dealer, Dad, on top of all the other crap I've been dealing with. And now you want me to lie for you."

"No," Jasper replied; now his whisper getting louder. "If you don't do this, I could be finished. I'll go to prison and you and your mom will likely lose everything we have. They'll come in and seize control of my assets, leaving you and your mom to figure out how you're going to live."

"I hate you for doing this to me," snapped Cindy.

Jasper said nothing in response. He merely kept his eyes locked in on her, waiting for her cooperation.

"If I do this," continued Cindy, "you're going to have to make some changes; first and foremost, no more drugs. That's non-negotiable."

Jasper nodded. "Understood."

A deep male voice from behind startled Cindy and she spun around to see a policeman standing just outside the ambulance.

"I'm sorry, Miss, but they really need to get your father to the hospital now."

Had she whispered low enough for him not to hear? How long had he been there? Her heart raced and she felt slightly nauseated. "Of course," she replied.

Before stepping out of the ambulance, Cindy felt her father's hand on her arm again. She turned to face him one last time.

"Don't let me down, Cindy," pleaded Jasper. "Our family's future is resting on you."

She glared at her manipulative father and pulled away.

THIRTY-TWO

Cindy watched Darlene Bedford enter the lobby of the hospital. Their phone conversation had been brief, with Cindy sharing only a few sketchy details of what happened.

Upon eye contact with Cindy, Darlene immediately sped up to greet and embrace her daughter. "Oh, baby, are you okay?"

"Yes, Mom, I'm fine."

"Are you sure they didn't hurt you?"

"I'm fine. I promise."

Darlene moved in for another hug. "Where's your father?"

"They have him on the third floor," replied Cindy.

"How's he doing?" Darlene asked.

"He's going to be fine," answered Cindy, taking hold of her mother's arm. "I need to talk to you before you go up there."

"Before I go up there? Aren't you coming up with me?"

"I can't right now. I need to talk to you though, somewhere private. Let's go outside."

"Okay," Darlene agreed.

The two of them walked into the stillness of the late night.

"What is it, Sweetie?" Darlene asked as they passed under the entrance canopy to the edge of the parking lot. "What's wrong?"

Cindy faced her mom and took a breath. "I know about Dad."

"What about him?"

"You don't have to cover for him anymore, Mom. I know."

Darlene hunched her shoulders and held her hands out to the side. "I'm sorry, Cindy. I'm not sure what you're talking about."

"The drugs, Mom," replied Cindy, momentarily wondering if her mother had been kept in the dark, too. However, upon the reference to drugs, Darlene's demeanor changed, revealing knowledge. Cindy pressed her. "So you did know?"

"Of course I know. I'm married to him."

"How could you let him do this and keep it from me?"

"Baby, I was trying to protect you. We both were."

"Mom," began Cindy, desperately frustrated. "Dad is a drug dealer. He's a criminal. How can you condone that?"

"Cindy, your dad is going to do whatever he wants. I couldn't stop him no matter how hard I tried."

"How hard did you try?" Cindy asked.

Darlene sighed, but didn't answer.

"How long have you known? Did you always know?"

"No, I didn't. He was trying to get his business started and he needed some money to keep him going. That's when he started. He put together two or three deals before I found out."

"When was that?"

"It was before you were born."

"My entire life? My father has been a criminal my entire life? Oh my god. How stupid could I be? How does someone live a quarter of a century and be that clueless?"

"Cindy, you're not clueless. Your father and I, especially your father, worked hard to keep that part of his life away from you."

Cindy turned and took a few more steps into the parking lot. Darlene followed and put her hand on Cindy's back. "Like I said, we were trying to protect you."

"So I guess my car, my education, my apartment are all fruits of my dad's lucrative drug-pushing business?"

"That's not true," defended Darlene. "Your father's company is very successful and it's completely legitimate."

Raising her voice in protest, Cindy argued. "If it's so successful, then why is he using it to peddle drugs?"

Immediately Darlene shushed her daughter. "Keep your voice down. None of that affects you."

"Oh really," replied Cindy. She stepped toward her mother and argued in a loud whisper. "I beg to differ with you on that one, Mom. Tonight, I lied to the police. I let that lying, manipulative man up there talk me into lying to the police."

"Keep your voice down," repeated Darlene.

"I can't believe you're condoning this," said Cindy. "You grounded me when I was sixteen for sneaking a lousy wine cooler. And now I found out Dad is the go-to guy for heroin in Chicago. That's kind of ironic don't you think?"

"Will you please keep your voice down?" Darlene begged.

"You're such a hypocrite."

Darlene said nothing as Cindy paced in front of her.

A young couple passed by them and stared. Cindy ignored them while Darlene's eyes drifted away. Once the couple had passed, Darlene stepped directly in front of her daughter and grabbed hold of her arm. "Listen to me," she demanded. "Your father has done everything he could to give you the best life possible. You owe him a little loyalty."

"A little loyalty? That's what you call this? Did you not hear me? I lied to the police. That makes me an accessory."

"Cindy, nobody has to find out."

Cindy looked at her mother in disgust, void of any sense of security in her life. "I have to get out of here," she said.

"Where are you going?" Darlene asked.

"I don't know. I have to be alone for a while."

"Sweetie, if you stay calm, all of this will pass and everything will return to the way it was."

"Mom, I've got news. Nothing will ever return to the way it was. It blows me away you would even say something so absurd."

"You know what I mean," defended Darlene.

"I've got to go," said Cindy, walking out into the parking lot.

Carter stirred a little and opened his eyes. Greeted by the dim light and steady hum of electronic equipment hooked up to various spots on his body, Carter soon realized he was in the hospital again. Half of his body ached and he felt like he weighed a thousand pounds; no doubt from medication he'd been given.

Wondering about the time, he glanced around the room looking for a clock.

As his head turned to the right, he noticed Cindy propped up in the chair beside his bed with her head against the wall, taking long deep breaths as she slept. The image of Cindy running toward his car with Tate Manning pointing a gun at her from behind popped up in Carter's mind. The last thing he remembered was shooting Tate.

"Hey," he whispered.

She didn't respond.

"Hey," he repeated, louder.

Cindy jumped into consciousness, slightly incoherent at first. She saw Carter and smiled. "Hey."

"Are you okay?" Carter asked.

Cindy nodded. "Yeah, I'm fine. How do you feel?"

"I feel a little weird at the moment. They must have me pumped full of meds or something. How long have you been here?"

Cindy looked at her watch. "Since late last night. I told them I was your sister so they'd let me in."

"What time is it?"

"It's few minutes after six," she answered. "Do you remember much about last night?"

"I remember rolling the car and shooting Tate Manning; after that, nothing." Carter paused for a moment. "Is he dead?"

Cindy nodded.

Carter expelled a long sigh, not really pleased with the news.

Cindy explained the events of the evening, filling Carter in on the history between Louise Conway, Tate and her father. Finally, she ended with the standoff between Jasper and Tate, with her and Tyler as the hostages.

"So, Tyler and your dad survived?" Carter inquired.

Cindy's head dropped. "Dad did."

Despite the three years of lies and betrayal, Carter saw the heartbreak and grief Cindy held for the man she had given three years of life. "What happened?"

"My dad said as soon as Tate drove off with me, Tyler tried to overtake him and the gun went off, killing Tyler."

Carter said nothing, but was immediately suspicious of Jasper's side of the story.

"I don't believe him, though," added Cindy. "I think he purposely killed Tyler."

Tears began to trickle down Cindy's shamed face. "I think my dad probably killed Tyler in cold blood. As a matter of fact, I'm sure he did."

Cindy clinched her teeth together as the emotion grew more intense, her face contorting to where it appeared she'd burst in sobbing at any moment.

Carter wished he had something to say to ease her pain, but he didn't.

Regaining her composure, Cindy wiped at her eyes and resumed talking. "And yet, in spite of the fact that I now know my dad is a lying, drug-dealing, adulterous killer, I still stood there in front of the police last night and covered for him."

"What do you mean you 'covered' for him?"

"I did exactly what he wanted me to do. I told them only what he wanted them to know; only what would keep him out of trouble. Why would I do that?" Cindy asked.

"He's your dad, Cindy. Yes, he's everything you just said, but up until recently, you didn't know any of that."

"I knew about the affairs, or at least I had my suspicions."

"Okay, but overall, you still thought your dad was just another business and family man."

"Yeah, but I know now and I can't do this."

Carter remained silent, giving Cindy an opportunity to vent and work things out on her own, without him pushing her. Yes, he wanted to see Jasper be held accountable and justice served, but he also realized the heaviness of Cindy's circumstances.

"I called my mom to let her know Dad was here and what had happened. When she got here, I told her that I knew about Dad and the drugs. I thought if I gave her the opportunity to give me some guidance, she might encourage me to do what was right." Cindy grabbed a tissue from the generic box on the nightstand. "She stood right in front of me and said if I did what my father told me to do, everything would go back to normal. She told me I owed him a little loyalty. The two people who have been my moral compasses in life have turned out to be hypocritical losers who are only concerned with saving their standard of living."

Considering his early perception of Cindy as a rich, spoiled, self-centered daddy's girl, Carter was impressed by her display of conscience.

"I'm worried what he might do to you, too," said Cindy.

"Me?"

"Yes. If my dad thinks you could be a threat, I'm afraid he'll do to you what he did to Tyler."

"I can take care of myself, Cindy."

Cindy stared Carter up and down in his hospital bed. "Yeah, I can see that."

Carter could not help but grin at Cindy's stinging sarcasm.

"I have to turn him in," said Cindy.

"Really?" Carter questioned.

"Yes, really. Do you think I'll be in serious trouble for not telling them the whole truth from the beginning? Could I go to jail?"

"Slow down and stay calm," advised Carter. "If you're serious about this, I can help you."

"How?"

"I have a lot of friends on the force. For that matter, I have a good friend at the FBI. As a matter of fact she's the one looking into Tainan Cement for me."

"You really went to the FBI about my dad?" Cindy asked with a hint of betrayal in her voice. "When were you going to tell me about that?"

"Relax, I didn't say anything about your dad," replied Carter.

"What does she know about Tainan?"

"I haven't heard back from her yet. She said it could be a couple of days. But if you're sincere about turning in your dad, I could set up a meeting between the two of you."

"How much trouble will I be in?"

"Cindy, the police and FBI are not going to be concerned with you, especially considering the bigger picture here."

Cindy's demeanor eased a little.

"Have you considered how your mom will react if you do this?" Carter asked.

"I've thought about it and quite frankly I'm not sure. Part of me thinks she might be relieved. My parents don't have the best marriage. But then a big part of me thinks she'll be devastated, disown me, and speed up the process of drinking herself to death."

"What if it's the latter of the two?"

Cindy shrugged and sniffed. "That's her choice. I have to do what I think is right. I certainly can't count on my parents for that."

"Should I call my friend of the FBI then?"

"You think the FBI is the better route to go over the police? They're the ones I lied to."

"Considering your father's crimes, yes, I'd say the FBI is the way to go. And they'll work with the police to keep you out of trouble."

Cindy took a long deep breath, staring at the floor as she nervously chewed on the inside of her cheek. Finally, after a fair amount of deliberating, she nodded. "Call her."

"Okay," said Carter softly.

"When do you think she'll be available?"

"Knowing Shawna, she's probably already there this morning. I'd say she'll make time to meet you today."

Cindy expelled another long breath. "That soon, huh?"

"The sooner the better, don't you think?"

"Yes, I suppose."

THIRTY-THREE

Later that afternoon, Cindy walked into her father's hospital room.

"Cindy," he said, trying to sit up in his bed.

Darlene stood and approached her daughter. "How are you? You look like you've been crying."

Avoiding direct eye contact with either of them, Cindy simply nodded.

"The doctor said your father's doing well," assured Darlene.

Cindy offered another nod.

Jasper spoke softly to his little girl. "The police were here earlier this morning. They told me you confirmed everything that happened last night. I can't tell you how much that means to me."

A wave of emotion and guilt slammed full force into Cindy. She wanted to turn and walk out of the room without saying anything.

Darlene lovingly wrapped her arm around Cindy's shoulder. "That's what families do. We stick together."

The complete lack of remorse in her mother's voice reminded Cindy of what had prompted her decision earlier in the day.

"How's your detective doing?" Jasper asked. His tone carried a certain false sincerity, or was it that Cindy had completely lost all faith in her father's character?

"Have you seen him?" Darlene asked. "Is he awake or talking yet?"

There it was, the self-preservation factor. What had been a suspicion regarding her father's interest now seemed crystal clear in her mother's questioning. Suddenly, Cindy pondered the possibility that her folks had been discussing Carter's condition and how it may affect them.

Cindy offered a shrug of uncertainty, fishing for some sort of reaction.

"What are the doctors saying?"

"I haven't talked to the doctors."

"Have you seen him?" Darlene asked.

"I'm not a relative," replied Cindy.

The reaction from both of her parents reflected a level of frustration. Cindy suspected now that they were secure in her loyalty, Carter Mays was their only threat.

"Hopefully, he'll come out of it okay," commented Jasper.

Cindy marveled at how different she now viewed her parents; the people she had loved and depended on for her entire life. How had this happened? How had she gone from loving and respecting them to feeling completely uncomfortable and distrusting around them? Yet, in spite of her present feelings, she dreaded the words about to leave her mouth.

"Mom, Dad," she began.

"Yes," responded Darlene.

"I came here to tell you something."

"We're listening, honey," said Darlene.

"This is the hardest thing I've ever had to do," continued Cindy, as a tear escaped down her cheek. "But I wanted you to hear it from me first."

Jasper and Darlene remained quiet.

"You two have always provided for me and given me every opportunity I could ask for. I've never gone without anything, even to the point I realize how spoiled I've been. When I think about my childhood and my life growing up, it's filled with great memories."

Darlene began to tear up as she listened.

"But what has recently come to light, about the things you've kept from me, has overshadowed that. I can't ignore what I now know. I can't look at you, Dad, and not think about what you've done. What I've seen and learned scares me. You're not the man I thought you were."

"Sweetheart," pleaded Darlene. "You don't mean that."

Jasper's face tightened. Cindy couldn't tell if he was mad, hurt, or scared.

"Last night I stood in front of those policemen and lied for you. I turned away from the truth and covered for you to keep you out of trouble."

Cindy's glance shifted to her mother. "And then, Mom, I stood in that parking lot last night looking for some moral guidance from you. I told you how I felt and you completely glossed over it, trying to convince me that everything could go back to normal."

"It can," argued Darlene.

"No, Mom, it can't. Stop telling me that."

Jasper spoke up. "What are you saying, Cindy? Are you disowning us? Are you writing us out of your life?"

With her gaze fixed on her father, Cindy swallowed hard before she spoke. "I talked to the FBI today."

Jasper's jaw dropped open and his eyes narrowed.

"You did what?" Darlene asked.

"I talked to the FBI."

"Why would you do that? Talk to them about what?" Darlene pressed.

"You went to the FBI?" Jasper asked, clinching his teeth.

Cindy saw the same intense look of rage she remembered seeing when he was beating Russell with the chair. She began to weep.

"You ungrateful little bitch!" Jasper yelled.

The words stung Cindy like she never could have imagined. At that moment her father looked as if he could actually kill her on the spot.

Darlene approached her only child, her chiseled cheeks flushed with anger. When Cindy cast her wet, heartbroken eyes toward her mom, Darlene struck her hard across the face with an open hand. "How could you?"

A nurse rushed in from the hall. "What's going on in here?"

"Get her out of here," Jasper demanded.

The nurse responded, "What seems to be the problem?"

"Are you deaf?" Jasper yelled at the nurse. "I said get her out of here."

"Congratulations," snapped Darlene. "You've betrayed your family."

The pompous manner in which her mother was playing the role of the victim infuriated Cindy.

The nurse gingerly tried to nudge her toward the door, but Cindy lashed out. "I betrayed you? You've lied to me my entire life. You two are the biggest hypocrites I've ever seen."

The nurse labored to neutralize the situation and tactfully remove Cindy from the room.

Cindy addressed the nurse, using her to vent. "My parents have lied to me for my entire existence. All this time of thinking my dad was just a successful business man, I find out he's a major heroin dealer."

The nurse's eyes grew wide and her mouth gaped open.

Darlene immediately turned red with embarrassment.

The veins in Jasper's neck bulged as he became more indignant. "Nurse, I demand you to get her out of here," he barked.

"I'm sorry, Miss, but you're going to have to leave," said the nurse softly.

Cindy looked back once more at the two closest people in her life. She shook her head in complete disappointment and walked away before the next wave of tears came.

THIRTY-FOUR

Carter was visiting with his friend Bobby from the police force when Cindy entered his room.

She stopped when she saw Bobby. "I'm sorry," she said. "I can come back later."

Carter could tell she had been crying and was still visibly upset. "No. You don't have to leave. I want you to stay."

"Yeah," added Bobby. "I've got to be going anyway."

Cindy offered a smile through the embarrassment of her obvious fragile condition. "Thanks, but I don't want to intrude."

"Cindy, this is my friend Bobby," introduced Carter. "We worked together on the police force. Bobby, this is Cindy."

Bobby took a couple of steps forward and reached out his hand.

She graciously accepted and shook his hand. "It's nice to meet you, Bobby."

"It's a pleasure, Cindy. Carter told me what you did today and I have to say it's one of the most courageous and admirable things I've ever heard. That took a lot of guts."

Cindy nodded her thanks.

"Well," continued Bobby, "like I said; I have to go. It was really nice meeting you, Cindy." Then he turned to look at Carter. "Get some rest, buddy. I'll check in with you later."

"Okay, thanks, man," replied Carter.

With Bobby out of the room, Carter looked at his heartbroken client. He felt so bad for her. He couldn't imagine how lonely she must feel at this moment. In a calm, compassionate voice Carter spoke. "I guess you went to see your parents?"

Cindy nodded.

"Didn't go well, huh?"

"No," answered Cindy. "Pretty much a disaster."

"I'm sorry," offered Carter.

Cindy shrugged. "I don't know what I expected. I did turn my own father into the FBI."

"They didn't know already, did they?"

"No. Shawna told me that they would start an investigation, but probably wouldn't confront my dad until they had more information."

"I don't know how he got away with it all these years," marveled Carter. "But I do believe it was a matter of time before it caught up with him."

"Thanks for trying to ease my guilt," said Cindy.

"How did your mother handle it?"

"She slapped me across my face and told me I had betrayed my family," answered Cindy, her voice breaking down before she could finish the sentence.

Her head dropped and she reached for the box of tissues on the nightstand.

Carter reached out and took her by the hand. "You did the right thing."

"Then why do I feel so guilty? Shouldn't making the right choice feel better than this?"

The gentle pulling of Carter prompted Cindy to sit on the edge of his bed.

He reached up and brushed her hair from her streaky wet face. "I'm sorry you've had this thrown on you," he said.

Cindy forced a brief but sincere smile. "Thanks."

"It'll get better," promised Carter.

Resting her hand on Carter's forearm, Cindy said, "I don't want to talk about them right now."

"Okay. What do you want to talk about?"

Cindy glanced away for a moment and appeared distracted.

"Is something on your mind?" Carter asked.

She offered an awkward smile. "Yeah, I guess there is."

"I'm listening," said Carter.

"I was thinking," began Cindy. "I know we've had some moments where we drifted beyond a professional relationship and we said we'd address it when everything blew over."

"Yeah, we did."

Cindy took a deep breath and exhaled. "I guess I was wondering where we were with that whole thing."

"Hmm, I see."

Cindy waited a few seconds to see if Carter was going to elaborate more than his initial response.

Finally he did. "I can't say that I'm not really attracted to you, Cindy. I definitely am. However, the time that we've had has been the most traumatic time in your life. You've had a lot thrown at you all at once and I guess I'm a little reluctant to start anything now."

A look of relief came over Cindy's face. "Oh, Carter, I am so glad to hear you say that. That's exactly how I feel, too. And I'm very attracted to you as well, but I'm going to need some time to get my life in order before I get involved with someone again. I am emotionally drained right now."

"I think that's a smart idea," replied Carter.

"Maybe six months or a year down the road, who knows? We'll see where we are in life and possibly entertain the idea. But I still want you in my life right now," she said adamantly. "I consider you a good friend, Carter. And quite frankly, I'm going to need some good friends in the weeks to come."

"Absolutely."

"I anticipate more changes to come. I may have to move. I don't think I can afford to stay in my apartment on what I make. God knows my dad isn't going to pay my way anymore, which is fine. I've depended on my folks long enough."

"You're a smart girl, Cindy. You won't have any problems making it on your own."

"Thanks."

"I'll help you move," offered Carter.

Cindy raised her eyebrows and took inventory of Carter's busted body and jokingly commented, "Oh really? I don't think you're in any condition to move anything at the moment."

"What? This? This is nothing. I'll be back on my feet in no time."

"Yeah," came Cindy's doubtful reply. "But hey, when you get your house replaced, I'll help you move in."

Carter scoffed. "Move what? I don't have anything."

"You will," insisted Cindy. "You'll get all new furnishings. That's when I'll help you."

"If I'm buying it new, I'll just have it delivered. Besides, you're a girl. Girls aren't any good at moving furniture," he joked.

Cindy held up her toned arm and flexed her bicep. "Shoot, you'd be surprised how strong I am. You didn't think I could scale that fence either."

"That's true," admitted Carter, grinning. "You definitely proved me wrong on that one."

Cindy smiled. Even with her red puffy eyes, and smudged mascara, she still had one of the most beautiful faces he'd ever seen.

"Well, I should probably get going," said Cindy, seeming more at ease than when she entered the room.

"Are you going to be okay?"

"Yeah, I'll take it one day at a time. That's what I've learned to do lately."

"Take care of yourself, Cindy."

"I will. And you do the same."

Before she left, Cindy bent over and gave Carter a slow tender kiss.

He licked his lips and smiled. "What was that for?"

"Just making sure you don't forget about me," she said with a grin.

"That's impossible."

Cindy turned and walked out of the room.

Carter sighed and allowed his head to fall back into the pillow. After a prolonged, exaggerated yawn, he did his best to get comfortable. He had endured the most physically demanding week of his life. The sleep his mind and body longed for was coming quickly. He hoped to dream of better days; having a mended body, a restored home, and a possible relationship with Cindy six months from now. Maybe three months, he thought.

THIRTY-FIVE

Three weeks after talking with the FBI, Cindy's life was not getting much better. In spite of all he had done to her, she still grieved over Tyler's death. Those few moments they had the night he died proved to be greatly inadequate to answering her questions. Her closest friends made themselves available to listen, advise, or completely ignore the recent dramatic events, depending on Cindy's desire to talk about them.

Jasper Bedford had yet to be formally charged, but it was coming. The FBI and police were very upfront with Jasper about keeping extremely close tabs on his whereabouts at all times, discouraging any thoughts of fleeing the country. Needless to say, he had absolutely nothing to say to his daughter. The bulk of his time was spent with Dylan Fitch, forming his defense.

Though she had softened a little during the three weeks, Darlene remained rather distant with her daughter. She had sent a couple of brief emails, but there had been no conversation between the two.

This had proven to be the biggest adjustment for Cindy. Never had she and her mom gone more than three days without speaking. No doubt, much of Darlene's time was being spent coping with the help of a steady supply of alcohol.

Returning to work had been Cindy's saving grace. It offered her a distraction from the train wreck her life had become. It gave her purpose. She discovered a new drive to succeed and advance her career. Perhaps it was the knowledge that she no longer had the safety net of her father's money. She started working on a budget based only on her income and it was going to be a significant adjustment.

Carter sat on the stoop of Cindy's building, waiting and holding onto a large bouquet of flowers.

She smiled when she saw him. "Hey, Carter. You're looking better."

Carter stood up, his left arm still in a sling and faint traces of bruising remained down the left side of his face. "I'm feeling better," he replied, holding out the bouquet.

"Thank you. This is a nice surprise visit. What are the flowers for?"

"No reason. Just wanted to get you some flowers," he answered.

Gently, she hugged him and invited him in. "You'll have to excuse the mess. I'm still getting settled in."

As they entered her apartment building, she stopped to check her mail, en route to the elevator.

A married couple from the building entered the elevator at the same time. Everyone offered their customary smiles and neighborly greetings. The doors closed and they began their ascent.

Carter noticed Cindy watching the couple holding hands, the way happy, loving couples who are more at ease together than they are apart, do.

Arriving at her floor, Carter and Cindy smiled as they passed by them.

Carter followed her inside the apartment past stacks of boxes waiting to be unpacked. "Nice place," he said. "I like it."

"Thanks. It's not as spacious as the other place, but I think I like it better. It feels like mine."

Cindy dropped the keys on the kitchen counter and began examining her mail. "Let's see," she said, "two credit card offers, cell phone bill, and a mystery envelope with no return address."

Carter glanced at the plain brown bubble envelope. "Can you tell where it's from?"

"The postmark is from Miami, Florida," she replied.

Opening the envelope, Cindy removed a letter and a tiny cardboard holder with a key inside. "Well this is weird," she said, holding up the key.

Carter reached out and took possession of the key. "It looks like it goes to a padlock."

Cindy unfolded the paper and began to read out loud.

Dear Cindy,

I'm sorry for everything you've gone through over the last several weeks. You didn't deserve any of it. I can't imagine everything going through your mind right now. I'm sure you feel betrayed and used by Tyler and I can't say I blame you. As a matter of fact, I can relate. What he did to you is inexcusable. But I had to write you to let you know some things.

First of all, I had no knowledge that Tate had any intentions of bringing you into that whole fiasco that happened the night all hell broke loose. I know Tyler didn't either. I never would have gotten involved if I had known you were at risk. I'm sorry.

Somehow, much to my amazement, I managed to get out of there alive. In the process, I crossed paths with Tyler. As I understand it, he had just left you moments before. I knew he was hurt, but I didn't know how badly. He acted like it wasn't serious, but at the same time, I could tell he was worried.

We agreed that I would get to my car and come back for him. Before we separated, he told me that if anything happened to him, there were things I should know.

He said that in spite of the fact he used you, he did care about you and wished that the circumstances had

*been different; that maybe the two of you could have had
a good life together.*

Cindy's voice cracked and she stopped reading. Handing the
letter to Carter she said, "Here, you read the rest."
Carter took the letter and continued from where she left off.

*The second thing he told me was about the money.
He gave me the number of an offshore account. He said
the account was in his name and mine. It shocked me to
find that out and helped me not to be so pissed at him.
When I heard that you turned your father into the FBI, I
was completely blown away. I couldn't believe it. You've
got more guts than I do. Your father can be one cold-
hearted bastard.*
*Anyway, I thought I would give you some of the
money back. I know Tyler would have wanted me to.
Your money is in a bin at A&G Storage in Nashville. It's
unit 23. The key will unlock the padlock I have on the
door. Inside you'll find a gym bag with $800,000. I
know it's only a small portion of the money Tyler stole
from your father, but it's something. Sorry, but I'm keeping the rest and disappearing to a life of luxury. You've
got until the end of next month to get it. That's as long as
I rented the space. Don't try to find me. I didn't leave a
trail. Have a good life.*
Billy

Carter handed the note back to Cindy, who had tears escap-
ing her eyes. "Are you okay?"
"Yes," she whispered, carefully attempting to wipe the tears
without smearing her makeup. She sniffed. "It's nice to hear that it
wasn't a total fraud."
Carter wrapped his arm around her. "I don't know how anyone could be with you that long and not have feelings for you."

Cindy put her hand against Carter's chest, looked up and smiled. "Thanks, Carter."

"It sounds like you just came into some money."

"That's an absurd amount of money to have sitting in a gym bag at a storage unit."

"Yes, it is."

"I'm going to need a protective escort," said Cindy, smiling at Carter. "Are you up for a trip to Nashville?"

READER'S DISCUSSION GUIDE

1. Which character do you sympathize with the most?

2. Should Carter and Cindy pursue a romantic relationship? Why or why not?

3. What would you like to see happen with the future of West Lake Property & Development?

4. What are your thoughts concerning Tyler's motives?

5. Did your initial opinion of Cindy change any by the end of the book?

6. If you were conducting the investigation, is there anything that you would have done differently than Carter? Why?

7. What are your thoughts concerning Billy's actions at the end?

ALAN CUPP

Alan Cupp loves to create and entertain, whether it's with a capti-vating mystery novel or a funny promotional video for his church, he's always anticipating his next creative endeavor. In addition to writing fiction, Alan enjoys acting, music, travel, and playing sports. His life's motto is, "It's better to wear out than rust out." Alan places a high value on time spent with his beautiful wife and their two sons. He lives his life according to his 4F philosophy: Faith, Family, Friends, and Fun.

Don't Miss the 2nd Book in the Series

SCHEDULED TO DIE
Alan Cupp

A Carter Mays Mystery (#2)

Carter Mays' newest client, Dana Carrington, has been given a year
to live. Her prognosis didn't come from a medical professional, but
rather the handsome, charming man she met while on a business
trip. After an evening with charismatic stranger, Mike Sweeney,
filled with potential and intrigue, things quickly deteriorate into the
most frightening and traumatic experience of Dana's life.

Presented as an opportunity to be envied, Sweeney instructs Dana
to spend the next year living life to the fullest, pursuing every ex-
traordinary opportunity she ever dreamt about. When the year is
up, Mike intends to reconvene for a romantic evening that will end
with Dana's death. However, if Dana dares to contact law enforcement, her impending death will come much quicker and be far
more brutal.

Paralyzed by fear of the seemingly ever-present Sweeney, Dana
hires Carter to protect her and stop her psychopathic suitor.

Available at booksellers nationwide and online

Visit www.henerypress.com for details

Henery Press Mystery Books

And finally, before you go...
Here are a few other mysteries
you might enjoy:

THE AMBITIOUS CARD
John Gaspard

An Eli Marks Mystery (#1)

The life of a magician isn't all kiddie shows and card tricks. Sometimes it's murder. Especially when magician Eli Marks very publicly debunks a famed psychic, and said psychic ends up dead. The evidence, including a bloody King of Diamonds playing card (one from Eli's own Ambitious Card routine), directs the police right to Eli.

As more psychics are slain, and more King cards rise to the top, Eli can't escape suspicion. Things get really complicated when romance blooms with a beautiful psychic, and Eli discovers she's the next target for murder, and he's scheduled to die with her. Now Eli must use every trick he knows to keep them both alive and reveal the true killer.

Available at booksellers nationwide and online

Visit www.henerypress.com for details

CIRCLE OF INFLUENCE

Annette Dashofy

A Zoe Chambers Mystery (#1)

Zoe Chambers, paramedic and deputy coroner in rural Pennsylvania's tight-knit Vance Township, has been privy to a number of local secrets over the years, some of them her own. But secrets become explosive when a dead body is found in the Township Board President's abandoned car.

As a January blizzard rages, Zoe and Police Chief Pete Adams launch a desperate search for the killer, even if it means uncovering secrets that could not only destroy Zoe and Pete, but also those closest to them.

Available at booksellers nationwide and online

Visit www.henerypress.com for details

KILLER IMAGE

Wendy Tyson

An Allison Campbell Mystery (#1)

As Philadelphia's premier image consultant, Allison Campbell helps others reinvent themselves, but her most successful transformation was her own after a scandal nearly ruined her. Now she moves in a world of powerful executives, wealthy, eccentric ex-wives and twisted ethics.

When Allison's latest Main Line client, the fifteen-year-old Goth daughter of a White House hopeful, is accused of the ritualistic murder of a local divorce attorney, Allison fights to prove her client's innocence when no one else will. But unraveling the truth brings specters from her own past. And in a place where image is everything, the ability to distinguish what's real from the facade may be the only thing that keeps Allison alive.

Available at booksellers nationwide and online

Visit www.henerypress.com for details

DEATH BY BLUE WATER
Kait Carson

A Hayden Kent Mystery (#1)

Paralegal Hayden Kent knows first-hand that life in the Florida Keys can change from perfect to perilous in a heartbeat. When she discovers a man's body at 120' beneath the sea, she thinks she is witness to a tragic accident. She becomes the prime suspect when the victim is revealed to be the brother of the man who recently jilted her, and she has no alibi. A migraine stole Hayden's memory of the night of the death.

As the evidence mounts, she joins forces with an Officer Janice Kirby. Together the two women follow the clues that uncover criminal activities at the highest levels and put Hayden's life in jeopardy while she fights to stay free.

Available at booksellers nationwide and online

Visit www.henerypress.com for details

FATAL BRUSHSTROKE

Sybil Johnson

An Aurora Anderson Mystery (#1)

A dead body in her garden and a homicide detective on her door-step...

Computer programmer and tole-painting enthusiast Aurora (Rory) Anderson doesn't envision finding either when she steps outside to investigate the frenzied yipping coming from her own back yard. After all, she lives in Vista Beach, a quiet California beach community where violent crime is rare and murder even rarer.

Suspicion falls on Rory when the body buried in her flowerbed turns out to be someone she knows—her tole painting teacher, Hester Bouquet. Just two weekends before, Rory attended one of Hester's weekend painting seminars, an unpleasant experience she vowed never to repeat. As evidence piles up against Rory, she embarks on a quest to identify the killer and clear her name. Can Rory unearth the truth before she encounters her own brush with death?

Available at booksellers nationwide and online

Visit www.henerypress.com for details

SHADOW OF DOUBT

Nancy Cole Silverman

A Carol Childs Mystery (#1)

A dead body in her garden and a homicide detective on her doorstep...

Computer programmer and tole-painting enthusiast Aurora (Rory) Anderson doesn't envision finding either when she steps outside to investigate the frenzied yipping coming from her own back yard. After all, she lives in Vista Beach, a quiet California beach community where violent crime is rare and murder even rarer.

Suspicion falls on Rory when the body buried in her flowerbed turns out to be someone she knows—her tole painting teacher, Hester Bouquet. Just two weekends before, Rory attended one of Hester's weekend painting seminars, an unpleasant experience she vowed never to repeat. As evidence piles up against Rory, she embarks on a quest to identify the killer and clear her name. Can Rory unearth the truth before she encounters her own brush with death?

Available at booksellers nationwide and online

Visit www.henerypress.com for details

THE RED QUEEN'S RUN
Bourne Morris

A Meredith Solaris Mystery (#1)

A famous journalism dean is found dead at the bottom of a stairwell. Accident or murder? The police suspect members of the faculty who had engaged in fierce quarrels with the dean—distinguished scholars who were known to attack the dean like brutal schoolyard bullies. When Meredith "Red" Solaris is appointed interim dean, the faculty suspects are furious.

Will the beautiful red-haired professor be next? The case detective tries to protect her as he heads the investigation, but incoming threats lead him to believe Red's the next target for death.

Available at booksellers nationwide and online

Visit www.henerypress.com for details

CPSIA information can be obtained at www.ICGtesting.com
Printed in the USA
LVOW04s1542310315

432751LV00016B/866/P